BOY
RELEASED

JD SPERO

Immortal Works LLC
1505 Glenrose Drive
Salt Lake City, Utah 84104
Tel: (385) 202-0116

© 2021 JD Spero
http://www.jdspero.com/

Cover Art by Ashley Literski
http://strangedevotion.wixsite.com/strangedesigns

ISBN 978-1-953491-22-0
ASIN B098NG55GX

For my boys, especially AJ

CHAPTER 1

Summer 2001

Part of Hen couldn't wait to be an adult. Another part felt like he'd always been an adult. Even when his young life was shaken like a snow globe and all the flecks still floated in the water, taking their sweet time to settle, paying no mind to the proper order of things. And in a few months, as soon as he became a legal adult, his whole world would change.

And the changes would be epic.

For one, he'd become a millionaire.

And two, he'd have to figure out what to do with the money.

Kids shouldn't have to worry about this kind of stuff. Not with so much work to do.

Hen knocked on cabin number two before using the master key to let himself in. He'd blitz this place in no time, before the renters got back from breakfast or wherever. Then he could take his time with the vacancies.

Yeah. Motel life.

Part of the shakeup. Four years ago, his little life in the sleepy town of Severance was upended when Mom and Bernie bought Blue Palms Motel in Lake George Village. And Hen, at thirteen, made it his summer job to clean the cabins. Why? Mom needed help. It had taken his every summer since.

But Hen knew Mom had worked her whole life for an opportunity like this. Bernie stumbled on the motel-for-sale in a thriving tourist area at a bargain. A "dream come true," according to Mom.

"It's only a half-hour south," Mom had said, at Hen's initial reluctance.

And then, "Look, the Queen of American Lakes is right across the street from your new school!"

On his tippy toes, Hen saw a sliver of the lake a half-mile away, past the other dozen motels and restaurants and T-shirt shops. "You're right. I can see it."

Key word: *see*.

Nature teased them from afar. It was too expensive to go out on the water by boat. Needed a car to get to hiking trails. Wildlife lived elsewhere. So much stuff blocked the way, and the animals stayed hidden in the woods. Hen hardly blamed them. Streetlights, not trees, surrounded their motel on the outskirts of Lake George Village.

Hen's childhood was filled with trees. And he missed them.

"Oh, Hen. What do you mean, there are no trees? We're surrounded by mountains. Trees are everywhere."

Mom didn't feel their absence, but he did.

Oddly, cleaning cabins seemed an extension of what he'd been doing the past ten years. Helping Mom. Making things better. Wiping away the dirt of their past. Putting a shine on the ugliness that plagued their family. That ten-year nightmare still haunted him. Compared to that, toilets were pristine.

So, if she needed him to be the maid at her new venture, he'd be the dang maid.

Still, he'd place his bets he was the only kid in his high school who cleaned toilets for a summer job. Even his best friend Wesley, whose folks owned the fancy waterfront resort down the street, had been spared housekeeping chores.

Leaving the cabin door open as he worked, he switched on ESPN to catch the Yankees' highlights from last night's game. Ever since

Bernie splurged and took him to Yankee Stadium shortly after moving here, he'd faithfully rooted for the "heroes in pinstripes," as Bernie called them. But his true love would always be basketball. One of his best-kept secrets? He was a Celtics fan.

Hen caught his reflection in the mirror as he Windexed. His shirt read: *I'd rather be playing basketball.*

How true. He tossed the paper towel in the bin. *Swish.* Two points.

This might be his last summer helping out at the motel, anyway. Next summer was graduation. And, of course, the millions. Sally Hubbard's inheritance had been hanging over his head for the past decade, like a gray-green cloud. Whenever Mom talked about it, she got so emotional, Hen avoided the topic. Seemed unreal, anyway. Like a story in a book.

Sally Hubbard. *Miss Sally.*

A hollow ache crept in at the thought of her. Even with her long gone. Hen focused on concrete things like the layout of her house, the blue willow dishes she had used, her polka dot socks. It was no use. Lots of unhappy feelings clouded his memories, his brother Tyler taking up a lot of the space. Maybe that was why the hollow ache.

A family-size box of Cheezits sat next to the TV. Hen's mouth watered. The clock told him he had at least another hour before any reasonable human ate lunch. Hen's stomach paid no mind to the clock, though. Always begging loudly for food.

He'd gotten fast at bed-making, especially when he didn't have to switch sheets. As he tucked in the last corner, a shadow blocked the doorway, giving him a start. A woman—sudden and silent—wearing, of all things, a Red Sox cap.

"Oh." Hen quickly shut off ESPN.

Though she seemed a similar age, she had none of Mom's beauty or softness. She frowned accusingly. "Do you work here?"

Hen glanced at the bin of cleaning supplies at his feet. "Yup." He checked himself. "Sorry. I'll be out of your way in a few minutes."

The woman clicked her tongue. "No, no, this isn't my room. I was just in the office. No one's in there. I rang the bell. Still no one. I was hoping to get a room. Could you help?"

Hen pulled off his gloves. "Sure. When were you hoping to stay?"

"Tonight? And through the weekend?"

"You want a room for *this weekend*?" Hen's incredulous tone was a reflex. Memorial Day weekend kicked off the summer season—always booked solid months in advance.

"Is that a problem?" Her demeanor matched the offending sports logo on her cap.

Hen checked himself again. His gaze swept the cabin, which would have to pass for clean. He gave the woman a smile. "Why don't we go to the office to check the register?"

Locking up cabin two, Hen left his cleaning bin on the stoop and made his way across the parking lot, the Red Sox lady quick on his heels. The empty office was expected. With a full book of reservations, Mom caught up on planting annuals while Bernie had gone out for pool supplies.

Hen made a big show of studying the register. "Sorry, ma'am. We're full."

"Full?"

"That's right. No vacancies."

She looked out the window. "There aren't any cars. How can you be full?"

"All the cabins are reserved, ma'am. This is the first weekend of the summer. It's always a busy weekend in Lake George."

"What about just tonight?"

Hen faked a sigh. "Sorry."

An exasperated grunt, and she craned to look across the lot. She tapped the window glass. "What about that one on the end?"

Hen would've bet she'd ask that. Folks never believed the motel was ever totally full. Uncanny. And they always asked for "the one on the end," cabin eleven. As if being last made it somehow undesirable and therefore up for grabs. Truth told, it did look a little sad and neglected way over there.

Though he expected the question, he felt a jolt. Any mention of cabin eleven triggered that response. Hen swallowed and remembered his manners. Still, he couldn't help the wobble in his voice. "No, ma'am. That one definitely is not available." *And never will be*, Hen wanted to add.

A dark feeling swam in his gut, knowing cabin eleven was occupied indefinitely by none other than his brother Tyler, who was recently released from institutional rehab.

CHAPTER 2

Ty forced hot coffee down his throat as he stared out the window of cabin eleven. Windows. Microsoft had Windows. Very different from the one in front of him now. Computers had taken over the world while he burrowed deep within the state hospital. Incarcerated. Rehabilitation. A lot of time passed. Ten years. And by the end, everything blinked digital.

He got out a month ago, like he'd awoken from a coma. Bits of his brain held on to his life there in the hospital. Clung like barnacles. They had programmed it that way.

Computers worked in mysterious ways. He didn't know why he'd been programmed to come here, to this strange motel so far from the home he remembered.

It didn't matter where he slept or ate or existed. Shame followed him, colored him purple. Like a thick, toxic paint on his skin. Beneath that, he was numb.

He drank more coffee and stared at the world outside. Along the pool fence, Marcella—it didn't feel right to call her Mother—squatted at a flower bed, planting tiny pink flowers Ty recognized as impatiens. Sounded like *impatience*. They'd die over the winter and then she'd have to plant them again next year.

His gaze found the solitary cloud in the big blue sky, which looked the same here as from the state hospital. Every day, different variations of the same sky.

Computers programmed it that way. They controlled everything. He knew that now.

Used to be security cameras. Those tiny red lights like beady lizard eyes, watching his every move. Recording stuff. His life. An ongoing reality television show produced by aliens.

It took a long time to let that go. Until one day when he passed by the admin office and—through another *window*—he noticed computers everywhere. Every single person on a computer. Not only the big box ones that sat on desks with separate keyboards, but some smaller ones that opened like books. On one screen he saw his own image, right where he stood in the hallway. The security cameras linked to the computers! More evidence they controlled everything. Quite a learning moment for Ty.

Then, the terrifying countdown to the Y2K crisis. The news talked about how, when the calendar flipped to year 2000, all computers would explode. Or implode. Didn't matter, the result would be the same. And because computers controlled everything, *everything would be destroyed.* Systems would crash. Planes would fall from the sky. Social Security numbers would reconfigure randomly. Astronauts and all space travel would vaporize. Digital media would blink out of order.

The world would explode too. And all the people in it.

Ty still waited for the bomb to drop, even if the calendar already read 2001. They, all of them, tried to reassure him the news stations and the tech people had it wrong. That the Millennium New Year passed peacefully. Thanks to some pre-planning by some very bright programmers, the hardware and software that hard-wired our society was protected. No one talked about it anymore. Not on news stations either.

But Ty knew how sneaky those computers were. How smart. It would be too convenient to do it on the 2000 New Year. It would be late, the explosion/implosion that would mean the end of the world. Like, any day now. Impending doom still threatened.

A harsh reality. That's why Ty refused to have a personal mobile device. Also why he stopped smoking. Dr. Asner and his social worker Sheila both said it was because he'd been hypnotized at rehab, but Ty didn't believe in hocus pocus stuff. It was the computers. Programmers rewired his brain to take out the smoking addiction. Made it smell and taste really gross overnight.

Coffee was another story.

Kind of.

Another gulp of coffee, wincing as it went down, watching outside.

Hen emerged from cabin number two, giving Ty a start. Across the lot toward the office, some lady following. Still had to get used to seeing Hen all grown up. That teenager—almost a man—used to be his baby brother.

Ty searched the mini fridge and found a Gatorade. Took his pill with it. Tasted weird after coffee. He should eat something. Mini fridge was mostly bare. Out of food. He'd eat something at work. He pulled on khakis and a white collared shirt, his unofficial store uniform.

Another look out the window, his heart pounding. He had to go out there soon. He had to expose himself. Give in to the computers.

Marcella still poked and plugged at the flower bed. Was Hen still in the office with that lady? He didn't see her car anymore—the one with the Massachusetts license plate. He panned the row of cabins. Hen's bin of cleaning supplies abandoned outside on the curb.

He'd rather not run into his brother, but he had to get to Mini Chopper. Bill expected him there to stock the shelves.

A slight panic simmered deep in his spine. Had to hurry before it traveled to his head. Quick, he checked his pocket for his wallet and key. Double checked. Triple checked. His heart thrummed, fear taking root. He had to go now. *Go now. Go now.*

Whoosh. Outside. Door closed behind him, set to lock automatically. An auxiliary wave of panic made him recheck for the key. Okay. There, safe in his pocket. Wallet, too. All okay. It's okay. He paused to let his breathing settle and his heart rate to normalize.

One foot in front of the other.

"Oh, hi! Good morning." Marcella hadn't gotten used to having him around. Even if they had talked every day by phone for the past ten years he'd been away. Seeing him in the flesh seemed to startle her.

She smiled, squinting. A gloved hand shielded her eyes, and specks of dark soil fell onto her shirt.

"Hi." Ty looked at the ground. Kept walking.

"Have a good day." Her voice sounded sad.

He felt her eyes on his back. Should he turn and wave? His hands deep in his pockets, a simple wave seemed impossible. Maybe tomorrow.

Halfway across the lot, Hen charged out of the office. Almost ran straight into him.

"Oh, hey," Hen said, a man's voice.

Not their first meet-up since getting out. But this one took Ty by surprise. Silence filled the space between them. Ty stole a glance at his brother. And another.

Hen had visited maybe three times during Ty's stint at rehab. Long time ago.

"Hey." Ty slowed his steps but kept moving.

"Going to work?" Hen sounded like a child again—angelic and kind.

Ty's heart quivered. "Yup."

"See ya."

"Yup."

Not a big deal. Pleasant enough exchange. Dr. Asner might call it progress. Still, Ty battled a lump in his throat the rest of the way to Mini Chopper.

Ty PUT on the royal blue apron and his nametag, and felt instantly transformed. Like a superhero cape, even though his nametag screamed **TYLER T.** in all caps.

"Good morning, Tyler." Bill, Ty's boss, ran a tight ship. But he liked Ty for some reason. Not Savannah, though—with the tattoo of a dolphin on her arm—who got yelled at for smiling wrong to a customer. She quit the next day. That stuff happened a lot here, Bill told him. What did he call it? *Turnover*. Like the pastry.

"Mornin'." Ty wasted no time getting to work. Every shift started the same way. First, to the delivery dock for new shipments. Then collect items on Bill's inventory list and stock the shelves. Everything had its place on the shelf. Ty took pride in knowing where to put what, placing the items just so. Better than a computer. Well, maybe not. But almost.

About twenty minutes into his shift, Ty felt woozy from hunger—a side effect of his medicine. A drug so powerful it rippled through his entire body just to calm his brain. He couldn't wait to be over and done with the meds so he could get on with life.

Bill allowed him as many breaks as he needed. He craved a bagel. Fresh from the bakery: sesame with chive cream cheese. Washed it down with another Gatorade.

After break, he rolled along his shift in a pleasant fog.

Until he stocked cereal boxes in aisle four and a familiar voice echoed through the store.

"Here we go. Breakfast of champions." A girl. Near the ice cream case by the registers. Where did he know that voice?

Another girl, unfamiliar: "Really? Didn't your mother teach you breakfast is the most important meal of the day?"

"Didn't your mother teach you ice cream is actually good for you?" Like a knife into his brain, that voice.

"It's not even real ice cream."

"What constitutes *real* ice cream? It's cold, and it's creamy." That sultry tone, flirty.

A wave of heat came over him, pinpointing the voice. Almost

dropped a box of Fruity Pebbles. But no, couldn't be. Ty should hide, just in case. But his legs wouldn't move.

Laughter. Girly giggles. "Why is it called a drumstick? It's ice cream, not a turkey leg."

"Because! You can play the drum with it?" Laughing, laughing.

"You can *not* play the drum with that thing!"

More laughter. A picture—clear as day—came to him. Open mouthed grin, her crooked tooth visible, her dark hair swaying. Freckles near her ear.

"Sure, you can."

Cracking up now. Paper wrappers tearing.

...Her glossy polished nails. Her smooth, perfect skin.

"Aren't you going to pay for it?"

"I will. I am! Geesh."

A raw heat moved from Ty's chest out toward his limbs. He *knew* this girl. Or he used to know her, before. His heart raced. The memory surged to mind. He had obsessed over this girl for years back in high school.

Before.

Questions flew through his mind. What was she doing here? Thirty-plus miles from Schroon Lake? Didn't she move to New York City after graduation? Wasn't that her plan?

These questions mixed with the memory of her—vivid and painful and real.

Wow. Plans don't matter when computers control everything. Clearly, she hadn't been programmed to live in New York City. And now, here?

He could smell her perfume. Feel the heat of her. His chest spun with the violent whirr of his heart. Sweat made his fingers slip.

Fruity Pebbles fell to the floor. On reflex, he turned to grab it.

And there she was. At the end of the aisle, she stood watching him, her mouth on her ice cream—bold and sensuous and innocent. Ty froze, unable to tear his eyes away.

She wore shorts and a sweatshirt, her face bare of makeup.

Sunglasses perched on her hair, which was pulled back with an elastic. He drank her in, forgetting himself. Roxanne Russo—more gorgeous than he remembered.

Recognition alight in her eyes, yet she couldn't place him.

"What kind should I get?" her friend called from the front.

Roxanne pulled off a bite of ice cream and rolled it in her mouth. Nuts and chocolate bits coated her lips. Ty trembled, staring.

She stepped closer, the torn wrapper like a ribbon in her hand. Her eyes, sharp and smart and sober, narrowed in on his nametag.

Hot lava pooled in Ty's body. His mouth gaped for air, but the store had none. He suffocated as she studied him.

"Oh," she said, ice cream warping the sound.

Direct eye contact now, Roxanne placed him. She knew exactly who he was. *TYLER T.* covered in purple shame no fancy blue apron could disguise.

Like his eyes had rolled back into his head, his mind zoomed back to high school. A computer's memory doesn't lose an ounce of data. Mrs. Finley's class. A mythology project. Laughing in study hall, flashing her snaggletooth. Then, dark. Nighttime at the bonfire. No, Leon's Diner. No, the bonfire. No, on his street...near his house... what happened...

He tripped over the timeline of his memory, terror muddying details.

Was she there that night? Did she know what happened?

Of course she did. Everyone knew. Ty deflated, like his organs shriveled.

Everything came back in a flash. Diner. The high. Derek's truck. Miss Sally. The lamp. Miss Sally. Her potpourri house. Miss Sally. Alien UFOs. Miss Sally.

Miss Sally. Miss Sally. Miss Sally.

Computer shorted. Maybe a virus.

No, no, no.

Here in the middle of Mini Chopper, a dismal reunion. Pity in Roxanne's eyes—her lovely, clear eyes!—told him. She knew everything, even what happened after. Where he'd been the last ten years. Shame flared, coloring his face.

Abruptly, she turned away. Pivoted on her flip flop and strolled back to the front, graceful and confident. Her friend's voice filled the silence, "I'm thinking ice cream sandwich."

Roxanne mumbled something like *let's get out of here*. But Ty wasn't sure. He couldn't hear. His ears didn't work.

Down on the tiles, his heart hammered and his vision blurred. Cereal boxes became huge, rising to the ceiling. Tony the Tiger. Toucan Sam. Trix Rabbit. Fred Freaking Flintstone. All laughed at him. Encryption failed. A total hack.

No, no, no. This can't be happening. He took his medicine. It's not supposed to happen anymore. He's *better*.

Bile climbed his throat. Would he puke?

"Tyler, are you all right?" Bill's voice.

Huddled, hugging Fruity Pebbles to his chest. He squeezed the box tight, trying to make it burst. His chest. It would explode any moment. He knew.

His mouth opened, and he heard his own voice. "I'm better." So quiet. But he heard it. It gave him strength. He tried again, louder. "I'm better."

Bill again. "Tyler? Come on. Get up. It's okay. Come on."

His boss gripped his elbow, and an electric current—hot and sharp—shot up Ty's arm. "No. No. *No!*" he shouted.

Oh, no. He yelled at Bill. *No, no, no.* He didn't mean that. Too late.

Fruity Pebbles crushed against him. He could smell it. Manufactured cherry and orange and lemon aromas infecting the air. Flakes rained onto the tiles *tap, tap, tap...*

Ty shoved the box away from him. It slid across the aisle into Bill's feet.

"I'm better," Ty said again, and covered his face in his hands, sobbing. Curled in a ball, he rocked and cried on the tile floor, his body lurching with sobs. Until there was nothing left, inside or out.

CHAPTER 3

Marcella watered her freshly planted annuals, feeling creaky and in need of a massage after digging in soil on her knees for the best part of the morning. The project took way longer than anticipated and she probably should have been sorting bills or touching up the porch paint rather than planting flowers. But so overwhelming was her need for cheer and color and vibrant, living things she could easily care for, she had no choice.

When she and Bernie first purchased Blue Palms Motel, it seemed like the opportunity of a lifetime. She'd finally taken charge of her life as a bona fide business owner. How could folks not take her seriously when she owned a resort in one of the most thriving tourist towns in upstate New York? Still, it nagged at her. Every aspect of it. The season hadn't even started, and they were already in the red after paying Pedro's Plumbing Co. an exorbitant sum to stop shower leaks and toilet malfunctions in six—no seven—out of the eleven cabins. Pouring salt on that wound was the mandatory mold removal and remediation afterwards. Of course. It's not enough to fix the darn leaks, the water damage had to be zapped into oblivion—by law—so no one got sick. God forbid another lawsuit entered their world. Over ten years had passed since Tyler's trial but the wound still throbbed, raw and bleeding.

Marcella bent down to drink from the hose like she used to do as a little girl. Harsh, cold water spluttered on her face and hair, her shirt. She drank and drank, feeling it down to her toes. Glorious. Righting herself, dripping from the jaw like a drooly Bloodhound, she almost jumped seeing Tyler walk into the parking lot, his apron slung across his shoulder.

"Tyler!" she called, her chest ballooning through the gloom.

She shut off the hose and ran to him before she thought better of it. Wary of surprises, she assumed the worst. She'd never stopped worrying about her firstborn—a debilitating kind of worry. For the past ten years, it lingered on the edges of her psyche. And she had been able to feign her way through life borrowing time against it. Because, at the state hospital, he'd been safe. Incarcerated, but safe. Their daily phone calls more a confirmation that the professionals in charge kept up with their important work rather than a deep dive into his true state of mental health. Now, with Tyler home, it walloped her straight in the chest, full force. Now, the important work fell on her shoulders.

As she approached him, her steps faltered. A stark reminder the years had not been kind. Though he held onto qualities of his late father's good looks—his strong jaw and Paul Newman eyes—his medication made him swollen. Gave him extra flesh on his otherwise lanky physique. Another reminder how sick he was.

Nerves made her mouth go. The verbal vomit of questions ran together with no room for answers. "What are you doing home? Didn't you have to work today? Did you get your schedule wrong? Or they didn't need you? Are you feeling okay? Did they send you home sick?"

As if he didn't hear, Tyler went right by, his face blank.

"Tyler?"

Marcella walked alongside her son, studying his profile. He looked pale. Stricken. Something must have happened. Despair exposed itself, an old file fanning open.

"Tyler, please. Let me help. What can I do?"

"Nothing," he mumbled.

A response! Marcella forced a breath. Told herself to calm down. Why did she pounce on him like that?

"I'm sorry about the twenty questions." Marcella swatted at her shirt, wishing away the wet streaks that made her feel childish and small. "I'm glad you're home," she added quietly.

No response.

At cabin eleven now, Tyler unlocked the door and started inside—

"Wait. Tyler? Listen, I was hoping we could... How would you like to come to the house for dinner tonight?" Verbal vomit resumed. "I mean, things will get crazy here starting tomorrow and really won't let up until after Labor Day. Can you imagine? I know how that must sound, but we have to pack in a year's worth of income in a few short months so there's a good reason to be busy. We are blessed to be busy! And have bookings! Reservations are solid. We're at full capacity through most of July, which is so great."

Tyler, inside his cabin, held the door so it obscured half his face.

But he hadn't shut it yet. A good sign.

Marcella took a breath and tried again. "Anyway, we'd love for you to come to dinner tonight. We can sit and catch up and eat together. Around a table. As a family." The last word sounded strange, even to her.

Tyler mumbled.

"What's that? I didn't hear, honey. I'm sorry."

"I'm better."

Was that a tear in his eye? "I know. I know you are. You're doing so well. I'm so—no *we're* so prou—"

The door started to close between them.

"Wait, Tyler. About tonight? Can we expect you? Around six? That okay?"

Only a sliver of his face visible, he shook his head really fast, a horrified look in the one eye she could see.

"No?" she said, stupid shock made the word sound defensive.

He wagged his head as the door closed. She imagined he kept

shaking his head afterwards, in the dark aloneness of his room. And her heart fell apart, right there on the stoop.

MARCELLA'S FOREARMS were dusted with flour like twin white-powdered crullers. She'd never been the neatest cook. With her hands busy, her mind spun.

Sheila Farris (aka social-worker-Sheila) had been clear as she went over the details of his release plan. To spare Tyler being sent to a heavily regimented group home, Marcella had strict legal obligations. If Tyler resided on her property, she was responsible for him as his official caretaker. Although Sheila's definition of "caretaker" sounded more like a babysitter. Due to not only his mental illness but also his violent history, he had to be carefully supervised. Watched at all times—like a toddler. And, in addition to his mandatory weekly meetings, Tyler needed additional support to integrate into society in a healthy way. A grand stroke of luck got him stocking groceries at Mini Chopper, on a trial basis. Sheila worked with Dr. Asner, his psychiatrist, to pull some strings in hopes Tyler might be allowed to attend a day program in Hudson Falls (all the way in Hudson Falls?), to no avail. Not yet, anyway.

Still. What did they mean? Tyler had come *home*. And Marcella had taken great pains to ensure "home" was not the same town where demons of his past would swallow him up. She had uprooted her family for a fresh start in a new area, for all of them, sure. But mostly, to give Tyler a second chance. He deserved as much.

What more needed to happen? Well, apparently, lots. And Marcella was getting a first-rate education in mental health policy and advocacy campaigns and Kendra's Law and...

What can we do for my son?

A simple question with no real answer. How could that be? The numbers astounded her—how many millions of people like her son suffered without treatment, or were thrown into prison unjustly. Just to be rid of them? How many thousands became homeless, dying on the cold streets. Was the system any better than when insane asylums shut people up in padded rooms? Had we fallen so short as a country that we have abandoned those who were clearly and dangerously ill and in desperate need of help?

She would never abandon Tyler.

Marcella's frustration was so great, she agreed to whatever social-worker-Sheila or Dr. Asner asked of her. She wrote to legislators, lobbied Congress...

What else can we do? How can I help?

Until Dr. Asner asked for her to prepare for mental health court. She'd already started the petition with the doctors who'd treated Tyler at the state hospital and had a mental health attorney lined up. Would Marcella meet with him?

She'd already said yes, hadn't she? She'd agreed to whatever, right? But she had a visceral, knee-jerk reaction—*rejection*—at the thought of working with an attorney and dealing with any kind of trial in any kind of court system. After Tyler's nightmare ten years ago, she couldn't bear it. She just couldn't.

She hated that she—of sound mind and body—didn't have that kind of mental strength. So, she'd put off meeting with the lawyer.

She'd made an absolute art of procrastination.

Instead, she cooked chicken cutlets for her son.

"What are you doin'?" Bernie asked, coming in after working on the pool.

"I'm cooking. For Tyler. Something's wrong."

A hand on the small of her back, warm and strong. He kissed her cheek. "You worry too much."

She glared. "Don't say that. He came home early—too early—from the store. He didn't look right."

Bernie stared into the fridge. "Is he sick?"

Her face fell. The question stuck. Tyler's illness still confounded her. How cruel, that no cure existed? That he'd have to struggle and suffer his entire life because the wiring in his brain kept glitching and turning against him.

Bernie astutely read her silence. "No, I mean. Does he have a fever or anything?"

A laugh choked out. "I didn't take his temperature, Bernie. He's a grown man."

"Right. He is a grown man. And he'll figure all this out." The fridge door remained open.

Marcella nudged Bernie aside and retrieved the cranberry juice for him. His smile went to his eyes, grateful and adoring.

"I asked him to dinner." She poked the chicken sizzling in the pan. If it tasted like it smelled, she'd done well.

"And?"

"He said no. That's why I'm bringing him food. He needs a home-cooked meal. I have no idea what he eats in there. Only so much you can do with a microwave and a mini fridge." On a pie plate, she arranged the green beans and chicken cutlet on a bed of rice. Zipped a square of aluminum foil to cover it. A rare bubble of pride crept in.

Bernie finished his juice. "Marcella."

"What?"

She felt his patient gaze, waiting for eye contact.

"You can't coddle him like that."

A buzz of anger flared. "Oh, stop. Let me do what I want. What that boy has been through? He deserves—"

"That boy's a man. And, you want to talk about what he's been through? No offense, but he got what he deserved."

Marcella's jaw dropped. Bernie clamped his.

"I can't believe you just said that."

A hint of a chuckle, and then his eyes grew serious. "He killed my mother."

Marcella stifled a gasp. She clasped her shaking hands together in a dust cloud of flour. Her therapist's warnings floated to mind. Bernie had to process what happened in his own right. He'd lost his mother. Miss Sally wasn't the only victim. Neither was Tyler.

"Don't say that." She couldn't help herself.

His face was drawn with grief. "I have to."

"No, you don't." Her voice shook. "Not to me."

He turned away. "Okay. Not to you, then. But I have to say it. For me."

Her lips trembled against tears. Bernie half-sat on the kitchen table, his entire being drooping with misery. He needed her love right now. For her to remain on his side, as steadfast as she'd been the past decade.

Tyler being home, though, mixed everything up in her heart. The right thing to do was to take care of her son. The fleeting thought held an undeniable truth: Bernie can take care of himself. A bitter dislike soured her against him—a strange, unwelcome feeling. She picked up the pie plate, held it like a shield. "This conversation is over."

"Tyler, open up." She balanced the pie plate in one hand while knocking on cabin eleven's door with the other. Not a sound from inside. Marcella forced a count to ten before knocking again. One, two, three...

Wet streaks dried on her shirt but soil stains remained. Also, flour.

Four, five, six...

She brushed off the flour and then ran her fingers through her hair—a nervous habit.

Seven, eight, nine...

Agh-ick! Now she had flour in her hair. A groan escaped.

"Tyler, I brought you a home-cooked meal. Please open up."

She heard a rustling inside. Or did she? Curtains blocked the windows, giving her no view to the room. She'd installed new curtains over the winter. Every year, she did some small improvements. She rolled her eyes at herself. Seemed frivolous now. If she'd known the mega-expenses they'd face for plumbing and mold removal, she'd have skipped the esthetics.

The least of her worries with cabin eleven, its tenant notwithstanding. That sad little cabin was more vulnerable to wear and tear because it sat on the end. With its sagging roof, it seemed to cower, sheepish. Primed to crawl into the ground to hide from the world. Always the last cabin to be rented, Hen mentioned once that folks thought it bad luck to rent an end cabin. Like, haunted or something. Now, she wondered if the superstition had merit. Or if it felt that way only now because Tyler lived there.

Social-worker-Sheila was the mastermind with the grand idea to plop Tyler into a motel cabin.

"A good compromise," she'd said. "To ease him back in."

Translation: as a twenty-seven-year-old man, he should have a place of his own. Not crashing with his mother. But he wasn't a normal twenty-seven-year-old man. Far from it. He would probably never live on his own, but he wouldn't exactly be welcomed with open arms into Marcella's home, would he? Not as long as Bernie lived there, anyway. Hence the motel cabin.

But Marcella questioned the whole idea from the start. Still did today. Was Tyler ready to have even that much independence? How closely did she have to watch him? Who's to say he couldn't be hurting himself right now. Maybe she should install security cameras...

She gasped at the thought, knowing his sordid history with those devices.

Panic blossomed anew.

"Honey, I can't leave the plate outside. Please. It's still hot. If you aren't hungry now, you can heat it up later." Trailing off, she sat on the doorjamb.

She surveyed her property. The expansive, mostly empty parking lot. The pool in the back. Her newly planted impatiens looking a bit pathetic in the grand landscape of it all.

Sigh. Was she up for this? Could she take care of him in the way he needed—when here she couldn't even get him to open the door?

As if miles separated them, and not just a door. He felt so far away. More so than when he'd been in rehab, and for a precious hour, her visits were accompanied by a team of professionals. People who made a career of dealing with people like Tyler. Even during her daily phone calls to rehab, she'd spend more time speaking with those professionals than her own son. Regretfully, she relied on those people. Why wouldn't she? But now the painful truth rose to the surface. She simply didn't have the tools. Or the training.

How to close the gap between them? Something to connect them. Some common ground, maybe. Eyeing the pool, she blurted out the first story that came to mind.

"You know, when I was a little girl? I was scared to swim in the lake. But growing up in the Adirondacks, lakes were more common than swimming pools. Oh, I thought pools were so fancy. I loved them. The smell of chlorine and how clean they were. Lakes seemed slimy and scary to me." She paused, took a breath. "Then, one day when I was about eight or nine, my stepfather—Jon was his name—decided it was time for me to get over my fear of lakes. And he threw me in." Her smile dropped. Perhaps this wasn't the best story to tell. Especially to Tyler. But she didn't want to stop. Besides, Tyler might not be listening. He could be asleep or in the bathroom or hiding in his headphones for all she knew.

She went on, submerged in reverie. "Now, it's no secret my stepfather Jon wasn't the kindest soul. That's putting it lightly. But wouldn't you know his trick worked? He threw me off the dock at his friend's camp at Schroon Lake. I screamed and kicked and somehow stayed afloat. After that, I was more scared of my stepfather than any kind of water. But that's another story." She shied away from that darkness, and focused on the sparkling pool at the back of the property, freshly shocked, skimmed, and vacuumed by Bernie earlier today. "I always dreamed of owning a home with a pool." A slight chuckle. "Didn't dream of all the work that came with it or all these cabins surrounding it, but..." Deep breath. The pie plate, warm on her knees, got heavy suddenly. As did her eyelids.

Just as she closed them, the door clicked. She shot up, alert, ignoring the ache in her lower back from the sudden movement. In the doorway, Tyler slouched in his grungy sweats and tube socks. He looked so much like he did in rehab. Marcella shook off the mental image. Maybe he'd just woken up?

"Tyler. There you are. Were you...did you hear?" Part of her wished he hadn't.

He nodded, held out a hand.

She gave him the pie plate.

"Thanks," he said, studying the aluminum as if it showed his reflection.

"It's chicken cutlet."

He glanced at her—a split second—a flash of brilliant blue. Something ignited in Marcella's heart. He shut the door without another word. But the warmth remained, and Marcella cherished and protected it. She slowly made her way back to the house, her face relaxing into a smile.

She wouldn't let Bernie or anyone extinguish that flame, she decided. Tyler was her son. And if nothing else became clear in her messed-up life, there were two truths she knew for absolute fact: she loved Tyler no matter what, and he desperately needed her.

CHAPTER 4

Hen usually borrowed Marcella's car for his family therapy appointments, but today she insisted on driving him. Should have been old hat by now, being six years into therapy. Hen knew it helped. Believed in the system. Still, at times he felt he should be at the other side of the table asking questions. His therapists, all of them, seemed inherently troubled.

"We can go to lunch after," she'd said.

Now they sat in awkward silence while Mom drove him two towns over. Trapped between childhood and adulthood, Hen was not quite comfortable in the passenger seat.

Uncharacteristically quiet, Marcella seemed preoccupied. She kept running a hand over her hair. Hen chalked it up to the season ramping up. It was always a little stressful until they all got into their groove for summer.

When she stayed on the main road past that familiar left turn, it took a few seconds for Hen to speak up. "Where are we going?"

"Oh, I thought I told you. This is a different kind of appointment."

The street turned from residential to urban after the next traffic light.

"What kind of appointment are we going to, Mom?" Surprised he had to ask, he heard sass in his voice.

"Advisor." She attempted to parallel park. After two tries, the car's nose still blocked traffic. She pulled out, mumbling irritably. They would have to walk farther from the end of the lot where Marcella finally found a spot. She shoved the gear shift to park and shut off the engine. "Financial."

"What?"

"Financial advisor."

Hen felt himself slouch, a reflex. No wonder Mom insisted on coming. He wasn't going to family therapy to talk about feelings. No warm and fuzzy *How's Hen doing?* Today, he'd be thrust into a surreal type of manhood where Monopoly money would become real. And his mom tagged along.

It felt wrong that only moments ago he'd been cleaning toilets and now he'd talk to this financial advisor about his upcoming fortune.

Mr. Peter Edgerton seemed oddly eager to speak to Hen and his mother. Hen took in his sleek clothing and thought he might be the only person in town wearing a tailored suit. Then again, they were in the big city of Glens Falls, to which Mom's parking conundrum could attest.

They sat in a conference room, a thick folder on the long table the only sign of life. Mr. Edgerton made idle chitchat until his assistant delivered coffee and shut the door behind her. Hen's mounting misery kept him silent.

Hen noticed Marcella shiver in her leather seat. She wore loose clothing. Casual. Almost too casual, but this had been her style since quitting the diner.

As a kid, Hen saw his mom wear dresses every day. Glamorous, with her long dark locks and striking hourglass physique. Now, he realized, her fitted clothing hadn't been a fashion thing but a requirement of her job. The dress, a uniform. Her preferred attire seemed to be shapeless, unflattering cotton. Her long dark hair cropped at her shoulders. A bob, she'd told him. Hen preferred it long.

"So, we'll get down to it, I guess," Edgerton said. "Henry, you have been named—"

"My name is Hen."

Edgerton nodded and opened the folder. "Hen, as you know, you are the sole beneficiary of Sally Edith Hubbard's estate. According to her will, the trust will be put in your name one hundred percent when you turn eighteen which will be..."

"April twenty-six."

"Right. April twenty-six, 2002."

"That's almost a year away." The implied question—why have this talk now?—didn't need to be spoken.

"Right. However, your mother and I thought it best we have some of these meetings over the next few months to help you plan, as you'll be coming in to quite a large sum of money." He straightened his tie. "Though you'll legally be an adult, it's advised that certain controls continue for your estate."

Hen glanced at his mom, unsure what he meant. She'd abandoned her coffee and now bit her nails—a fairly new habit.

He turned back to Edgerton. "Controls?"

"So, Sally Hubbard—very wisely, I might add—put some stipulations in her will that dictated how the money would be invested over the years. Most of the funds were secure in a low interest-bearing account. But some funds were put into a diversified portfolio. This all was set up shortly after the will was executed, as you might remember, Mrs. Trout."

Marcella hugged herself and nodded quickly. Hen forced a cough, smudging out the words from the financial advisor. Because that's what they were at this point—words and nothing more. Hen didn't want to think about it. He didn't like how it upset Mom.

"We had lots of tech stocks which garnered you quite a lot of profit, and if you had cashed out a few years ago, you'd be golden. Unfortunately, no one can predict the future, although many experts saw it coming. With the Dot-Com bust of ninety-nine, you ended up losing money." Edgerton laughed, inexplicably.

Hen blinked at the man, who seemed to speak Cantonese. "I lost money?"

How could he lose something he hadn't yet been given?

"Well, all in all you're still sitting pretty with overall gain. But it's a pittance compared to what you would've had." He glanced from mother to son, cleared his throat. "It happened to everyone. Everyone lost money. No one's at fault here."

"Okay." Hen said, the word sounded like a question. "How much did I lose?"

"About fifty-thou." Cough. Then, softer, "Fifty thousand dollars."

Hen allowed himself a moment to let it sink in and felt nothing. How odd it didn't feel like a loss.

"What's the value of the trust now?" Marcella asked.

Edgerton shifted in his seat. "Right. As a reminder, the original value of the trust was $1.3 million. With the two percent compounded annually minus the ten percent of the diversified portfolio lost, the current value is a little over $1.6 million." His face flushed as he announced the number.

Hen looked at his mom, whose face reddened from the neck up.

The woman who never had it easy, working her fingers to the bone to care for her children. He remembered after the trial, after Ty went away to rehab, Mom cried all the time. It seemed like she'd never stop crying. She'd try to hide it from Hen but he always knew.

When Bernie moved in, it got a little better. That funny couple who eventually moved into Miss Sally's house offered some comic relief, with their pet pig Oscar who only went outside on warm days. And Hen would feed him carrot sticks and celery. That roly-poly oinker got Mom to laugh, but tinged with sadness. Only after they bought the motel and moved to Lake George did Mom seem to come alive a bit. And now this whole money inheritance thing set her back. Hen felt it wasn't worth it. He'd rather see Mom happy. Or, as happy as she could be.

"Yeah, one-point-six-mil. I'm sorry it's not more." Edgerton frowned.

"More?" Hen laughed. "That's more money than any of us could dream of."

Edgerton's eyebrows shot up hearing that, and Hen realized the man could and had dreamt of way more cash than a measly $1.6 million. Yet relief fell over his face. "You're right. Absolutely. It's quite a large sum, which is why we wanted to talk about controls."

"Right. Controls," Marcella chirped.

"Once you turn eighteen, Henry—I mean Hen—the estate will be in your name. It will be completely yours. One hundred percent. And you can do whatever you choose to do with it."

"But, Mr. Edgerton, you were saying. About the controls?" Marcella leaned so far forward, she nearly fell out of her seat.

"Well, sometimes the deceased names a trustee to manage the account, such as a parent or the bank. But Mrs. Hubbard didn't do that."

Marcella's high-pitched voice. "But we could set it up now?"

"N-n-n-not exactly. We can't make any changes to the trust until it's in Hen's name." Edgerton shrugged. Took a big breath. "So, Hen. Come next April, you have a big decision to make. What do you want to do with your money?"

Edgerton gave a wide grin. Hen, a pacifist by nature, felt an unexpected urge to slap it off his face.

CHAPTER 5

Marcella sat across from Hen at Olive Garden, nursing a bowl of minestrone and trying to resist the breadsticks. Though the restaurant always proved a good choice for Hen, Marcella pushed away slight revulsion at the gigantic portions served. Hen ate his chicken Alfredo with gusto, barely pausing to breathe.

She waited until he'd mostly cleaned his plate before asking, "What do you think? About what Mr. Edgerton said?"

Hen shrugged, reaching for a breadstick. Marcella marveled he wasn't yet full.

"No, seriously, Hen. It's my job as your mom to talk to you about this stuff." She cocked her head, an attempt at being stern.

Hen sopped up sauce so his plate shone. "I don't want you to worry about it. Any of it."

She grasped his free hand across the table and was struck by the sinewy strength of it. A man's. She let go quickly. "Oh, Hen. I'm not worried. I mean, maybe there's a little worry there. There's always worry when it comes to my child. And this is something we've known about for so long. Now that it's finally coming, I just think we should be prepared."

Hen nodded, chewing the enormous chunk of bread in his mouth. He wedged his hands under his thighs like he used to as a boy.

Marcella's heart swelled. Her soup long gone, she broke apart a breadstick in a dozen pieces, as if preparing to feed birds. "So, what do you think?"

"About?"

"About what he was saying. About what you'd like to do with your money. Have you thought about that?"

He held her gaze. The light coming in from the window made his wide eyes look so green, her breath caught. Such unconditional love in a single look. So handsome, almost unfathomable he held any of her DNA. She wondered how he saw her these days—not the heroic guardian of his childhood, but the broken, harried hack of a mom she really was, and continued to be. How could her heart be so full, loving Hen, while at the same time ache from the love he gave her?

His voice carried all that emotion and then some. "Can I give it to you?"

Marcella blinked at him. "Give me what?"

"The money," he said simply.

She palmed her chest, overwhelmed by a sudden rush there. "Hen, sweetie. You can't give me your money."

"Why not? You could use it. You probably need it, right?" He rocked in his seat, side to side, as if to a melody.

To Marcella, it was a song. "Oh, my goodness. That's not why I'm asking. I hope you don't think—"

"I know. I know you aren't asking me for it. Still, you can't tell me you don't need it."

"Hen, that's—"

"You certainly deserve it, after working so hard all these years."

Marcella's throat filled.

"For us," Hen added.

Silence floated to the table as Marcella realized Hen referred to Tyler too. Despite all that had happened, despite what Tyler had done, despite his incarceration for the past decade, Hen still included him in all this. He beheld him as a brother, honoring the bond of blood—even when that bond could have been severed years ago.

Sweet boy. Still sweet at seventeen. So different from his brother, it was heartbreaking. Here he spoke of what she deserved, while implicitly forgiving the person who upended his childhood. Never a harsh word for anyone. Bernie's voice inevitably came to her, unbidden: *Tyler got what he deserved.* A dark cloud flooded all the goodness and light Hen just gifted her.

Her lips parted. A noise came out—a start of something, but no words.

At this inopportune time, the waitress brought their check. Marcella slowly retrieved her wallet. As she put down her credit card, she couldn't meet Hen's bright, brilliant eyes anymore. Or hide the fact even this simple lunch was a splurge.

"Thanks, Mom," Hen whispered, respectfully turning toward the window, knowing.

After the waitress collected the billfold, she waited a moment before speaking. "Do you want to go to college, Hen?"

Hen propped his elbows on the table, his eyes downcast. "I haven't really thought about it."

"Okay, then. Is it something you *might* want to do?"

He chuckled. "I have no clue. Everyone's always asking about my future. I have my whole senior year ahead of me. I don't see why I have to decide everything now."

"You don't have to decide everything. But you're a good student. And you'd do well in college. If it's something you're interested in, then—"

"And the guidance counselor at school," Hen interrupted, picking up his string of thoughts. "He shoves these brochures at me and asks me what I might want to major in. How am I supposed to know what I want to do with the rest of my life? They say I should study science or maybe engineering. That a lucrative career will come from a major like that. All of a sudden everyone's concerned with how much money I'll make when I'm older." Hen shook his head.

Marcella smiled. "They don't know you have this gift—this inheritance, I mean."

"Well, what if I don't want it?" Hen sounded irritated. "What if it causes more problems than it's worth?"

A lifetime of struggle swirled in Marcella's memory like a destructive tornado. The constant fret over money, so strong it pulled her from everything else. How to pay the bills, how to keep the house warm and stocked with food, how to afford gas and keep her car running. She felt it in her entire body, for years, every muscle responding with cramps and tension. Maybe if she hadn't been so preoccupied about providing for her children, she would've seen the signs of Tyler's illness. She felt the darkness of depression threaten— right there in the restaurant booth.

She chose her words carefully. "No, Hen, it's impossible that the money will make things difficult. It will make your life easier, no matter what you decide to do with it."

"Even if I decide to give it to you?" Hen's eyes widened. Marcella hadn't thought they could get any bigger.

"I can't let you do that."

A shrug. "Mr. Edgerton said himself it was mine one hundred percent and I could do whatever the heck I wanted with it."

Was he testing her? He couldn't be serious. "I know but—"

"I could travel to Vegas and blow it all at the casinos, if I wanted."

She played along with his game now. "Right. But. That's why he spoke about those controls. You could appoint a trustee."

He flicked a hand at the window. "I could buy a fancy car and a boat and a penthouse, if I wanted."

Enough of this nonsense. "Hen."

"What?"

She forced a breath. "Nothing. That's all true. It's your money. You choose what you want to do with it."

"Would you rather me do all that zany stuff than give it to you, my mother who raised me? The person who deserves all the money in the world for all she's been through?"

Marcella kept her trembling hands under the table. "I just want you to give it some serious thought. It's your life and your future. This is an opportunity. You can go to college and travel and all of it— anything you want. You want to be smart about it, though. And I know you will be."

Hen leaned back, studying her. Marcella, self-conscious, broke eye contact. Until Hen's voice reached her. "Can I ask you a question, Mom?"

Mom. She'd never grow tired of hearing it.

"Of course."

"Does Tyler know?"

She raised up a smile. "Does Tyler know—what?"

"That I'm getting a bunch of money. From Miss Sally."

Heat climbed her neck as she searched for an answer. The words Tyler and Miss Sally didn't belong together. She'd worked hard to block their pairing from her psyche. Sickness filled her throat. Seconds ticked by in silence.

Hen tried again. "Does he know that when I turn eighteen, I'm basically a rich man?"

Marcella swallowed what felt like a tennis ball. "No."

She wanted to say it didn't matter if he knew. Assure Hen this had nothing to do with Tyler. The money was his and his alone, and Tyler shouldn't be a thought around it. But, of course, they both knew that wasn't the case. Tyler intruded on every thought, on each particle of their lives. It would be naïve to think he wouldn't be affected by whatever Hen decided. Tyler's existence alone colored their every reality.

Minestrone churned in Marcella's stomach, realizing the true weight of Hen's burden. It wasn't just his future to consider, it was Tyler's too—even if Hen took the money and ran. Tyler had to be considered in all this. They all did. As much as she wished it weren't true, she and Bernie could desperately use that money. Despair pressed hard on her shoulders.

In the next few beats, Marcella felt the roles reverse. She the teen and Hen the adult, an anchor of integrity giving more weight to the wiser one.

The billfold returned. Marcella quickly scribbled her name and stuck the receipt in her purse, feeling like an impostor.

"I wonder what he'd think," Hen said, and got up from the table, leaving so much unsaid.

After a moment, Marcella dutifully followed him out to her car, that fraudulent feeling stalking her.

CHAPTER 6

Ty awoke in complete darkness to what felt like a huge wet blanket smothering him onto the bed. Couldn't move.

A woman spoke to him—cooing and seductive one moment, lashing out at him the next.

Loser, she said. *You can't get away from what you did. It's stained you. Forever.*

When he was younger, it used to be a man's voice, gruff from years of smoking. Now, this woman. Not Marcella's voice. But one he recognized from his past. Even if she'd never use such language—on principle. Their old neighbor, Sally Hubbard, certainly had an ax to grind.

Ty turned on the lamp. He used only one inside the cabin. Artificial light reminded him of rehab. Fluorescent lights everywhere. So bright, they'd almost stung. Buzzed too. Like static. Sometimes, he heard Sally's voice in the sound.

You are evil. Scum! You will never be good. The devil is in your blood.

Got louder and louder. Until she became real and Ty knew she was real and listened. A big feeling grew inside him.

"I'm not a monster. I got help," he shouted, a sob erupting from his chest. "I'm better."

Cycles of laughter, in haunting echoes.

She left him only when the sun peeked through the curtain gap.

Then he slept.

He awoke four hours later, late for his shift.

"It's okay," Bill said on the line, his tone unusually gentle. "I figured you needed a couple days. I spoke to your social worker, Sheila Farris, and it's all set. Take the rest of the week. Maybe call me when you feel better and we can get you back on the schedule."

"You don't need me?"

"No, you're fine."

No, I'm not.

He took a cold shower and shaved quickly, nicking his chin. Pulled on his white collared shirt and khaki pants even though he didn't need his uniform. Had he left his superhero cape at the store, along with his nametag, **TYLER T**?

Ty had stretched the chicken cutlet over two days. Now out of food, he had to go out. Had to get food.

Through a two-inch gap in the curtains, Ty watched the world. There was Hen, shooting hoops on the ten-by-ten-foot square of cracked cement by the pool. He made it look easy. Ty began to count his shots. How many baskets could he get in a row?

One...two...three...four...

Miss.

Ty didn't like that, seeing the ball bounce off the rim. Hen seemed unfazed, dribbling and tricking it between his legs, dodging invisible defenders, and then shooting at foul-line distance. *Swoosh!*

Ty had never played sports, really. Clearly, Hen had basketball skills. He looked like a star athlete out there on that rinky-dink court. When did he start? Did he play on the team at school? Ty tried to picture it, Hen wearing a sports uniform.

"Yeah?" Hen shouted abruptly. Ty stepped back on reflex.

Marcella's voice, disembodied, calling to Hen from inside. Ty couldn't make out what she said.

One last shot, *swoosh*, and then Hen wedged the ball at his hip and headed inside, wiping his brow with the seam of his T-shirt.

With Hen gone, Ty watched other stuff. Marcella had been right. It had gotten busy. Real busy. Noise seeped into his cabin—holiday revelers and whatnot. So far, no one tried the pool. Probably not warm enough yet.

How long had he spent at the window? The big pane of glass, a computer screen. Everything wired from within. Too dangerous to go outside. Could trigger a circuit breaker. People will look at him. He might have to talk to someone.

A young girl—maybe five or six—carried a hula hoop to the pool fence, whining to her father, "Why can't I go swimming?"

"Because it's too cold."

"But I want to go swimming."

Over and over, back and forth. The girl had soft curls down her back and wore tiny shorts and a tank top. Her voice got louder as she stepped on the plastic tubing of her hula hoop, pinching it closed. Ty bit his lip. She was breaking the hula hoop. Didn't she know it would break if she kept stepping on it? She wouldn't be able to hula or swim. What would she do? Whine and complain forever. Maybe tears. Definitely a tantrum. Part of him felt like yelling at her to stop. Part of him really wanted to. But that meant opening the door and going outside.

Her foot pressed harder, and the plastic bent beyond the point of no return.

Ty closed the curtain gap and slunk into the gloom. Maybe he could go without food.

Knock, knock, knock.

How long had Ty been out of it? Had he slept? Did he take his pill? A sharp thirst sidelined him, and he scrambled to the mini fridge for a Gatorade. Of course, he was out.

Ty fell onto the bathroom sink, his mouth under the faucet gush. He drank and drank, filling his arms and legs and up into his brain.

Dizzy after, he slid into the armchair by the closet. Closed his eyes. Felt the water slosh through him.

Knock, knock, knock.

A computer glitch? Someone hacking in?

Knock, knock, knock.

Was that his door? His mother? Hope lifted. Did she bring him another hot meal? His stomach lurched. He sprang to the door, but stopped short—almost forgot it led *outside*.

Deep breath. Open just a crack.

What the—

Hen?

"Hey." His little brother held a brown bag of groceries, pushed the door open with it. "I'm sneaking you some food." With Hen all the way in now, the fourth wall collapsed. The wiring exposed. Ty stepped back, feeling lost.

Hen stood the bag on the dresser near the TV and went back out for a case of Gatorade. An entire case! Hen had an air of authority about him, like he did when he cleaned the cabins. Like he belonged.

Hen unpacked the groceries, calling out each item like an auctioneer.

"Ramen, yogurt, bagels, apples, peanut butter, bread, Pop-Tarts..."

As the items filled a corner of the room with color, Ty remembered the store. Hen spun around, folding the bags under his arm.

Ty watched him, agape.

Hen flicked the curtain, reinstating the gap. A laser beam shot through the room. Ty ducked from it.

"Dr. Asner told us we weren't supposed to do this, bring you groceries. You know, to empower you or whatever. But Mom couldn't help herself." A laugh. "You know Mom."

A fuzzy feeling came over Ty, hearing Hen casually refer to their mother. As if they were still yoked together as siblings.

You know Mom.

As if it were a magic word, Ty locked eyes with Hen. And his chest filled. Like little computer screens, a whole world lived inside Hen's eyes. Like Marcella's hazel color, but not.

A second passed, and then his eyes changed. Pity flooded the room and brought back the shame. Ty ripped his gaze away as a wave of heat rose from the floor.

"Speaking of Dr. Asner," Hen said softly. Urgently. "You know your weekly meetings with her are mandatory, right? Like, it was part of the deal when you got out. She's overseeing your treatment but also kind of like a probation officer."

Ty nodded, kind of.

"So, you can't really skip."

"Okay."

"Mom wanted me to remind you," he added, almost bashful.

And again: *Mom.*

Hen held his arms out, as if sizing up the place. "So, are you good? Is there anything else you need?"

Ty gave a brusque head wag. It answered both questions.

Hen only registered one. "Okay, then. You sure?"

Ty couldn't look at him anymore. He stepped deeper into the cabin. In the mirror, Hen dropped his polite half-smile as he surveyed the room that encompassed Ty's life. The sheets told most of the story. Unmade, unclean, turbulent, and cold.

Hen left quickly, mumbling a sort of goodbye.

Ty felt a loss instantly.

But at least now he had food.

CHAPTER 7

Though Bernie's legs felt heavy as lead, he helped Marcella clear the table. It had been a long day and Bernie spent most of it on his feet. He wanted to collapse on the recliner and watch sports but Marcella's silence through dinner told him she wanted to talk. He'd gotten used to that paradox.

She stacked the dishwasher aggressively, her mouth a tight line. Bernie slumped back into his seat. "What's wrong?"

"Nothing."

He waited, weighing his options. After a few minutes, he decided motel business would be neutral enough.

"After the Paulsens leave cabin five, we can't rent it."

Marcella twisted to face him, a platter poised to slide into the rack. "Why not?"

"Just for a day or so. I have to get in there and fix a clog in the tub."

Steam rose from the rush of hot water at the sink, misting around her hair like fairy dust. "Can't you do that as we turn it over? You know, while Hen cleans?"

"I have a feeling it's a bigger issue than a hair ball."

Marcella slammed off the water. "Great. Well, we're not having the plumber back. He charges eighty dollars just setting foot on the property."

"I'll take care of it."

She dried her hands on a dishtowel, her face taut. "Thank you."

Was that sarcasm in her tone?

Bernie nodded and searched for an escape. Uncanny how many of their fights played out like this. If it were a movie script, it would read fine. The words themselves, harmless. By now, Bernie knew better. She wasn't happy with him, and although he could guess as to why, he'd have to coax it out of her like tweezering a splinter.

He found what might be a balm out the window. "Let's go out to the pool."

Marcella's laugh held no mirth. "It's cold."

"We're not going to swim." He grabbed two Miller Lites from the fridge. "Come on."

Relief doubled down as her footsteps followed him out to the pool deck. The cool air felt good on his skin. He drew in a long breath.

Marcella rolled up her pants and dunked her feet at the edge. "Oooo, chilly."

He chuckled. "You knew it would be."

"Renters are complaining."

He joined her, wincing as his feet went in. "They do every Memorial Day weekend."

Marcella half-grinned. "I know. It's hardly ever warm enough to swim this early."

"It's warmer than the lake, though." He didn't speak his next thought, which of course Marcella shared: they needed a pool heater. It would be a good investment, if they had any money to invest. Maybe next year.

Slow kicks made the water clap.

"It's not so bad after a while," he said softly.

"Yeah." She sounded sad.

He glanced over to cabin eleven—the only unit with a clear view to the pool. The lack of light inside did not mean its tenant slept, Bernie knew. Tyler could very well be watching them. Aware of how water carried sound, he kept his voice low.

"I'm sorry about the other day. What I said."

"Oh, Bernie." She sighed and said nothing more. No forgiveness, apparently.

"Do you want to talk about it?"

She glared. "What do you think?"

What kind of question was that? Every bone in his body told him she wanted to talk. If it wasn't about Tyler, then what—

"Hen and I went to see Edgerton the other day."

"Ahh." He should know what that was. Or *who* that was. He should know the name. Edgerton, Edgerton...

She caught him. "Edgerton Investment Services?"

"Oh. Right." A punch to the gut left an ache no sip of beer could soothe. *This* was what she wanted to talk about? Hen's money? The money his own mother left to someone else? For years, they'd had an unspoken agreement not to talk about it.

He had always told himself it didn't matter. No amount of money could compete with his relationship with Marcella, not only the love of his life but actually his *life*. That never changed, how strongly he felt about her, how much he valued their relationship, which had been solid and strong and, frankly, quite beautiful since moving in together nine years ago.

But now, certain truths he felt best ignored came to surface. Hen would acquire his inheritance in a few months. An inheritance that, really, should be Bernie's. Another truth? One that only showed itself after Ma's death? Bernie had been kept from the family business for years, well after the death of his father, well into his adulthood. Even as he continued to prove more than able-bodied and willing. He'd always been a worker. Yet, his own ma kept him out of it. Kept him on the payroll, managing the piddly multi-family in Lake George while the bulk of their empire was run by—who?—*Ma*. That sweet old lady turned out to be quite the real estate mogul. And Bernie stayed on the fringe, ignorant.

Hard to push away resentment at that. First toward Ma, now toward Hen. He prayed he'd never feel that way toward Marcella.

He swigged more beer, but the ache persisted.

Marcella hadn't touched the drink he brought her. She watched him, waiting.

He had nothing to say.

"Don't you want to know what happened?" she asked.

It took him a moment to come back to the conversation string. Right, Edgerton Financial Services. Hen's fortune that should be his.

He tried to take a deep breath. "Not really."

Her eyes hardened on him. Reluctantly, he looked at her. Not good. All kinds of accusations hid there. "Do you all of a sudden hate my kids?"

That word—hate—hung in the air. She'd said it with such ferocity. Most likely, Tyler heard it too, all the way in cabin eleven.

Taken aback, he blurted, "No. No. Not at all."

Anger simmered. How could she ask such a thing? He had been there for Hen since his birth. And Tyler? Well, that was complicated. Shouldn't it be enough he respected how she felt about him? Respected the fact he was her son? It had been easy to love Hen, but he may never learn to love Tyler. It didn't mean he wouldn't try.

Regardless, Bernie had shown time and time again the extent of his dedication to her and her kids. If that wasn't love, he'd been a fool all these years.

He used his pet name for her, "Em—" but couldn't follow it, the warm feeling that typically accompanied it had cooled. "Please. That's a terrible thing to say."

Her words were quick. "You've said some terrible things lately."

After a moment, he tried again. "You're angry."

In a sudden gust, tears spluttered, and Marcella sobbed into her hands.

Shock made his movements slow. He wrapped his arm around her, and to his great relief she melted against him. The warmth of her went through him—and at once his feet in the pool seemed foolish and unseemly. Her body pulsed, each sob quaking through her. His heart broke as he held on tight. His love for her surged so strong, it could move mountains. He wanted to lift her up and take her away, magically smudging out all their problems forever.

Rather than try to shush her or say anything, he waited—how many torturous moments?—before she calmed, wiping her face on her sleeve.

Tyler had to hear all this, he thought fleetingly, secretly glad. Part of him believed Tyler was responsible for it.

"Do you know, when we went to lunch after? Hen said he wanted to give it to me."

Something swooped inside his gut. "Give you...the money?"

"Yeah. Can you believe that?"

Bernie rubbed her back, letting it sink in. Any bitterness he felt fell away, replaced by a bloom of affection for Hen. What a kid. What a great kid.

He chuckled to himself. "Wow."

"I know. At first I thought he wasn't thinking it through. Or he didn't realize what kind of doors it might open for him. But then he asked about Tyler. If he knew."

"Oh." Darkness returned, and Bernie's hand froze mid-caress.

"Once again, he's smarter than I give him credit for. He knows what this money can do. He knows it will change everything. And Tyler—"

Tears started again. Bernie hugged her to him.

"It's supposed to be a good thing," she said brokenly.

He held her. Said nothing.

"It's supposed to help. We should be thankful. Grateful. It should make all our lives easier."

His jaw set, he turned toward the pool. The water, so crystalline blue earlier today, seemed a liquid shadow. He waited. She wasn't done.

"But, you know what? It's going to be a problem." Tears started again. "It already is."

He held her and said nothing, feeling his own troubles like chronic pain.

CHAPTER 8

F riday night, Hen took his bike down to Wesley's place near the Bolton Road turnoff. They planned to play some basketball and then hang out in the village—hit the arcade and get some pizza. Typical Friday night stuff.

Staying on the right side meant he had to cross busy Canada Street twice, but he'd gotten good at navigating traffic over the past four years. It was easier than driving, sometimes. As he pumped the pedals under the streetlights, he remembered how Tyler taught him to ride a bike. Like a trailer for a movie, images came through. Colorful fallen leaves blanketed the earth. Sun high and bright, but not giving much heat. Shedding his backpack and saddling the bike, knowing Tyler would make it safe. Hen laughed into the wind as he found his balance—a miracle with no training wheels. What a day. Halloween, if Hen remembered it right...

That's when the memory soured.

Hen shook it off and crossed Canada Street again. Almost to Wesley's.

The fact that Wesley's folks also owned a motel had bonded them as friends when Hen first moved to Lake George. The new kid at a small-ish school (though not nearly as small as Schroon Lake), he had an automatic in with a group of kids whose parents owned businesses in the village. When Wesley found out Hen's family purchased Blue

Palms, he high-fived him, and that was it. Aside from the huge, obvious difference in their situations.

Wesley's motel, Lakeside Inn, sat directly on the water and had not just a pool but a hot tub, tennis court, and—Hen's favorite—a regulation-size basketball court. Clearly a major step up from Blue Palms. Heck, all the tourism brochures called it a *resort*. Most of their renters came from New York City and tipped an entire twenty dollars just for bag delivery. It attracted wealth, which showed in Wesley's clothes and his never-ending spending money and the blue sports car he shared with his brother.

"'Bout time." Wesley waited by the neon motel sign. He wore jeans, a button-down, and loafers.

"Thought we were playing hoop first."

"Yeah, but then we'd get all sweaty and gross. And all the girls would run from us."

"Girls?" Hen laughed, but Wes didn't smile. As Hen got closer, he caught a whiff of cologne. Clearly, Wes had certain ideas about how the night would go. Hen considered his T-shirt and gym shorts as he pulled his bike into the breezeway, hiding his disappointment.

They headed toward the village on foot. Wesley nearly skipped, hopped up on adrenaline. "Look at this! After that long suck of winter, everything's alive. Man, I love it. Everything's open and lit up, like it's a legit city."

Wesley had the gift of gab, more energy than AA batteries, and could make a miser laugh his head off. Which all helped him get attention from girls, making up for his saucer-like ears that stuck out. He walked with gusto, throwing in a random dance move. He was a constant source of amusement. Hen's grin never let up.

With Hen his captive audience, Wesley talked nonstop. "How crazy is it we're still in school? I mean, there should be a rule. No school after Memorial Day. How are we supposed to get anything done now that the weather is sunny and warm and the village stores are open and tourists are coming in and pretty girls are lining the streets?"

Hen laughed. "Girls aren't lining the streets."

Wesley whopped his chest. "You know what I mean."

"Yeah. School seems kinda pointless right about now." In more ways than one, for Hen. With Miss Sally's inheritance hanging over his head, everything that made up his life—school, basketball, cleaning cabins, helping Mom—seemed about to disappear. Like a bad prank, a fortune waited for him, yet he had only seven dollars in his pocket.

The arcade felt like a casino. Bright and noisy and intoxicating, even if it smelled like the inside of a sneaker. Hen spent four dollars exactly, saving the rest for pizza. He played his usual pinball, then Pac-Man, and contented himself to watch Wesley play the more high-end, expensive games. Then they headed back up the strip to Capri for a slice.

Too busy to sit inside, they took their slices on flimsy paper plates across to Shepard Park, and ate on a bench facing the beach. Salty pizza made Hen thirsty. His mouth watered as Wesley chugged his Mountain Dew.

"Man, what kind of music is that?" Wesley wiped Dew from his peach fuzz mustache.

Hen shrugged. Shepard Park hosted live music every Friday night. Usually a throwback band covering seventies tunes, this one seemed too punk for the village crowd. The lack of any identifiable beat kept the dance area empty.

"Well, look at you two. How romantic."

Hen saw her before Wesley, and his partially digested pizza cut into his sides. Bianca Chase, who lived on the back streets, made it her mission to not only know the goings-on but *be* the goings-on. As if she owned the village. One of those girls who knew she was cute but needed people to keep telling her, she'd developed somewhat of a reputation at school. Guys who gave her attention expected something in return—something in private Hen was glad never to witness. But it seemed a pitiful, never-ending cycle, and Hen wanted nothing to do with it.

"Bianca." Wesley sang, leaping from the bench.

She sauntered to him, tugging on the strap of her tank top, which looked more like a bathing suit. Hen fought an uneasy feeling.

A few years ago, when Hen first moved to Lake George, this same girl showed off her pink Tamagotchi pet to anyone who'd listen. She took it so seriously, this pixelated, imaginary creature. Like, she fed it and gave it medicine if it were sick, cooing at the tiny screen. At the time, it seemed childish and a little pathetic—her best friend a digital pet. Now, he saw it as innocent and kind of sweet.

She'd changed quite a bit since then.

Bianca took Wesley's soda, screwed off the cap and drank, a challenging look in her eyes. Wesley didn't stop her. Hen felt an incongruous loss. He would've killed for a sip.

"What's going on tonight?" Wesley asked, his suggestive tone making Hen want to disappear.

"Some people are up on the catwalk. Keith said he was bringing beer."

"Ah."

Hen's spirits lifted, hearing that name. It was their out. Keith, Bianca's latest conquest, could win a ribbon for Biggest Jerk on the Planet. He and Wesley agreed on that much.

But when Wesley reached for his soda, Bianca yanked it away, and he accidentally touched her breast. Hen's breath caught, seeing it. Not entirely Wesley's fault. Bianca had large breasts. Another big change since the Tamagotchi days...and the other thing people talked about at school.

"Sorry, sorry." Wesley's face went red.

Bianca cracked up as if he'd told one of his famous jokes. Hen felt his own face go flush as the laughter went on and on. No longer an inkling, he felt downright uncomfortable now.

Bianca back-stepped, putting herself at a distance to simulate a stage, and began to dance. The punk music immaterial, she found her own beat. She swayed and pulsed and gyrated, waving Wesley's soda around like she was flag dancing.

Hen and Wesley exchanged a look. Hen pleaded with his eyes, *let's go*, but Wesley had other ideas. Just as he'd danced along the street earlier, he sashayed to Bianca as if they were at a school dance. They had a strange sort of privacy. There were probably a hundred people out by the amphitheater, yet they had the beach strip totally to themselves.

Hen's mouth fell open as he watched his best friend not only dance with this girl, but actually put his hands on her hips. A kind of relief came when she shoved him away. Short-lived, though.

She said, "I want you to watch."

Now, Hen was a pawn in her game. He had no choice but to watch, too, and that's exactly what she wanted. Dread closed in as she moved before them, gliding the plastic soda bottle seductively across her cleavage, at her waistline, at the zipper of her shorts. Wesley whistled next to him, a catcall of sorts. Hen tasted bile. This was not how he thought the night would go.

"Show me what you got," Wesley said, in a voice Hen didn't recognize.

Bianca licked the air, then the bottle cap. Hen's eyeballs quivered. How did he end up here, doing this, watching this girl, feeding into all the yucky stuff that built her reputation at school?

A few years back, she was a cute little kid with a pink Tamagotchi. And now she was big-breasted, humping a bottle of Mountain Dew?

"Oh, yeah, baby," Wesley called, in one of his comical voices. The way his hips rocked the bench, it was no joke. Hormones had taken over his best friend, making him some kind of drooly ogre, obsessed with Bianca's boobs.

The music shifted and kicked up a notch, and Bianca danced faster, tossing her hair like a wild animal. It had to stop. Hen had to do something. His pulse raced, and an urgency filled his veins.

Before he thought it through, he was on his feet, dancing and spinning and tossing what would be his hair if it were long enough. He flapped his elbows and thrust his chin, leaping around in a circle.

Bianca saw an opportunity—a dance partner! His sensors keen, he felt her moving closer, oozing sex and breasts and musky perfume. Hen spun away from her, dancing and flailing like a maniac. Until she gave up and froze on her feet.

The stage had shifted to Hen. He kept dancing like a fool, not caring about anything except diverting any hint of sex from the atmosphere. A puzzled half-grin made Bianca look like the young girl who loved digital pets all over again.

Abruptly, the music stopped. A loaded silence filled the air. Then, the squeak of feedback from an amp, a muffled announcement about the band. Whatever. No one listened. Hen was breathing hard. The other two stood nearby, the trio making an obtuse kind of triangle.

"So, are you going to the catwalk?" Wesley asked Bianca, more curious than suggestive.

Her eyes flicked to Hen, then to the ground. "No. I don't really want to see Keith right now. Or ever, really."

Hen wanted to say *I don't blame you*, but he kept quiet.

"I think I'm just gonna go home." She looked up at Hen and held his gaze. Her round brown eyes shone in the street lights, her full lips slightly open, and they all seemed transported to more innocent days.

Hen and Wesley exchanged another look, one softer than before.

"Come on," Hen said, still out of breath. "We'll walk you home."

CHAPTER 9

Ty's threadbare khakis were slick with grease inside and out. Yellow stain near the collar of his white shirt. The shower hadn't been used for days. Maybe three? Since Hen brought food.

Days passed behind the glass, in his own personal computer of cabin eleven.

A vague recollection of Sheila coming to see him, standing in the doorway, backlit like a mirage. She stood there longer than he liked. He didn't remember what she talked about but could hear her voice. A woman's voice unlike the other woman's voice—Sally's—who called him names.

Sheila wouldn't do that.

Motel was busy on the other side. Must be Friday. Another weekend underway. Renters loaded and unloaded beer and suitcases from their cars. People swam in the pool now. Always people hanging around. Lots of noise. Music and loud talking and lots of traffic. No hula hoops anywhere anymore, though.

Ty took his pill with faucet water, craning to drink. And almost gagged on it. Stuck in his throat. Watched the clock, kept swallowing, but it stuck. Twenty minutes. Thirty. Still felt clogged.

Panic set in. Ty pulled at his hair. Would it work if it didn't go down? He shook the bottle near his ear and that sinking feeling he ignored yesterday returned. He shook it again. No rattle. He shook it again. Empty.

Out of meds. That was his last pill. And it didn't even go down.

No fighting it anymore. He'd have to go out into the jungle. He'd have to leave cabin eleven.

His movements were sloth-slow, peeling off his clothes and stepping into the shower—the water hot-hot-hot. But he stayed, burning in the rush of it.

Shaving hurt after so many days. He wondered how he'd look with a beard. It never grew in evenly. Did his dad ever have facial hair? His gut hitched, thinking of his dad. Like someone he had seen on TV as a sitcom guest star. When did he see him last? He was long dead now. Killed himself by accident, they said. His father was lost in those dark memories, before Ty got help.

Ty pulled on his old sweats.

The sun high in the sky reminded him of the overhead lights at rehab. One big dome of light in the middle of the room made things too bright with no place to hide. The sun was like that sometimes.

Safer to wait. Maybe in a little while he'd go and figure out how to refill his prescription. Computers had the answer. Marcella had filled the first and only bottle he'd had since his release. At a pharmacy where special computers had all the information about medicine and his illness. Dr. Asner said to trust those computers because they helped keep him safe. She said it was the best way to make sure no one gave him the wrong kind of pill by accident.

His dad had an accident like that, with pills. Ty didn't want that to happen to him so he had to believe Dr. Asner. But he didn't think he could really trust any kind of computer since the Y2K crisis still loomed.

Then, an idea.

Maybe he didn't need his meds anymore. He'd been feeling pretty good. Then he wouldn't have to bother going anywhere.

Out the window, he saw Marcella's car parked in her usual spot. Bernie's truck too. No trace of Hen's cleaning bin.

People went in and out of the office without bothering to close the door. Mosquitoes surely flew in every time. The office was probably full of them. Marcella too busy to swat them away. Bites on her ankles would itch at night and she would scratch subconsciously, maybe with her toes. Tomorrow, red welts would appear above her shoes.

Beyond overwhelmed, he decided to lie down just for a minute...

HE AWOKE IN COMPLETE DARKNESS. But could hear no voice. And no wet blanket weighed him down. He bounded out of bed in a kind of celebration. Short lived. Darkness meant night, which meant pharmacies were closed. Computers powered down—the ones that held all the information about his medicine. A sign from the universe he was okay. Better. He didn't need meds anymore.

He already felt more alert, more alive. Lots of energy. He shoved the curtains open all the way. Gazed out, fists on hips, a roiling heat rising in his chest. He wanted to crash through the window and holler at the stars.

His breath made a circle of steam on the glass. He wiped it away and noticed Bernie's truck wasn't in the parking lot. Marcella's car was there. Also some other—a rundown two-door, an old Mazda maybe—parked in the visitor spot, the one reserved for check-ins and stuff.

Something about the car made Ty perk up. His hair stood on end. Something about that car bugged him.

From cabin eleven, he saw through the tempered glass window to the office, which was attached to the home where Marcella and Hen lived with Bernie.

Only shadows visible. Two. One, a huge black mass—some guy. Definitely a guy. A big dude. The other? Slight. Thin. A pouf of hair. Had to be Marcella. A stirring in his chest, seeing the shadowed wisp of her.

Like a computer on the fritz, the screen showed ghost-like images. Digital waves trying to form into something meaningful.

Seemed like they talked—the shadows. Maybe about reservations? Though quiet settled on the property, Ty knew the motel was fully booked. The talking went on a long time. Too long? The motel had been buzzing all day but now seemed too calm. It must be very late.

Ty's pulse raced, blood pumping his veins.

What's this person doing in the office?

Marcella raised her voice, pointed to the exit behind him. *Please leave*, he imagined her saying, in a firm voice she'd use on Ty, back in Severance. Back when he was a kid. When she'd try to be stern.

But the guy didn't budge. Moved in closer, even. His shadow looked like a gorilla's. A dark, hulking mass in that small office. He took up all the space.

Ty should go out to help.

His legs were stuck.

A sudden movement made the tempered glass shimmer—grays and tans and blacks morphing together and splitting apart. Light peeking, shining through the angled glass.

Marcella flinched back with a yelp. Ty heard it all the way in his cabin. Was she surprised? Or scared?

Was she in trouble?

Her shadow cowered behind the counter.

Then, the computer got hacked. Programmers hadn't planned for this.

So familiar, Ty had been there before.

The gorilla towered over his mother, blocking his view of her. A thick arm raised—Thor with his giant hammer—and came crashing down.

The trembling went through Ty's limbs. No, he hadn't been here. But at Sally's. At Miss Sally's when—

Blood-curdling screams. Marcella's, echoing across the lot.

Definitely not the work of programmers. Something had shorted. Was this the Y2K crisis? Was he witnessing history? Was his mother the target?

A death-cold chill went through Ty.

No, not Y2K. Wildlife had taken over. Gorilla hunched over her, arms flailing. What was he doing?

Wild animals cannot be tamed just as computers cannot have feelings.

Gorilla was helping himself to a meal. Greedy and hungry and wild.

A feral energy raged inside him, his blood pulsing hot. Ty felt it so acutely. His shoulders swelled with strength as primal heat and sweat built beneath his clothes. Like he'd become the beast himself. His breathing got ragged, ready to roar.

Everything swirled. Ty felt dizzy. Images of Sally on the floor. A frantic voice nearby: *What the heck did you just do?*

What did he do? What did he do?

Was this real? Or was his brain tricking him again?

He blinked and blinked. Rubbed his eyes. Still, the gorilla loomed over his mother.

Oh, no. That pill never made it into his bloodstream. His mind had spun loose. His personal computer on the fritz. His sickness made him see things. Made him see *this*. This gorilla shadow thing.

Not real. Not real.

But he felt it still. That beast inside him—a raging bull. Miss Sally was a victim. And now Marcella, too.

Gorilla shadow made small movements, clunky through the tempered glass.

He waited. His crackly breaths cut through the quiet.

Still no voices. He expected them to come, but no. Quiet felt wrong, after what he'd seen.

Nausea made his knees buckle. The window fogged with his breath again. A sour smell. He hated himself so much right now. A fresh, new kind of hatred. But why? Why now?

Gorilla shadow walked out the door, to the outside. And turned into a guy. A large guy with a black hood, folding himself into the Mazda. Like he had to stuff himself in.

Wait. He was real?

But, what happened? Where was Marcella? Where did her shadow go?

He blinked and blinked, trying to think. Staring at the shimmery window, wishing it were a clear, smooth pane of glass. The Mazda zoomed out of the parking lot, a flash of orange at the rear. It turned toward the village, leaving skid marks on the pavement.

In a moment, the beast left Ty's body. Like it never was there. A hollow panic filled his body now.

So...

He thought hard.

Was it real, then? Who was that? Wait—

Ty couldn't make sense of it. But the ache in his chest and limbs signaled bad news. And he couldn't get the image of Miss Sally out of his head. On the floor, in a puddle of her own blood.

Calm settled over the property again. Quiet.

Okay. Quiet was good. Right? Everything's okay?

Still, he couldn't tear himself from the window. Eyes wide. He stayed there, sweating and panting and shaking all over—his vision going fuzzy from not blinking.

Flashing lights. Siren—loud and long buzz through the airwaves. Computer reboot.

Ty blinked like mad. His heart rate picked up in a different way.

Two police cars pulled in to the lot, which triggered Ty, like unearthing a dead root. They parked. Siren cut out. Programmers had identified the problem, caught the hackers, working the code to fix it.

Lights flashed and rotated, spinning disco colors—blue and red— against the wall of motel cabins.

Two officers rushed out of their patrol cars. Seeing them in uniform ignited something within Ty, and his heart went to his throat. Heat shot up and down his legs, which itched to move.

Outside. The cool air hurt his eyeballs. Cabin eleven's door closed and locked behind him. Did Ty have his key? Didn't matter.

He had to mitigate the Y2K crisis. Help the programmers. They had sent their signal. It blazed across the lot.

He ran, shocked at his behavior—seeing himself as if from a bird's-eye. His ankles throbbed and the pads of his feet stung. He'd forgotten to put on shoes. No stopping now. He ran toward the lights with his hands in the air.

"Hey!" he called, a grunt.

One of the two officers paused, turned to him—hand on his holster.

"It was me!" Ty shouted, his voice croaky and hoarse from underuse. "It was me!"

CHAPTER 10

Hen walked beside Wesley, sluggish with fatigue. It was late. They'd been on their feet for hours, covering the same square mile of the village. Bianca thanked them about a hundred times as they escorted her home, surprised anyone would make that kind of effort. To be kind. To her.

"Don't you ever get curious?" Wesley asked, the village far behind them. Even his voice sounded tired.

"About what?"

A snicker. "About sex."

Sleep, not sex had not been on Hen's mind. "Sure. I guess."

"I mean, Bianca would have."

"Would have what?" Their time with her had already become a memory.

"You know, fooled around with us. I mean, you know, one of us."

A few steps in silence. Hen contained his shock and disgust, and kept his eyes on the sidewalk. Almost to Lakeside Inn.

"I'm not interested in fooling around with Bianca," he said.

"Yeah, but. She would."

Hen dug deep to find the right words. "Exactly why I wouldn't want to."

Wesley studied him. "You're funny."

"No, I'm not. You're the funny one."

"No, I mean. You're different. Anyone else would have taken Bianca to third base tonight. But you? You walked her *home*."

"So did you. We both did."

"Yeah, but." Wesley didn't have to finish. Still, Hen didn't want to hear that Wesley wanted to hook up with Bianca just because people said she was easy. He didn't want to believe his best friend would do that.

"We both did," Hen said again.

Neon lights on the Lakeside Inn sign made Hen squint as he retrieved his bike from the breezeway. Wesley yawned through a high-five goodbye and then went in to his house without another word.

Hen thought to call home but his cell was out of charge. Just weighing down his pocket now. He sighed and started the jaunt home. Felt like the Tour de France up the hill to Blue Palms. At least he could stay on one side and not cross Canada Street—

What the—?

Blue and red lights flashed as he crested the hill. At first, he thought—car accident. But the lights came from the motel's parking lot. Blue Palms.

His heart thundered as he pumped faster, different scenarios popping to mind. He pushed away the worst and told himself it was nothing. A renter got rowdy, maybe broke something or got in a fight or—

"It was me! It was me!"

He knew that voice. Sleep far away now, Hen zoomed his bike into the lot. Just in time to see Tyler standing beyond the patrol car with his hands in the air.

"Sir, stay where you are, sir," the cop said to Tyler. "Do not come any closer."

Tyler obeyed, keeping his hands up. He looked like death warmed over, standing there in his socks and grubby clothes. His eyes were sunken craters, his skin ashen and waxy-looking. An ambulance siren sounded in the distance, getting louder, coming closer.

Hen hopped off his bike. "Officer? What's going on here?"

Now to Hen. "Stay where you are. Do not come any closer." The cop had both arms airplaned out, panic on his features.

"I live here," Hen said, his hands up too. Blood roared in his ears.

"Hen!" Tyler called, wide-eyed-alert. "Go to her!" A side nod toward the office. "Go to her!"

Hen's stomach sunk. "Who? Mom?" His voice cracked. "Officer, please."

The cop waved him through as the ambulance pulled into the lot. The siren was deafening now. Everything spun with sudden chaos. He rushed to beat the paramedics in to the office.

"Mom? Mom!"

Curled on the floor, cradling the cordless phone, Mom held a blood-drenched towel over one eye. The other streamed a river of tears. She gazed up at Hen, unseeing.

Another police officer stood behind the desk, mumbling into his walkie-talkie.

"What happened? Who did this to you? Where's Bernie?" Fury sliced through Hen. Tyler's voice echoed in his mind: *It was me! It was me!*

"Move aside, son." The paramedic shoved him to the wall. While another snapped open a gurney.

"Wait." Panic shot through Hen's chest. "She needs a stretcher? What the heck—"

As a medic eased Mom onto the gurney, she handed Hen the cordless phone. "Bernie's at the Johnson's up in Severance." Her voice surprisingly calm. "Finishing some deck work. Call him. Tell him what happened."

"What happened?" Hen hadn't meant to shout, but it burst out. "What happened?"

He followed, frantic, as they wheeled her toward the ambulance. So focused on his mother, he missed Tyler getting handcuffed. But Mom saw—

"Wait. What's going on? Why is my son being arrested?" She pushed up on her elbows. The medic eased her back down.

Hen looked from Mom to Tyler, the cordless a pointless prop in his hand. He wanted to throw it in the pool. *What the hell?*

The first police officer led Tyler toward his patrol car. "This young man confessed."

"What? No!" She tried to get up again. No use. Medic strapped her in—across her shoulders, hips, ankles. "He didn't do it," she said miserably, wagging her head, trying to kick.

Tyler didn't resist. The cop opened the door, and he climbed into the back seat.

"He didn't do it!" Mom, hysterical now. "Listen to me! I can give a statement or description right now. Stop this. Please! I *saw* my attacker."

Her words cut through Hen. Her *attacker*? He felt like he might puke.

His mother was attacked? Right here at the motel? While he was hanging out in the village with Wesley? Walking Bianca home? Guilt stung and rendered him immobile.

"Please. He didn't do it." She repeated over and over, fading as she tunneled into the ambulance.

"You riding with us?" the second medic asked. It seemed a different language. Hen blinked at him. Oh, would Hen ride with Mom to the hospital? Every cell of his body wanted to. If he weren't holding the stupid phone, he would have. But she wanted him to call Bernie. Stay here at the motel. Smooth things over. Already, renters lingered outside their cabin doors, stunned curiosity keeping them up.

Hen wagged his head, his heart breaking into pieces. "I'll be there as soon as I—"

"Stop it! I mean it!" Mom's voice cut out as they closed and locked the back door of the ambulance.

As it pulled out of the parking lot, siren starting up again, Hen noticed black tire treads marking the pavement at the entryway. His gaze pinned there, he almost missed the cop car rolling past him. Where Tyler sat in the back seat. They met eyes, and Tyler's went wide. His lips moved. Trying to tell him something. Hen couldn't make it out. Part of him didn't want to, his thoughts darkening toward his brother. Tyler nodded urgently and mouthed it again, whatever it was.

Hen tore his eyes away as they filled. A shock of rage, like a branding iron on skin, came over him. The cop car pulled out, following the ambulance toward the highway.

An eerie calm fell over the motel grounds.

Hen forced a breath. It took every ounce of his courage to turn and face the cabins, and the tenants standing there, watching.

"So sorry for the disturbance, everyone." He hoped no one noticed his voice tremble. "Everything's going to be just fine. You can all go back to bed now."

Pivoting away, Hen made a beeline for the office. His hands shook as he looked up the Johnson's number in Mom's paisley address book. It rang for ages before anyone picked up. He had no idea what to say to whoever ans—

"Bernie. Something's happened. It's Mom. She's hurt. Come home."

Miraculously, Hen managed to hang up before the tears came. But they didn't let up the rest of the night.

CHAPTER 11

Marcella continued her rant the entire way to Glens Falls Hospital. "They can't arrest Tyler. He didn't do it. He's my son." But the EMTs completely tuned her out, as if she were a barking dog. So, she barked louder. And promptly vomited all over herself. Only then did she get their attention. But not the kind she wanted.

By the time she was admitted into the emergency room, her voice barely worked—sore and hoarse from overuse and stomach acid. All the people in scrubs told her to rest.

Fine. For now. She'd been barking up the wrong tree, the thought finally struck her. The police who handcuffed Tyler and took him away—that's who she needed to talk to. Where did they take him? Why did they arrest him?

Fatigue sapped her fight. Her eye hurt. Blood still seeped from her wound. Incredible how quickly they stitched her up. Even more incredible it only took a half-dozen stitches. Judging from the amount of blood, it seemed her head had nearly been severed.

"You'll have a scar," the doctor said after, unmistakable remorse in his voice. Even the nurse gave her an apologetic look as she cleaned her up.

Marcella wouldn't have it.

"I don't care about a stupid scar." Her words barely audible, she pressed on. "Who can I talk to about my son?"

No answer.

"Is there a detective? Someone investigating?"

The nurse patted her hand. "We're taking care of you first, honey. Don't worry about anything else."

Infuriating, people telling her not to worry. Always people were telling her that—her therapist, Bernie, even Hen sometimes. Dr. Asner and Sheila. What the hell? She was a MOM. A mom with a mentally ill adult son whose recent release from institutional rehab now seemed a temporary reprieve, seeing him taken away in handcuffs. All the warnings Dr. Asner had given her. All those strict obligations as his caretaker. She'd failed. Miserably. How could it be so hard to keep your adult son safe? How could he so quickly slip back into the iron arms of the legal system—a system which had no understanding of who he was or how his brain worked?

Worry rippled through her whole body, a stinging torture.

No, please no. Not again.

Pain shot through her midsection. It had nothing to do with her head injury.

Without warning, she vomited again. The nurse, quick with the basin, caught most of it. Still, it accelerated her admission to a room where they changed her into a hospital nightie as if she were an invalid.

"No getting out of bed, honey." To reinforce, they put up the side rails and hooked her up to an IV and some other beeping machine. What—did they really think she'd make a run for it? Even her bones felt sluggish. Her blood thick and heavy. She couldn't move if she wanted to. And—gosh—they must have stitched her too tightly up there on her forehead because she had a searing headache. The laser beam they shot into her eyes didn't help. Marcella flinched from it.

"It's just light. I'm checking your pupils, honey."

The nurse went on to say something about having to wait for the equipment to be ready. The doctor ordered some sort of scan to check her for a concussion. Apparently, vomiting after a head injury was a symptom.

No, she wanted to say, *I'm upset. I got worked up. That's why I barfed. Totally understandable, considering...*

But she didn't say a thing. Frankly, she feared getting sick again. They got her to drink some sugary water, gave her a painkiller, and told her to rest. Somehow, the room still buzzed with activity after everyone left.

I'll never sleep, she told herself as her eyes grew heavy.

"Tyler," she whispered to the ceiling, a prayer, before her eyes closed and sleep came for her.

MARCELLA WOKE to Bernie hovering over her bed. It took a moment to realize she wasn't home but in the hospital. Then, all the pieces of the puzzle flew together in a mad rush—the attack, Tyler's arrest, the awful ride to the hospital.

Her heart raced with panic. "Oh, Bernie. Where's Tyler? We have to get him out—"

"Hush now, Em. No one's going anywhere. Tyler is safe."

"But they arrested him."

Bernie looked pained. "You have a head injury, Em. They take that stuff pretty seriously around here. As they should." He leaned closer. She smelled paint and turpentine on his skin. It stung her nose. "I'm so sorry, Em. I'll never forgive myself for not being there." When he stroked her hair, it felt like a rubber mallet to her skull.

She groaned in pain, and Bernie reared back. He shot out of his chair to call the nurse.

"No, it's okay," she managed. "Sit. I'm fine."

"You are not fine." He flicked tears off his face. He was crying? "I can't believe someone did this to you." He spoke to his fists.

"I'm okay." She softened toward him, taking some water from the cup he held out.

A tray of food materialized. "Let's get some food in you."

"I'm not hungry. Where's Hen?"

"He's keeping an eye on things at the motel."

"What's happening at the motel?"

He spooned some applesauce. "Normal stuff. Don't worry about it. Hen's got it all under control."

A tart-sweetness slid down her throat. Made the words easier. "Did he speak to the police?"

"Not sure. I think maybe."

Another spoonful. "What did he say?"

"Probably exactly what he said to me. But I don't want to talk about that." Putting down the spoon, he spoke quietly. "I don't want you to either. I don't want you thinking about anything but getting better. Then, you can tell me everything. And we can figure out what to do about it."

"I need to talk with the police. Where are they? Why haven't they come to talk to me?"

"They were here, but the doctors sent them away."

"Why?"

A sigh. "Em, you have a head injury. They're not going to—"

"It wasn't Tyler."

He shifted, grimacing. "I don't want to hear it." His voice sounded strange.

"They arrested him and they shouldn't have. It wasn't Tyler."

His eyes went wide as they met hers. "He confessed, Em! He came out saying, 'It was me!' to the cops. What were they supposed to do?"

"No, he didn't."

A heavy sigh. "Yes, he did. That's why they took him."

"Why would he do such a thing?"

He clamped his mouth shut, his eyes going dark.

She scrambled to find reason. "He was confused. He didn't know. Maybe he was trying to protect me."

Bernie shook his head, jaw clenching.

It smacked her consciousness. "*You* don't think...you wouldn't.

Don't you dare." Marcella fought against her own tears. "And don't tell me no. You weren't there. It wasn't him."

"I'm not telling you no. I just—"

"We have to do something about it. Now!" She wanted to scream. "I can't wait for the doctors to figure out I'm fine. I don't want Tyler spending a second in jail. Not a single second."

He let out a long breath. "Okay. I'll go see what I can do."

"No. I want to do this. If they won't let me out, bring the cops in here. Or detectives, I guess. I have a statement to make."

"Okay. I'll see what I can do."

Something snapped inside of her. "Not good enough. *I'll see what I can do.* Do it."

Bernie paused, his eyes flatlined. She'd never spoken to him in such a way. Even *she* heard the cruelty in her voice.

He left without another word. Incredible how soundlessly he could move, how uneventful his exit could be. Marcella couldn't care less he didn't say goodbye.

CHAPTER 12

"For three hundred M&Ms," Ty mumbled, his brain firing. Hack gone wild. Flash of orange. Lights blazing, siren howling.

The room in which he sat felt familiar. Not a comfortable feeling.

Last night, the cot he'd slept in also felt familiar. Used to be his lifeboat. It had saved him from sharks back then. Now, just a cot.

The whole night, he held on to the secret code, waiting to deliver it to the appropriate person. He didn't know how to code. Computers eluded him. Other people would know what to do.

After he'd eaten some oatmeal, they'd brought him here, in this square room with no windows. A few wooden chairs around a wooden table. Sparse. Not very clean.

He'd been arrested for his mother's assault. He understood this. This wasn't the important thing, though.

He hadn't taken his pill today. It had been over twenty-four hours since he had his meds. Maybe longer. He knew the upshot—the dire result—of this fact. Waiting for what might happen in his mind—or what already happened?—overwhelmed every thought. Concentrating on the questions from the guy in a brown suit proved difficult.

But maybe this was the tech guy who knew what to do. How to fix the hack.

He said it again. "For three hundred M&Ms."

What can you tell me about last night? Do you remember when you left your motel room? Did you hear or see anything that made you go into the office?

In between the questions he sang inside his mouth, humming a few notes like a song stuck in his head. Maybe this wasn't the tech guy after all.

Finally, exasperated: *Do you know what's happened to your mother?*

That last question felt like a knife through his chest. But he still couldn't answer. Not yet. His mind wouldn't go there even if he wanted it to.

Crucial information hid in his memory. The programmers needed this special code to fix the hack. He couldn't forget this information. If he did, something bad would happen. Or something good *wouldn't*.

He mouthed it to Hen from the cruiser as they drove out of the motel parking lot. But it didn't compute, he could tell by his brother's face. Of course, it wouldn't. Hen wasn't a tech guy either.

"For three hundred M&Ms," Ty said again.

Suit guy jutted his chin. "If we get you some candy, you'll talk? Is that what you're telling me?"

"For three hundred M&Ms."

Suit guy sang inside his mouth again. Tall, with lots of gray in his blond thinning hair. His mud-colored suit made him look super pale, going red as the questions piled up.

Experience told Ty he was in legal trouble. But unlike his last go-around, they had skipped a step. They went right to the arrest without any investigation. Now, the questions came from a guy in a suit, not a cop. A tiny tape recorder sat on the table. Like in movies. Old timey. Not digital, which would imply involvement in Y2K. Solidified the fact that suit guy was no techie.

Around and around went the little tape. So tiny, it looked like it could belong to a family of raccoons. Ty couldn't help grinning at the thing.

Suit guy didn't like that.

"You're being charged with a serious offense. You know that, right?" he said, a flush of scarlet rising on his neck. He wasn't humming his song anymore. He clicked off the tape recorder. "I'll be right back." He hoisted himself out of his chair and went out, leaving his stuff on the table.

For three hundred M&Ms. For three hundred M&Ms. For three hundred M&Ms.

Ty heard scratching. From the other side of the wall. Those raccoons. Scavenging for food? Their claws. Agile paws. So adept, those critters. They could get into a locked safe, he heard once. Maybe Hen told him that? But they were nighttime animals, right? What time was it?

He got up and put his ear to the wall to hear better.

Suit guy stormed back into the room and tossed five bags of M&M candies on the table.

"I don't know if there are three hundred in there, but I'm guessing we're covered."

Ty glanced at the candy, then back at the suit. "What time is it?"

He raised his eyebrows. A million wrinkles appeared on his forehead. "Eleven thirty. Eleven thirty-seven, to be exact. Why do you want to know?"

"At night?"

A pause. "No. It's mid-morning."

"Ah." The raccoons might be rabid. That would be a bad thing.

"Tyler, would you please take your seat?"

"Take it?"

"Please sit down."

Ty sat. But kept his eyes on the wall. Raccoons on the other side. Could they scratch their way through?

Big sigh. "Tyler, it would behoove you to take this a bit more seriously." He shoved the candy toward Ty. "Aren't you going to have some, then? So we can get on with it?"

Ty blinked at the M&Ms, beyond puzzled.

Just then, none other but social-worker-Sheila burst through the door—a flash of a police officer behind her.

"Excuse me. Stop this right now. Tyler has a right to an attorney."

A sight for sore eyes, Sheila reminded Ty of one of his old teachers from high school whose name escaped him. Her round face always seemed kind. Except right now, she seemed mad. She turned sharp eyes on him. "Tyler, tell this man you want a lawyer."

Tyler hesitated. Brown suit guy was no techie. Not a lawyer either.

"Now!" she said.

"I want a lawyer."

She nodded once. Then, she set her razor-like gaze onto the non-lawyer with all the questions. "Shame on you. Are you aware this young man has a serious mental illness?"

That reminded Tyler. "I'm out of meds," he blurted. "But it's okay. I don't need them anymore. I'm better."

Sheila palmed the table. "Tyler, stop talking."

"No. No. No. I don't need them anymore. I'm better."

"Tyler, *hush!*"

"I figured something was up," said suit guy. "With all the talk of M&Ms. Now he won't even eat them. You his lawyer?"

"I'm his social worker. Also, his guardian...of sorts."

Suit guy gathered up his things. A look of relief crossed his face. "So, what's wrong with him?"

"Excuse me?" Sheila's eyes went wide behind her glasses.

He hummed some more and gave a shrug. Then he smiled at Ty, friendly-like. "I'll be speaking to you later, Tyler."

After he left, Sheila took his seat. Rubbed her face like trying to get something off it. "Tyler, what did you say to Detective Randolf?"

"He was a detective?"

"Yes. What did you tell him?"

Ty rewound to find some things. He knew the human brain was a super computer and could never be replicated even by the most brilliant programmers. Dr. Asner told him his brain had been wired differently than other people's. Not good or bad just different. And he needed to do exercises and take medicine to help his brain so hackers couldn't give it a computer virus. Dr. Asner didn't say that but didn't have to. Ty didn't know everything about the intricacies of the human brain and that was the point. Still, he wished he could click back and find memories and other information he needed.

When he tried to remember in order to answer Sheila's question, he saw Roxanne eating ice cream in the cereal aisle. Sticky shame fell over him. For the first time, he didn't want to go back to the store. He didn't want to work there anymore. A great sadness enveloped him.

"Nothing," he said.

Sigh. She shut her eyes for an extended blink. "This is not good. This will set you back in the system, after we've worked so hard to get you into that program... Are you really out of meds?"

Nod.

"How did that happen?"

Shrug.

"How long have you been without them?"

"Since yesterday. Before yesterday? I don't know. I don't remember."

"Not good." She typed into her phone. "I'll have Dr. Asner get in touch with Bernie. He can pick up your prescription. He's the one who called me. I got here as soon as I could." She put her phone down next to the bags of candy. "What did you say about M&Ms?"

Ty stared at the candy—the red cartoony guy with Mickey Mouse appendages. "Huh?"

"Detective Randolf mentioned you talked about M&Ms. 'With all the talk of M&Ms' is how he put it. What did you say?"

Something clicked. "Oh. For three hundred M&Ms." He was proud to have remembered.

Sheila waited, her face blank. She made that face a lot.

"But I wasn't talking about candy."

She brightened. "Oh? What were you talking about?"

He looked away from the table. All the color distracted him. *For three hundred M&Ms.*

That's what mattered. Who did he need to tell? Not Sheila.

Sheila had other valuable information. "How's my mother?"

She closed her eyes for a second. "She's healing. It will take time. I went to see her this morning. About the paperwork for the mental health courts...to get you into that transitional day program. Looks like the process will take even longer now since we can't really count on her help any time soon. And of course," she palmed the sky, "whatever comes of *this*, for you."

A long pause. In a soft voice, she added, "Marcella's got a bad concussion. But she's going to be okay."

Such warm relief bubbled up in Ty, he laughed aloud. Love for his mother flooded his entire being, and he laughed some more. All that blood gushing from her head didn't hurt her brain-computer. Not seriously. She'd be okay, Sheila said. Just a concussion. She would heal. Whatever happened to Ty, didn't matter. Marcella would be okay. Even if Ty wouldn't.

A childlike giddiness made him bounce in his seat. He tore a corner off one of the bags. Hard candy shells clicked together in a pile in his hand. Such happy colors. The aroma of chocolate filled the small room. He tossed a few in his mouth and—*zing!*—went his salivary glands. He crunched down and grinned at Sheila, whose mouth hung open a little. Maybe from hunger?

He held up the bag. "Want some?"

CHAPTER 13

On autopilot, Hen cleaned cabins in a mad blitz, unable to get Mom off his mind. Everything in him said to be at her side, yet he was stuck here at the motel. Over twenty-four hours had passed since the attack and he hadn't been to the hospital since that first night—and Mom had slept through his entire visit. Since then, with the motel so busy, he hadn't been able to sneak away. Maybe this afternoon after he finished up?

No, not maybe. Definitely. He would get there, come hell or high water.

Thoughts of that night haunted him. It kept replaying, his mind filling the gaps where his memory lagged. Still, he had a hard time reconciling the fact that Tyler had been arrested for assaulting his mother. Hen's gut told him Tyler wouldn't do such a thing...no matter how sick he was.

But still. Tyler's voice rang in his ears.

It was me! It was me!

A sinking dread weighed on him. Since his brother's diagnosis, he'd learned how frightening schizophrenia could be. How unpredictable, the treatment unreliable. He had heard more than one horror story which scared him senseless. Like, a young executive out in the Midwest forgot to take his medication and killed his girlfriend of three years with a kitchen knife. Stabbed her fifty times in the stomach. His explanation? He thought he *had* to. Hen could hardly wrap his mind around it. Stuff of nightmares.

He glowered at cabin eleven. Even vacant, it exuded bad energy. He didn't want to be like this. Pissed off. Suspicious. But he couldn't help it.

He took his fury out on the toilets.

Between cleaning cabins seven and eight, a man approached. Hen hadn't noticed him pull up.

"Detective Randolf." His badge flashed in the sun. "Mind if I ask you a few questions?"

Hen grabbed his water bottle, sat on the curb, and chugged it. Detective Randolf could wait. In the pause, he hummed a tune— almost subconsciously. Though his lips stayed closed, Hen heard an impressive vibrato. Irksome. But it seemed the guy didn't realize he could be heard. Didn't seem to mind waiting, either.

Hen cleared his throat. "This about the other night? My mom's attack?"

Song cut out. "Yes. I understand you were here?"

A wave of regret deflated him. He didn't have a right to be so ticked. He was partially to blame. If only he had been home.

"No. I wasn't here when it happened. I came home right after the cops showed up."

Despite having rolled-up sleeves, Detective Randolf seemed overheated. Beads of sweat gathered on his forehead. He flipped over a page of his small notebook. "Right. Okay, then. Could you tell me anything about that night? Any observations?"

Hen quickly recapped his version of the awful night. Facts only. The occasional time-stamp. Detective Randolf nodded blandly. Bored.

"Can I ask you a question?" Hen wiped sweat from his brow. "Wasn't there a confession? Why investigate? Doesn't that make it a case-closed kind of thing?"

Randolf slapped his notebook. "Your brother's confession is on file."

Your brother. Hen's mouth went dry. "My mother insists he didn't do it."

"I'm well aware."

Hen pointed toward the road. "And you saw the skid marks. From that night." His words felt loaded. He hadn't realized he would say them aloud.

A hint of a smile. "I did. Are you also a detective?"

He took more water. "My brother doesn't drive."

"I'm aware of that also."

They both stared at the black tire marks on the pavement. "Then it has to be someone else, right?"

Please, let it be someone else.

Still personally conflicted, Hen definitely did not want to see Tyler in trouble. Not again. Even if his mind made him do something awful, Hen couldn't stomach the legal trouble and what it would do to his mother. Suddenly, he was seven years old again—David against Goliath—pulling out every hope and belief and lucky star to will his brother's innocence.

But in his heart, Hen knew the tire marks were a straw-grasp. Any random car could've skidded out two weeks prior and those marks would still be there. He couldn't prove it was Mom's attacker who sped away. He didn't see it. Bernie didn't see it.

Only Tyler saw.

And all Hen saw was Tyler, confessing to the cops in his dirty socks.

Of course, Detective Randolf must have had these same thoughts —tire marks were flimsy evidence. He didn't speak them, though. And why would he? To a kid, no less. Son of the victim.

He didn't answer Hen, either. *Then it has to be someone else, right?*

"Do you have a record of the tenants who stayed here that night?" asked the detective. "Looking for potential witnesses."

Randolf followed Hen into the office. The room felt tainted after what happened.

A family at the pool splashed and played out back. The laughter and squeals that filtered inside seemed so out of place they were borderline insulting. Hen fought an urge to apologize to the detective.

He mechanically opened the register listing renter names and numbers to date in Marcella's waitress-trained shorthand. Legible, but barely so. Randolf took a picture with his digital camera.

"Any of these folks still here?"

"Cabin one. The Platts. They stay for the whole week. Have every year since we got the place." Mr. and Mrs. Platt had stayed in their room that night, Hen had noted. After the ambulance left and Hen had encouraged everyone to go back to bed, their cabin remained dark and quiet. They probably wouldn't be any help. But he kept this to himself. "They're not here right now. Out for the day."

Randolf glanced out the window. "Beautiful day."

"Yes, sir."

"Thanks for this. I'll let you get back to work." He handed Hen his business card. "If you think of anything else."

As the detective pulled away, Hen's cellphone rang.

Bernie: "Your mother's coming home this afternoon. Would you—"

"Of course." Hen's heart soared. "I'll have her room ready. And straighten up. Everything will be all set for her."

A pause. "Thanks, Hen."

He snapped his phone shut and fist pumped the air. Three more cabins to clean but, more importantly, he had to tackle the house. Dishes overflowed in the kitchen sink and he wanted Mom to come home to fresh sheets on her bed. Will she be bedridden? What will her recovery look like? Gosh, if he had time, he'd get some fresh flowers for her nightstand. That would make her smile. He'd have to work fast.

Such a different kind of adrenaline this time. Still, he cleaned cabin eight in record time. On to number nine. Almost done...

A royal blue sports car pulled in, heading straight for Hen. Its stereo boomed across the lot.

Wesley.

He didn't bother getting out of his car, just turned down the radio. "Jay's got the boat this afternoon. A bunch of us are going up to Calves Pen. Come on, grab your suit."

Hen waited, agape. Wes asked him to go cliff jumping? Today? "Is that a joke?"

"No. Why? Let's go. It's a stellar day. They're waiting at the dock."

"I can't go." He couldn't believe he had to say it.

"Why not?"

"Wes, you know what happened to my mom. How could you even think—"

"Yeah, but you said she'd be all right. So..."

"So, I'm not going anywhere. She's coming home this afternoon."

"And? Hen, you have to live your life."

Hen scrunched his face. "What's that supposed to mean?"

"You can't always worry about everyone else. It's your life too. You have to do your own stuff."

A bolt of irritation made him start. In a split second, the little things that made up his life folded together like a batch of jambalaya. He flung his arms out toward the motel property. "Dude. This *is* my life."

In saying so, the truth of it came clear. This was his life. The motel, his mom, Bernie, Tyler, and all the junk that came with it. The overhanging fact of his inheritance tormented him. Like the mechanical hare now forbidden to chase, it seemed unethical. Or in bad taste. He couldn't leave today and go out on the lake. He couldn't go off to college in a year and leave Mom. This was it for him. Money wouldn't reshape his life, even if he wanted it to.

Wesley narrowed his eyes. Hen saw pity there. "Seriously?"

"Seriously. And I have a lot to do before Mom comes home." Hen felt something rise up in his chest. He had to show Wesley he was right. He struggled to find the words, the feeling was so huge. "I've got to get her flowers too."

As soon as he said it, he wished he hadn't.

Wes laughed hard. "My man, you are bonkers."

Heat built around Hen's eyes. How could Wes, his best friend, not understand? He couldn't go cliff jumping as his mom came home from the hospital. He shouldn't have to explain. Wes shouldn't have asked in the first place. So annoyed, Hen wanted to shove him off the property. He turned his back to him, headed in to cabin nine. Time was wasting.

"Okay," Wes called, his tone curt. "Sorry. Anyway. Have fun. Call me later. Or whatever."

Hen started on the beds as Wes's car peeled away, a loud screech of his tires.

No. Hen's stomach dropped. *Oh, no. No.*

He rushed out to check, hoping he'd be wrong. He blinked the view into focus, wishing his vision could correct what he saw.

Fresh skid marks from Wes's car on the pavement, playing over the tire tracks from before. Smudging them out.

CHAPTER 14

Marcella padded gingerly into the house, Bernie gripping her elbow. Still queasy from the ride home. The bright sun burned her eyes. She wished for sunglasses. Or a blindfold. Only a dozen steps to the house, but it seemed an impossible feat.

"Everything's all set. You don't have to worry about anything." Hen led them past the kitchen, straight to her bedroom. Marcella marveled at his confidence and strength, a stark contrast to how she felt. Hen seemed to have matured in the past twenty-four hours.

He presented her room Vanna-White style. Marcella took in a quick breath, feeling her chest fill. "Oh, Hen."

The room was immaculate. A clean, floral fragrance filled the space. Sun filtered through the blinds. Dappled light splayed across her fresh-sheeted bed, her side turned down just so. On the nightstand stood a glass of ice water and a jelly jar of bright pink flowers. She squinted at them.

"Are those...my impatiens?" The annuals she'd planted days before the accident. Had Hen actually plucked them out of the soil and brought them inside?

His proud grin told her yes, he did. He'd pulled up her flowers.

"Oh." She swallowed, tamping down a flutter of grief. And returned her son's smile. "Thank you."

"Nice work, Hen." Bernie's voice boomed behind her. Too loud.

She must've winced. Hen noticed.

"Come on, Bernie," he whispered. "Let's let Mom get some rest."

"Guys, I'm not sick. I'm fine. Really. Just a little tired." Even so, she ambled toward the bed, eager to feel clean cotton sheets on her skin. Rest her head on her own pillow. She felt heavy with fatigue.

"Want us to run you a bath?" Bernie forgot to whisper.

"Later," Hen said softly, bless his heart. "Come on. Let her rest."

Marcella slunk under the covers and breathed in the comforting smell of her favorite laundry detergent. Her entire body relaxed. The click of the door, like a closing bell, quieted her thoughts.

When she closed her eyes, though, sleep refused to come. On the contrary, her heart raced. Anxiety pricked. Worry for Tyler, the motel, the future, Hen. Her eyes popped open and roamed the familiar room. A sip of water failed to soothe the lump in her throat. This wasn't rest, this was torture.

That awful conversation with the detective had ruined her.

After all the insistence she'd finally gotten her chance and had lost her words. She stumbled through her statement.

"It wasn't my son," she'd said, a lame preface.

"You've said that," the detective had said, his eyes half-mast.

"No, it was...he was a man. A big man. Heavyset."

"What did he look like?"

Didn't she just tell him?

"Fat," she spat.

"Any other, more distinctive, traits come to mind?"

She'd wracked her brain. His physique polar-opposite of Tyler's, the other stuff seemed superfluous. Perhaps she could identify him in a lineup but to recall specific facial features from memory proved troubling. All that emerged were shadows. "He wore a hood. A black sweatshirt with a hood that covered his face."

"A hood doesn't typically cover one's face. A hood—"

"No, but. You know what I mean. His face was dark."

Detective's eyebrows raised. He wrote something in his notebook. "He was dark-skinned?"

"No. No, I don't think so."

"You don't think so?"

"No. He wasn't. That's not what I mean. His face was dark because of the hood. Like, a shadow. You know?"

"Oh." He scribbled out what he'd written. His pen clicked under his thumb. He hummed what sounded like an aria. After a few, he said, resigned, "So you didn't really get a good look at him then."

"No, I..." Marcella wanted to correct him but didn't know how. The halting noises from her throat embarrassed her.

The detective moved on. "You say the sweatshirt was black. Are you sure it wasn't gray?"

"It was a dark color." How many times had she said the word 'dark' in the last few minutes? Dark, dark, dark. It sounded funny now. Like, a made-up word.

"Right," he said. "It could've been a dark gray, say."

She frowned. "I said it was black."

"But it could've been a very dark gray."

"Why are you asking me that?"

Click, click, click with his pen. And the humming again. Maddening.

Marcella's head felt about to burst. A swooping queasiness came over her and she closed her eyes. So tired. Talking took too much effort. Maybe because he wouldn't listen? She willed her eyes open and forced a deep breath.

Suddenly, it fell into place. Why he'd ask her such a thing, insist on gray-not-black. A slow gasp came with her next inhale.

"Tyler wore a gray sweatshirt that night. That's why you're asking, isn't it?"

An image of Tyler sprang to mind. That night, he'd worn those grubby sweats from his days at rehab. The legs tucked into white tube socks at the ankles. She'd hated seeing him like that. It reminded her of where he'd been, how long he'd been away. Irrational, she knew, but the clothes seemed to trap his illness inside of him. She detested those gray sweats.

The detective shrugged, affirmative.

"Mr. Randolf, I thought I'd made myself clear. My son—"

"Ma'am, please take no offense. But your son has a record. And his mental illness, unfortunately, could be seen as motive."

Marcella pounced. "Motive? To attack his own mother?"

"My apologies. I shouldn't have used that word. It could be the reason for him to attack, is what I'm saying. Not you, per se. Anyone. We've seen this kind of thing before—"

Fury cut through her. Cruel mockery sounded from her lips again, atypical for her. "Oh, you have seen this *thing* before? Are you sure the *thing* you're talking about is the same kind of *thing*? Have you interviewed any witnesses? Surely someone at the motel saw the whole *thing* and could clear up a few *things*."

He held her gaze, his jaw cocked. His low voice held restraint. "We've been calling your tenants who were there that night. No luck so far. But we're still trying."

"And are you trying to exonerate my son as well?"

He stared—his gaze floating up to her stitches. "Let me remind you, Mrs. Trout, that Tyler has confessed. He has not yet rescinded his confession. Nor have we any other suspects."

"No. It was a large man..."

"In a dark gray sweatshirt."

"Black."

"Right. Black." He pretended to write something else in his tiny pad. "What else do you remember from that night?"

"What—they took me away in an ambulance while at the same time my son was wrongly arrested. And I freaked out." So hopelessly exhausted and nauseous, as if she'd been on a bumpy roller coaster. How could the simple act of *talking* make her feel so sick?

"No, I mean. Do you remember any specifics about the attack itself? Or before? What was said, etcetera?"

She opened her mouth to speak but made those annoying throat sounds again.

"Ma'am? Excuse me?"

She blinked in rapid succession, feeling faint suddenly. "Um, I'm not sure what you're asking. You've seen the doctor's report. You know what happened."

"Yes. But, do you remember?"

"Why...how could you ask me that?" Out of breath, she searched the room for an escape. Though she was the one pinned to the bed. She thought so hard, pain knifed into her skull. "The man came in and...asked for a room...and got very angry. I told him...full. Full!"

Sweat coated her in seconds. He did ask for a room, right? That's why folks come there. What else would he have said?

She pressed on. "We were full. And then. He struck me. I asked him to leave, but he attacked me instead. He wouldn't go even though we were full. And..."

Every time she ran through events of that night, there it was: a blank spot. A blip in time she couldn't remember. She'd opened her eyes and her attacker was gone. Like a magic trick.

"Mrs. Trout?"

She caught herself staring at the ceiling tiles. "Yes?"

"Are you having trouble remembering?"

No way. She remembered it all, didn't she? How could she possibly forget?

"No, just tired." Her eyes closed. Done talking. "Do you mind if we pick this up another time?"

He mumbled something on his way out. Marcella was flooded with relief to rest at last. As she felt herself slipping, she promised to figure this out. Remember all those pesky details. Something would trigger the memory. Then she'd go back and make it right with this detective or whoever she needed to talk to. One thing for sure, no one would ever know she'd blacked out that night.

No one.

CHAPTER 15

As long as Bernie kept moving, he felt some semblance of control. Task after task to keep busy so he didn't have to think about Marcella being so short with him lately. Something always needed fixing at the motel. For once, he was grateful for the endless projects and repairs.

Aside from committing to Marcella, purchasing this motel proved to be the smartest decision he'd ever made. He'd found his calling here, and took pride in making it one of the best-maintained, moderate-priced motels in the Lake George area.

Still, returning from Home Depot, even with his truck chock full of fresh supplies, his thoughts weren't on the next project but with Marcella—a lump forming in his throat.

He ached to feel close to her again. He knew he had to be patient as she continued her recovery. But even before the accident—it hurt too much to call it assault—he'd felt Marcella pulling away. To be honest, she'd been distant since Tyler moved in. Bernie didn't know how to be okay with it, after all the work he'd done in therapy, after all the effort he'd put into being a father figure to Hen. After all the love he'd poured into his union with Marcella. He didn't know how to be okay with Tyler. Frankly, he didn't want to be okay with him.

Was he a terrible person to feel relief when Tyler had been arrested again?

Maybe if he kept his head down and got things done, she would come around and life would go back to normal. Lots of laughs, dinner on the couch watching Jeopardy, holding hands on long walks to the lake, sleeping side by side. It pained him to think how long it had been since they'd been intimate.

These thoughts nagged as he drove, in the quiet of the highway. Pulling into his spot at Blue Palms, he shook it off. Ah, there was Marcella's car. That meant—

Hen sat at the kitchen table, the glow from Marcella's open laptop lighting his face. Opened envelopes stacked near the motel ledger nearby, the curls of the ripped enclosures aerating the pile.

Bills.

Bernie paused at the doorway, his Home Depot receipt wedged between two fingers. "What are you doin'?"

Hen palmed his forehead. "These books are kind of a mess. You guys don't even charge the same rates for rooms."

A tug of defensiveness. "Well, repeat tenants get a discount if they book before the end of the current season."

Hen flapped a hand at the screen. "Yeah, but it doesn't even look like they pay on time. It's all over the place. Some pay before. Some after. Gosh, it seems like one or two haven't paid at all."

"Now, wait a minute." Bernie leaned over a chair to see. Numbness climbed north from his shoulders. "Some people haven't paid?"

Hen pointed to a tiny Excel cell, its contents a mystery. "Right here. Last spring. Maybe just once it happened. As far as I can tell. Still, that's one too many."

"No, I agree," Bernie said, dumbfounded. And embarrassed. What else to say?

Hen tipped back in a kitchen-chair-wheelie his mother forbade. He raked fingers through his overgrown bangs. "Why is my mom doing the books, anyway?"

No answer seemed adequate. "How's she feeling?" he asked instead.

Hen's eyes stayed on the screen, rocked on the rear chair legs. "I guess the same. She did some laundry today. It's the one thing that doesn't make her queasy, she says."

Bernie felt himself grin. "She doesn't like sitting still."

He dropped his smile when Hen looked up. "Yeah, but in general, why is she in charge of the books for the motel? She's never been a financial wiz or anything. I mean, you're the one who has experience managing properties and stuff. Right?"

Bernie almost didn't recognize Hen's voice. So grownup and sure. Accusing, almost. He hated his sudden stutter. "Uh, your mom insisted. It-it was important to her she wasn't pushed off to do 'women's work' as she called it."

"Like laundry? Or housekeeping?" Hen chuckled.

"Well, yeah. I guess, yeah."

In one fell swoop, Hen righted the chair as he flipped open a manila folder. Tiny strips of paper floated up like tossed salad. "And what's with these receipts? I assume these expenses need to be recorded somewhere?"

Bernie folded the Home Depot receipt into his fist as his neck grew hot. He nodded slowly.

Hen chuckled again. "Well, this folder has some real artifacts. I mean, some of these receipts are from ninety-eight. Hey, what do I know? But don't you have to claim this kind of stuff on taxes?"

Holding his breath, Bernie carefully closed the folder. Hen's hand caught inside, he slid it onto his lap. At once, he seemed a child again. Bernie shut the laptop, and shadows fell over both their faces. Hen became that little boy who was scared of the dark.

Bernie spoke softly. "I'll take it from here, I think, Hen. You don't have to worry about it."

Could Hen hear the concern in his voice?

Hen held his gaze, uncertainty in his huge eyes. Then he sighed an "okay" in a "whatever" tone teenagers used. He mumbled about being tired, turning away from the mess of financials.

Bernie felt him slipping and scrambled to hold him there. Hen's trust was crucial. If he lost that, it would be the end of him in this family, with Marcella, the motel. He'd lose it all.

"I think the Yankees are playing. Against the Orioles, I think."

Hen stretched, scratching his stomach, totally uninhibited. "Nah. They're off tonight. Tomorrow they play the Orioles."

"Ah, right. Yeah. So, are you hungry? Did you eat?"

"Yeah, I ate. Did you?" Hen's eyes brightened. It made Bernie's heart ache.

"I had a late lunch. Not really hungry."

Hen nodded, turned away.

"Wait, Hen." But when Hen pivoted back, Bernie was lost. "Um...haven't seen you playing basketball much these days. Want to shoot some hoops?"

"When, now?"

"Sure."

"It's, like, nighttime."

Bernie tried a laugh. "Yahp, it is."

"I think I'm good. Kinda tired. Another time?" Hen smiled then, his eyes so sincere Bernie wanted to embrace him. But didn't.

"Sure thing. Goodnight, Hen."

CHAPTER 16

The buzz of activity around the motel, the momentum of summer's swing, seemed to emphasize Marcella's dreadful inactivity.

Amazing, the whirlwind of motel life. As if she only now truly saw it, she found herself awestruck at its pace. Bernie never stopped moving. Were there really so many things that needed fixing? Hen now took on most all the tenant interaction in addition to the housekeeping. So hard, he worked. And never complained. She really had to count her blessings with those two.

Marcella hated feeling so useless. And she hated herself for missing Tyler's arraignment, which seemed to happen seconds after his arrest. And then his bail hearing, where the judge set his bail at an astounding twenty thousand dollars—cash or bond. Until they could figure out how to get the money, he sat in the county jail, awaiting a trial date that hadn't even been set.

Every day she had to fight off concern for Tyler. Still, the calm her mind now required only made room for worry. Thoughts of Tyler constantly swirled. The heartbreaking image of him sitting in a jail cell was way worse than him at rehab in his grubby sweats.

Could it possibly be any worse timing? He'd been a free man for, what, a month before getting arrested again? They had just made some headway with that advocacy group. And just as people in power began to pay attention to Tyler and his unusual situation, he's back behind bars.

Not good.

Marcella's last conversation with Dr. Asner proved extremely unsettling. Given Tyler's record, it won't be easy to get him off. Given his confession or whatever asinine thing he did—why did he do it?—he's essentially guilty until proven innocent. Never a good position to be in. On top of the nausea from the concussion, Marcella was sure a stress ulcer grew inside her.

And what, for goodness' sake, went on inside Tyler? Was he sitting there, psychotic and suffering, left to rot? How the hell would he cope, after all he'd been through? Bernie had to pick up his prescription and get it to him somehow. How long had he been without his medication?

And as he sat in jail awaiting whatever came next, she couldn't even visit him. The mere thought of driving ten miles to the Municipal Center was enough to give her heart palpitations. Over everything, the constant fatigue and nausea—triggered by nothing and everything—that stemmed from her concussion.

It all seemed so hopeless, no wonder she wanted only to sleep. Sometimes, even awake, she'd be sleepwalking. Going through the motions. Barely able to do much but *be*.

After a week, she'd tried to check guests in, take reservations, do the books, but she quickly gave up. Her eyes hurt to read even her own handwriting. And the phone to her ear was like a needle to her temple.

Simply standing in the office, smiling and greeting people made her queasy. So ridiculous, her symptoms too silly to address medically. She'd quickly dismissed the options for treatment and referrals to various specialists. The doctor at the hospital told her time was the only true healer. Besides, they couldn't afford to pay their current hospital and lab bills, let alone fees from a physical therapist or, goodness gracious, a neurologist.

Most of her awake hours she spent on the back deck under the terrace, waiting for news about Tyler and watching activity in the pool as if it were daytime drama on television. Yesterday, Bernie had brought out her favorite armchair and hassock.

"Oh, please," she'd said. "I don't want to be seen as the kind of family who sits on living room furniture. You know, outside on the front lawn."

"You're not on the front lawn. You're on the back lawn." Cat-like grin. "No one can see you back here. Just try it."

Marcella sat and promptly decided she didn't care what people thought. Something had still made her uncomfortable. Beyond whatever an armchair could fix.

"We need to talk about the bail bond," she told Bernie.

He'd sat in the plastic lawn chair next to her, flimsy under his weight. "We do?"

"Yes, Bernie. I can't stand that I can sit out here in the fresh air while Tyler is stuck in the county jail when he didn't do anything wrong. I need you to call a bail bondsman or whatever it's called."

Bernie raised an eyebrow. "You know the only way to do that would be to have a bail bond secured by the mortgage on the motel."

"Well then. That's what we'll have to do."

He shook his head. The plastic chair wiggled from the motion. "We could lose the motel, Em."

"Only if he runs away or something. He's not going to do that."

"We don't know that."

Marcella stiffened. "I know it."

Bernie looked at her askance. "Em, no you don't. You know his behavior is unpredictable."

"Don't tell me what I know and don't know about my own son. I know he won't run away."

"Em—"

She raised her voice. "It's a risk I'm willing to take, okay?"

"Well, I'm not sure it's one I'm willing—"

"Listen Bernie, I don't want you to argue with me. I want you to do what I ask. Please. Just go and call a bond bailsman. You can look one up in the yellow pages, for crying out loud." She would do it herself but after that mess of an interview with the detective, she didn't trust herself to talk to anyone official. Talking in general gave her a headache. Talking about numbers gave her a migraine. Was talking with Bernie much better?

His eyes went all puppy-dog disappointed. Or perhaps pity.

She couldn't stop herself. "It's my motel as much as yours. You can't withhold my rights to do whatever I want with the mortgage."

Now he looked pained. "It's fifty-fifty, Em. Like our relationship."

Marcella held back from rolling her eyes. Would Bernie really turn this into a marriage proposal? They'd decided long ago they didn't need rings or a ceremony to prove their commitment. And part of her liked holding on to her own identity outside of Bernie or Miss Sally and the Hubbard estate. She wanted to have the same last name as her kids.

She sank further into the armchair, her eyes closing. "I don't want to talk about us. I don't want to talk anymore. Period. Call the bail bondsman and get my boy home."

She felt Bernie's aura assent, or maybe she willed it so. He took his time disappearing into the house.

Now, as she sat idly on the terrace, she wished she had been at his side as he made the call. What exactly did he say? And what was the status? Thinking about it now, she hadn't seen Bernie since that conversation. And all she knew was cabin eleven still sat empty and her boy still sat in jail.

Marcella glazed over, seeing but not seeing the young girl in the pool with an inner tube, her mother reading a magazine in a nearby lounger.

"Mommy, look!" again and again. Sometimes, the voice of one child jarred her more than a chorus of them.

The memory struck hard and fast. Young Marcella calling her mother, venturing into her darkened bedroom, hoping to show off a new dance move or her self-braided hair or an outfit she'd put together on her own. It didn't matter what, the answer was always the same.

Her mother wouldn't even open her eyes. "I don't feel well."

"But Mom, look."

"Leave me alone," she said, dismissive. "I'm sick."

"You're sick? What's wrong?" Stepping closer, Marcella reached for her.

"Don't you grab at me. Go on. Leave me be. Go find Jon."

Jon, her stepfather, was the last person Marcella wanted to find.

Shuddering from the memory now, Marcella wondered what had been wrong with her mother. So often, she'd hide away in her bedroom. For days, it seemed. Did she suffer from migraines? Depression? Or, had Marcella been right all these years, assuming she hated being a mother?

Marcella vowed she'd never be so cold. She would love fiercely, openly, with her whole heart. She would be the loving mother she'd never had.

"Mommy, look!" the girl with the inner tube snapped her back to the present. She fantasized an escape, though she felt glued to her chair. Her gaze went to cabin eleven, and before giving herself time to doubt, she began moving toward it.

It's just walking. One foot in front of the other. Not far, just across the parking lot.

When the knob refused to budge, she realized her mistake. Master key in the office. Or Hen's pocket?

She sat on the curb and weighed her options. Again, searched for Bernie, who constantly hovered when she didn't need him but vanished whenever she did. Her car gone from its spot—Hen had taken it out on some errand, she recalled. Strange that neither were home.

From the pool: "Mommy! Mommy, did you see me?"

She closed her eyes against the too-bright sun and felt her body temperature rise precipitously. Had to get into some shade.

Rather than go back under the terrace by the pool, she went to the office. Fully facing the sun en route, it seemed a much longer distance.

Finally inside, the shock of A/C iced her sweat-drenched skin. Fatigue made her molasses inside. Her bed beckoned.

But, oh look, there it was. The master key. A shot of adrenaline came out of nowhere. Also, something close to optimism. An about face, and she headed back to eleven, not quite sure why she needed to go.

Inside Tyler's room, a damp humidity smothered out any breathable air. She left the door open and ventured farther in. Not sure what she expected, but it wasn't this. His unmade bed held his shape, an imprint of his figure on the mattress. It seemed lonely and stained somehow—not so much dirty as dejected. Clothes strewn about the floor. Food packages stacked on the bureau by the TV, an open container of blueberry Pop-Tarts and a half-drunk Gatorade obstructed the screen. It seemed another lifetime when she'd cooked for him—chicken cutlets. The thought of preparing a meal right now overwhelmed her. Such a simple thing, cooking for your child, and she couldn't possibly muster the energy for it. Not a chance.

A putrid smell came from the bathroom, and she closed the door before detecting its source. When was the last time this unit had been cleaned? She ran a fingernail across the fabric of the chair, and dust floated from it. She caught her hand back in a tight fist.

She should make his bed for him. Clean his sheets and freshen things up. But even if she did have all the energy in the world, she didn't want to touch it—or anything in here.

The short walk across the parking lot back to her home took ages. The too-bright sun now felt like punishment. A deep yearning to weep weighed her down, but no tears came. Straight to her bed, skipping lunch. She donned a silk blindfold she swore she'd never use —a gift from Bernie after the accident—and slept the rest of the day.

CHAPTER 17

Ty got his meds from Bernie and took his pill right away because he had learned to be a good patient. Even though part of him believed he didn't really need it.

By the time the fog cleared, he'd been officially charged with assaulting Marcella. They made him stay at county jail because he had a record of being a violent criminal. Mr. Haas said he had to stay there until someone posted bail—which meant someone had to pay a bunch of money so he could go home. But only home and nowhere else.

His lawyer, Mr. Haas, also wore a brown suit but was shorter and chubbier than the detective. Bald with a goatee. Mr. Haas said they need to prepare for a trial even though a date had not yet been set. Very confusing stuff. Ty had been on trial before. Lots of big words flying around a courtroom. Cameras in every corner. Cameras he now understood linked to computers the government controlled and contained all the important information in the entire world.

Ty had important info too, that had to be input into the secret computer so nothing bad would happen. *For three hundred M&Ms.* Would Haas know what to do? Did he have tech skills? Some lawyers were old fashioned, he knew from television, and didn't like to use the internets but only those thick books with gold writing on the spines. Haas had written it down on his big yellow legal pad with his fancy pen. Haas promised he would "get to the bottom of it," which meant he would find tech to input the code and they would be saved.

Now, he waited for nothing bad to happen.

Ty didn't mind waiting in jail. Jail held no surprises. He didn't have to go to the store where Roxanne might be. He didn't have to rev himself up to go outside or talk to people. Unless he had a visitor, he didn't have to talk at all.

Apparently, Marcella wasn't well enough to visit.

But Hen was.

Ty found himself sitting across from his little brother as if plopped into a dream. Leaving his cell, following the policeman through the echoey hallway, entering the visiting room, all a blur. He stared at Hen, hot shame washing over him, wishing it were Marcella visiting instead.

Hen leaned back in his chair, crossing an ankle over a knee. Ty could see a trace of the little boy he used to live with back in Severance. But Hen seemed to be a completely different person. Ty could trust Hen, he told himself.

They sat in silence awhile.

"Hi," Ty said.

"Hey." Hen methodically tapped the edge of the table with his index finger, like he kept count of something. But he didn't talk numbers. "So, I thought we could talk about that night." Businesslike. No smile.

Trust Hen. "Okay."

Moments built in quiet.

Ty only thought of one thing. "How's Marcella?"

"Mom?" Hen let out a long breath, uncrossed his ankle. His face relaxed. Another glimpse of that little boy. "Getting better. She sleeps a lot."

"Good. That's good." Ty nodded and rocked in his seat.

"It might take a while, they say." Pause. "She's worried about you, of course."

Worried about me? Ty didn't know what to say, so he kept his mouth shut. He pressed his teeth together, hard, like trying to bite through them. Until his jaw ached.

Hen watched him evenly, the little boy disappearing. His voice rose in pitch. "So, about that night? How about if we talk about it, you know, brother to brother? Just, all honesty. Can you do that?"

Brother to brother.

Ty wanted to be brave.

Trust Hen.

"I talked to a lawyer," Ty whispered. "He has the information."

Hen kind of laughed. "I've also talked with Mr. Haas. And he doesn't have any information, really. All you gave him was some cryptic code that makes no sense."

Ty frowned hard, his eyes on the table between them. Shiny metal. Cold-looking. "No. No. No. The code—the secret code will make sense once it gets into the super computer. You need—*Haas* needs to get it to tech if he doesn't know how. The computer has all the information in the world and that code will go into it and then nothing bad will happen."

Hen unfolded a piece of paper from his pocket. "For three hundred M&Ms."

Ty straightened. "That's right!"

"Not candy, you said. But a secret code?"

Ty grinned at the ceiling. "You *did* understand. Through the window."

Hen grimaced. "What? What do you mean, through the window?"

Inexplicable joy coursed through him. Hen could help. Such great news. "I told you through the window. In the back of the police car, I told you through the window. I didn't think you heard me. But you did!" He beamed at the table, too shy to meet Hen's eye.

"No, actually. I *didn't* understand what you said." Hen made a thinking face. "But I do remember you trying to tell me something as they took you away. Honestly, I had forgotten until you just now said it."

"But then—how?"

Hen flicked the paper across the table with a shrug. "Haas gave me the code. What does it mean anyway? And what were you trying to tell me?"

"No. No. No. It has to get in to the computer. Like an equation, it had to link with other information and then…"

Ty heard a sigh on the other side of the table.

Oh, no. Hopelessness thwapped like a magnet to metal. Haas wrote it down with his fancy pen and that's all. The code was useless if it stayed on his legal pad.

Ty opened the paper to see. And it gave him a start. Hen had written it wrong. Or Haas did.

"No. No. No. See. It's not like that." Ty ran his finger over the ink, trying to erase it. "It didn't look like that. See…" His pulse raced as he searched for something to write with. Of course, guards wouldn't let him have anything. He'd have to get special permission, maybe. An anxious feeling grew. He felt it in his neck and throat.

That's why Haas hadn't done anything. He didn't hear it right. No wonder. It's been a communication error. A misfire. Faulty wiring. A severed connection. Computer shorted out. On the fritz.

Ty was breathing hard now. Sweating. He needed to make this correction. It was crucial.

But his heart pumped hard with hope now.

"I need to write it. I need a pencil. Need a pencil. Pencil. Pencil."

His ears stopped working as he zoned in on the paper. Hen went over to a guard. Then, a miracle, Ty held an oval-shaped ball with a tiny point of ink. Safe pens.

He turned the paper over to the clean side. Tried to stop his hand from shaking, and wrote:

4300MM

And he drew a rectangle around it.

CHAPTER 18

Hen watched Tyler carefully draw a box around the string of numbers and letters, as if for emphasis. He blinked at the paper. "That's the equation? The secret code to put into the computer?"

Tyler dropped the pen, not registering Hen's sarcasm. He seemed worn out. "Yes. Yes. Yes. It needs to be input into the super computer so nothing bad happens. Programmers know how. There are lots of programmers around who know tech. You need to find them and show them and they will put it in and then nothing bad will happen."

Gibberish.

Hen swiped the paper. Folded it into his pocket. "Whatever." His patience had run out. He didn't care about being polite anymore. Why did he come here? Haas told him it would be no use. And he was right. No use trying to reason with the unreasonable. Tyler's psychosis had forever changed his view of the world. Hen had thought if he tried to join him on his planet, he'd be able to understand. Fat chance.

He glanced at his watch. He didn't have time for this nonsense.

"Take it to Mr. Haas," Tyler said. "He'll know what to do."

Hen stood. "Really? You think?"

Tyler pinned his gaze on Hen's pocket that held the slip of paper. "Yes. Yes. Yes. He will. He said he could get to the bottom of it, which means he has access to tech. Take it to him as soon as possible."

Humor him, don't upset him more.

"Sure thing, bro."

Hen got out of there as soon as he could, feeling deflated. Tyler made zero sense. He would rot in jail because of the nonsense he kept spewing. And Mom's heart would continue to break apart. Hen wanted to fix everything. But, with Tyler, he was at a loss. It made him invariably sad—not being able to help his own brother. Knowing how much Mom hurt because of him. They were all stuck in a vortex of confusion—*Ty's* confusion.

In Mom's car, the radio boomed while he drove down to Glens Falls for the other errand he'd given himself that day. Music didn't help, though. His sour mood followed him into Edgerton Financial Services' driveway.

Hen didn't want to bring negativity into this meeting. Not when he'd be asking a favor to bend the rules. He took a moment in the car to breathe and turned the music off, leaning back on the headrest.

A bird's call made him come to. He scanned the lush greenery of a giant tree at the back of the drive. A beautiful tree, its leaves shimmered in the high summer sun. When the bird called again, it took Hen by surprise. He was determined to spot it. Only when it flew away did he see it. A bright red cardinal. His favorite kind of bird. He hadn't realized cardinals made such a pretty song.

If he couldn't reach Tyler, maybe he could help in another way. He found himself smiling as he climbed out of the car and skipped up the few steps to Edgerton's office.

"But you're not yet eighteen, Hen," Mr. Edgerton said.

"I know. But there's got to be exceptions, right? I mean, a case could be made for getting the money earlier?"

Edgerton grimaced, his eyes on an open folder on his desk. "I'm afraid you can't access your inheritance until you turn eighteen. Period. You aren't even old enough to talk about doing a loan."

Hen fought the beginnings of a headache. "No, I wouldn't want to do a loan." His head wagged slowly. Why couldn't this be easy? All this money sitting there doing nothing. So dumb. What's the point if he couldn't use it—

"May I ask why you want the money, son?"

Hen shifted in his chair. He didn't want rumors to spread. Besides, he hadn't fully formed a budget, and a numbers guy would want to see that. Why didn't he prepare better?

Edgerton's face grew serious. "Henry. If you're in trouble..."

"No, sir. That's not—"

He talked to himself now. "You know, I always advise clients—eighteen is too young. An entire fortune could be blown on drugs in a millisecond. But the legal adult age holds a lot of weight in people's minds."

It took a moment to compute. And Hen felt unseen. He'd worn his nicest clothes today. Combed his hair the way Mom liked. It was as if Edgerton saw a drugged-out tattooed kid with a mohawk, piercings all over his face—it stung.

"That's not me. Mr. Edgerton, please."

"Does your mother know you're here?"

"No. But, it's okay. I mean, it doesn't matter."

Now suspicious. "Why don't I give her a call, then?"

Hen stood abruptly, ready to explode. "It's for her, okay? The money is for her. She had a bad accident and the medical bills are insane and our insurance sucks and she can't work for a while. Probably all summer. She doesn't know I'm here and if she did, she'd *forbid* me to make this ask, okay?" Hen floated back to his seat. "So, please don't call her."

Another reason loomed. Tyler's bail had been set, and it was a whopping sum Mom could not possibly afford. Like, no way. Plus, Tyler's attorney. After only a few meetings, the bill from Mr. Haas exceeded five hundred dollars. No way did Hen want to tell Edgerton about Tyler's situation. One hint about his chronically delinquent brother, and Hen would have no chance of getting the money any time soon.

Mr. Edgerton received Hen's outburst in stride and retrieved a glossy trifold from a drawer. "Well, if it's truly for your mother, she may be able to take out a loan herself. Here are some options. Interest rates are high but you get money right away…"

Hen listened only as much as would be polite. He mumbled a thank you and got out of there as quickly as possible. He had practice with quick exits lately.

Hen didn't bother looking for the cardinal or waste a glance at the giant tree before reversing out of the drive. He'd rushed around this morning with lots of energy and hope, but now he felt sluggish. Part of him dreaded going home, having accomplished so little. Also, lots of work waited for him there. He took the long way along Route 9 to give himself time to recalibrate.

Not taking the highway seemed a good idea until he reached the Million Dollar Half-Mile. Outlet traffic slipped his mind. Who comes to Lake George to shop, anyway? Why aren't these people out on the lake?

Speaking of, he hadn't seen Wesley since he invited Hen to go on Jay's boat to Calves Pen. Later, Hen learned from Jay that Bianca had gone too. The only girl out on the lake with a bunch of horny teenaged guys, in her bikini with her large breasts. What happened out there in that boat? Hen cringed to think of it. No wonder Wes hadn't reached out since. He probably knew Hen would disapprove.

Still in gridlock, Hen groaned, frustrated, and punched the radio off. Turned up the A/C. Not only cars, but lots of tourists lined the streets—toting big paper bags from designer stores. At a turtle's crawl, he'd be here awhile.

On long drives when Hen was little, Mom entertained him by playing games. When I-Spy got tiresome, they made a scavenger hunt of license plates. How many states could he find? Being in the Northeast, he usually collected at least two or three from New England alone.

Deep breath, and Hen zoned in on the license plate in front of him. From Ohio.

"Aha. There's one you don't see every day," he said aloud.

He laughed for talking to himself. And stared at the Ohio plate until he had to blink. Nothing unusual about it, really. Like any other plate—some numbers and letters put together, inside a box. And then his fingertips went tingly as a slow realization settled like cold rain on his scalp.

Hen scrambled, pulling out the slip of paper Tyler had written on.

4300MM, with a box around it.

Hen's heart picked up, having unearthed a great clue.

He laughed, tenderness for his brother filling him.

Tyler was right. He had given them a secret code that could save the day. It had to be input into a computer to link with other information. Not really a code but...

...a license plate.

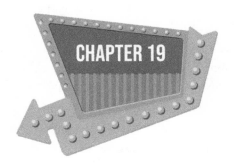

CHAPTER 19

Ty felt hope lift inside his chest, seeing his next visitor, Haas.

"Did Hen give you the paper? Do you have the code? Did you get tech to put it into the super computer?"

Haas didn't smile. And didn't answer any of Ty's important questions either. "Good news. Your mother and Bernie have secured a bail bond with the mortgage on the motel, so you'll soon be released on bail and we can start having these conversations in my office. Or your living room or wherever as we await the next steps from the DA's office."

...with the mortgage on the motel...

Ty's jaw came loose. "What about the motel?"

"Do you understand how a bail bond works? So, the motel will be used as collateral in order to get you out of here."

"The motel will be used...?"

Sigh. "Basically, they could take the motel if anything goes bad after you're free, as you wait for your trial."

An uneasy feeling pooled at the base of his spine. "She shouldn't have done that."

"Well, just don't high-tail it out of state or anything. Stay close. Keep your head down and stick around."

Ty glanced up at the security camera. "They watch all the time. My picture goes into a computer. The government has all the information."

"Yeah, well. There aren't any security cameras in your home, are there?" Haas didn't wait for Ty to answer. "I've notified the DA and am working on getting a psychiatric expert from your rehab to write an official statement. Dr. Asner is more than willing to cooperate but I'd like to have a second fighter in the ring, so to speak. You know?"

Ty stared at the table. He knew Dr. Asner. She could help. She told him a while ago it was her job to help him.

Haas had moved to another topic. "A plea deal looks promising, especially since your verbal confession occurred prior to your arrest. In this case, it's a 'statement of interest' rather than a confession. I'm correcting everyone who keeps saying it." He gave a crooked half-smile.

He waited, and Ty realized he was expected to smile back.

"You were smart not to put it in writing," Haas said.

"What?"

"Your statement of interest."

Ty went blank.

A subtle eye-roll. "Your confession."

"Oh." Ty inched forward in his seat. "Did you get the code? I wrote it down the right way and gave it to my brother and told him to bring it to you. I wrote it on a little piece of paper and he put it in his pocket but it really needs to go into a compu—"

"So, it's like this." It wasn't polite to interrupt, but Haas did it a lot. "I'm going seventy miles per hour in one direction. And your little brother charges into my office with this slip of paper and a theory on what it might mean. And now I have to figure out if I'm gonna make a U-turn or not. Not easy when you're going so fast. But at least I'm slowing down. Not going seventy anymore."

Ty blinked. "You're driving?"

Haas opened his hands. His gold wedding band seemed too tight on his thick fingers. Looked like sausages. "It's an analogy."

"Oh." It had been a long time since Ty drove. He kind of forgot how. He only had his license for a little while before all that awful stuff happened and the trial and then rehab. His desire to learn all over again had long faded. Made him anxious to think about it. "I don't—"

"Yes, to answer your question," Haas interrupted. "I got the paper from Hen."

He opened the folder and there it was, in Ty's scratchy scrawl, shiny inside a plastic protective sheath.

4300MM

Ty smiled inside. See, it *was* important. He knew it.

"Tyler, is there a reason you drew a rectangle around this?"

"Yes. Yes. Yes. That's what it looked like."

"What? That's what *what* looked like?"

"The thing. That night. On the car."

Haas shimmied his head like he waited for more. "The thing on the car? You mean, the license plate?"

Ty's eyes popped. "Yes. Yes. Yes! That's it. You got it. I knew you would."

Haas slammed the folder down. Fire blazed in his eyes. "Is this a game to you?"

Ty's grin dropped. "What? No game. It's the code that needs to be put into the computer where all the other important inf—"

"Why wouldn't you come out and tell me you had the license plate of the supposed attacker? Why wouldn't that be the first thing you say to me, your lawyer, whose job it is to get you out of this mess?"

"No. No. No. I didn't—"

"And why the hell would you come out of your cabin that night and *tell the cops you did it?*" He shouted the last bit.

"I tried to... I was trying to—"

"'It was me! It was me!' keeps getting thrown in my face. It's not an easy thing to erase from people's minds, you know. Especially the arresting officers."

Ty squinted at the table and then remembered the cameras watching him—watching them. "Computers have all the information. Did you know the human brain is like a computer? But computers can hold more information and access it faster. Did you know—"

Haas threw his hands up. "That's enough. I don't need a lecture from you about how smart computers are, thank you very much."

"...still need to protect ourselves from the Y2K crisis. It hasn't happened yet, but that doesn't mean—"

"Okay, okay. Can we get back on track here?"

Ty frowned. *Back on track*. Like a train derailed. That could happen, too, with the Y2K crash. Computers controlled everything, including high-speed trains.

"Can you tell me anything more? What did the car look like? If you could identify the make and model, even better."

Tyler shook the image of high-speed trains. "The car?"

"The car with the license plate." Sigh. "With the secret code?"

"Oh." Ty scratched his head, going back. He hoped to translate into words the picture in his memory. "It wasn't a very nice car."

"Okay." Pause. "Anything else?"

"It was all beat up. Black but real dirty. Dusty, you know? Two-door, small car. Like a sports car but not. Like one of those old Datsuns. Maybe it was a Datsun. Remember those?" Marcella had driven one when Ty was really little. She hated it but he liked it. He called it a racecar. That was before Hen was born.

Haas busily wrote. "Hardly. Go on. When did you first see it?"

Ty was somewhere else now. "No, it was a Mazda, I think. Not a Datsun. A Mazda."

"Mazda? Are you sure?"

Ty scowled. "Am I sure?"

Haas drew a big question mark, twice. "And when did you first see it?"

"I was in my cabin. Cabin eleven. Everything was visible from the big window there. Like a huge computer screen, looking out into the world. Except there aren't wires and circuits inside my cabin. There's a bed and a mirror and a dresser and a television. Televisions are kind of like computers except they're not as interactive and they're not as intelligent. They're made for different purposes."

"Okay, another tangent." Haas waved his big mitt around, his eyes on his legal pad. "So, getting back to that night. Did you get a look at the assailant?" After a pause. "Did you get a look at the attacker? The driver of the black car?"

Ty rocked in his chair. "The window to the office shimmered. Like the computer powering down, and then the wild took over. The gorilla casts a big shadow."

"Whoa. Slow down. Just describe what you saw."

"Guerrilla warfare. Spelled different. Still irregular and small and unorganized attack against the established calm and clean and good. Gorilla, like the animal. Like the wild."

"Tyler, please. What you're saying is not making sense." Haas pressed on his temples.

"Oh..." Something shorted out, leaving only the code. *For three hundred M&Ms.* "The numbers. The letters. The secret code. You got it, right?"

Haas slowly opened the folder again. Ty saw it anew, hardly recognizing his own handwriting.

"Yes. Yes. Yes. That's it. Did you put it into the super computer?"

"Wait a sec. You saw something else. You were about to tell me."

"No. No. No. The window shimmered. The glass is bumpy. Not like a smooth computer screen. Although those are curved. Still provides a clear image."

Haas lowered his voice. "What did you see through the window that shimmered?"

"I told you. It looked like a gorilla."

"A gorilla." Haas smirked. Didn't talk for a while. Wrote something in his yellow pad, crossed it out, wrote something else. "Okay. Maybe later we can talk about what happened. When you're ready."

Ty felt himself sweating. Smelled it too.

Haas turned back to the shiny plastic sheath that held the secret code. "I'm having my guy run the plate. Or as you'd say, put 'the secret code into the super computer.'"

"Yes. Yes. Yes! That's good. Very good."

"I'm assuming it was a New York plate?" Haas gave Ty an expectant look. "Was it a New York plate, Tyler?"

"New York?"

"What color was it, the license plate?"

Flash of orange. "Orange. Or a dark yellow. Like a school bus."

"Okay, good." He wrote something down. "Don't get too excited. I can't guarantee anything will come from this. It's problematic that you were the only witness—I still can't believe a full motel, and no one saw anything—and our only witness has *confessed.*"

Heat fell down on Ty's shoulders. Was Haas talking about him? Ty was the only witness. But Ty had helped. Was still helping. Right?

Who knows how much time had passed? Guards called. Haas held them off.

So tired. Ty could put his head down and sleep right there on the table. Hard, cold metal. Like in morgues.

"I think that's enough for today, then?" Haas turned up his lips. Not quite a smile.

Ty nodded. Yes, he was done. And craved the solitude of his cell. He didn't really want to be released on bail. Didn't want to go back to the store. Didn't want to go back to cabin eleven. He definitely didn't want to see the shimmery window.

In here was safer. The dank, stark concrete walls, the unyielding punishment of his cot. Where he belonged.

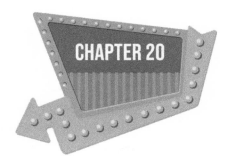

CHAPTER 20

Today she would bring her boy home. Marcella had to temper her excitement and save energy for the drive. She hadn't gotten into a car since her release from the hospital, and that ride nearly did her in. It boggled her mind, though, how a concussion could have this kind of impact on her life, even the mundane. Suddenly, in middle age, she was scared to not only drive, but ride in a car? Today, she had to find the strength. She would do it for Tyler.

Bernie came through. The bail bond was secure. On paper, it put the motel at risk. In her heart, she knew that was bunk.

Yesterday, she spent most of the afternoon folding linens, a chore she'd always avoided in the past. Since the accident, she took comfort in the warmth of the towels, the smell of bleach and fabric softener. She could take her time, even sit while she worked. And the cool, dimly lit basement eased her headaches.

This morning, she saved her energy. Forced herself to stay in bed until ten o'clock when she carefully showered and dressed as if she were going to a coronation. She wore a cotton sundress and parted her hair to cover up her wounded eye. Painted her lips a shiny pale pink. She skipped the rouge and mascara, though. Pointless.

"Ready?" Bernie leapt from his chair when she appeared in the kitchen.

A slight nod. "I look okay?"

"Beautiful," he said, grinning widely.

She tamped down a jolt of irritation. His standard response about her looks would not do today. She knew better. She would never be beautiful again. The scar that sliced through one of her eyebrows—still swollen with stitches—made sure of it. Her black eye now a putrid shade of yellow. Almost green. The eye itself still showed broken blood vessels. Not beautiful by any definition. She only hoped her looks were passable. Like, she wouldn't scare little children. Or Tyler.

She accepted Bernie's arm as they ventured outside. Hot and humid already, the sky full of clouds like a storm brewed. A boisterous summer thunderstorm. Wouldn't that be fitting?

She focused on breathing, which proved more difficult than it should've.

"We'll take your car. I have a bunch of stuff in the truck."

Of course. Marcella wouldn't dream of getting into his bumpy utility vehicle. Her head would explode. She settled into the passenger seat, fantasizing it was her favorite armchair with a view to the pool.

Bernie, kind as always, drove with utmost caution, staying in the slow lane of the highway. He kept the radio off and didn't whistle, thank goodness.

The lack of sun made her forget her huge black sunglasses, which acted as a mask more than anything these days. Not only hiding her wounds, but her emotions as well. Now, layering on her nerves, she felt exposed.

Marcella's breathing gradually regulated. She closed her eyes, but nausea swooshed through her core. Eyes back on the road ahead. Breathe.

Bernie broke the silence, jarring her. "So, what did Detective Randolf say?"

She didn't want to talk. Words seemed buried. She dug them up. "Another suspect."

"What's that?"

For goodness' sake, Bernie. Use logic. "There's a lead...to another suspect." She pushed the words out with effort. Her head throbbed.

Detective Randolf had been businesslike on the phone, asking whether she had remembered anything else of importance. He mentioned the possibility of another suspect besides Tyler almost as an afterthought. But he'd said it. She'd heard it. And it inflated her with hope, light and airy. Finally, another suspect! It had to come to light, eventually. Of course, Tyler didn't bash her head, the fat guy in the black sweatshirt did. Just a matter of time before they found him. Bittersweet relief.

The detective's call also brought fear, though, for she had no answer to his initial question—*Anything else come to mind from that night?* She couldn't remember anything new, so she'd repeated what she already told him. Even then, the details seemed to have faded or changed since the accident—and he kept asking for clarification. And then he'd asked, *Did you get a look at the car or the license plate, by any chance?*

She'd felt like a grade school student failing a test. Initially she thought her memory had gone fuzzy in a kind of defense mechanism. Now she believed her concussion was to blame. Also, whatever happened in those lost moments when she blacked out—she couldn't say. It terrified her to have lost even a second. What could her attacker, the bastard, have done in that lost time? Abused her? Robbed the motel? The notion chilled her. Kept her up at night. She had prayed it would come back, to no avail. That secret—her blackout—she kept tightly under wraps, praying the detective could not detect it.

"Another suspect," Bernie whispered.

They rode in silence awhile. Not until Bernie cleared his throat did Marcella realize this news affected him. He gripped the steering wheel so hard it squeaked. "Oh, Em. They have to get him."

She swallowed. "Please."

"I know. I know. One step at a time."

A sigh escaped her.

He pulled off the highway. "Almost there. Let's get Tyler home."

A swell of love made her reach for him. His warm, strong hand on hers felt safe. She held on the rest of the way to the county jail.

CHAPTER 21

Reluctantly, Hen pushed open the door to cabin eleven. He'd been avoiding cleaning it since his brother moved in. To be honest, he considered it outside of his responsibilities. For real. Tyler, at twenty-seven, could take care of his own room.

But Mom asked specifically it be cleaned today—a *deep* clean—in anticipation of his release on bail. Or as his ever-optimistic mom called it, his "homecoming."

Inside, the place stunk like garbage and dirty laundry and something else. Even with the door wide open, he could still smell it. Hen plucked all the clothes from the floor and piled them on the armchair. Stripped the bed without much thought, clumping the sheets outside the door. At least Hen didn't have to launder his linens. Mom insisted on doing that much. Did she plan on cleaning his dirty clothes too? He'd have to ask.

Following his routine, he saved changing bed sheets for last, lumping the comforter back onto the naked bed while he dusted around Tyler's crap, random stuff, on all the surfaces. He tossed out any opened food container. Emptied the overflowing trash by the desk that held a rotting orange peel.

Hen tried to pretend this was just another cabin to clean, and these things didn't belong to his brother but to some messy tourist. It didn't stick, though. With everything he touched, he felt Tyler's presence. He'd put on his disposable latex gloves like always but still felt Tyler through them. When he Windexed the mirror, he saw Tyler in it.

Visions of what Tyler did in here, how he might occupy his time —since he spent an enormous amount of time in this small space— popped into his head. Never pretty pictures. For Tyler, he knew, living wasn't easy. To simply exist proved a struggle.

Still, Hen couldn't find sympathy for him. And he had to push away mounting resentment because he had to clean his fricking room.

Vacuuming helped. He pushed the machine into the corners, heavy and loud. Bumped it into the armchair. Under the bed, scraping by the closet door.

Over the roar of the vacuum, Hen thought about Tyler's "secret code." Turned out he was right to keep repeating it. Puzzling and a bit disturbing, how Tyler relayed the information. Hen couldn't stop thinking about it. The way he mouthed it to Hen through the window of the cop car while being arrested haunted him. And then, at jail, the flat affect in which he repeated it, zombie-like. How he leaned over the tiny piece of paper, painstakingly writing it out, drawing the box around it with a shaky hand. He'd looked like a child who had recently learned his letters and numbers. It gave Hen chills.

But he had something, after all. Led to the car at the scene, which linked to a new suspect. This was good. Right? Hen never wanted Tyler to be in trouble again. Not after last time. Not after what it did to his mother.

So, why did Hen still feel angry toward him? Why couldn't he stop hearing Tyler's voice?

It was me! It was me!

Hen shut down the vacuum. Static electricity warmed his feet. The place started to smell better, anyway.

His cell phone rang in his pocket. Wesley.

"Hey."

"Where the hell ya been?" Wes shouted. "Get your ass over here."

A chuckle. "Hello to you too."

"Seriously. I have to babysit the vacancies and I need company."

Ah, Wesley's parents never gave him any chores around Lakeside Inn—except to watch over the place if they had to go somewhere.

"What's it this time?" Hen asked. "They go out to lunch or something?"

"Who knows? But I'm bored stiff. Come over. We'll play some hoop or something."

Hen's smile faded, knowing he had to say no once again. He'd love to play ball on Wes's pristine basketball court right now. More than anything. But Mom would want him here when Tyler got home. Even if she didn't come out and ask, he knew. But the fact was she didn't come out and ask. Maybe he could sneak away to play some hoop.

"Yeah. Yeah, okay. I'm just finishing up. I can be there within the hour." He could take his bike down. Why should he have to wait here? It's not like Tyler cared. Mom shouldn't either. And it had been so long since he'd seen Wes.

"Hurry up. I might die from boredom by then."

"Don't die. I'll be there."

A giddy spring in his step now, he was psyched to hang with Wes. Just the two of them. Goofing around Lakeside Inn like old times. After a little one-on-one, they could swim in the lake. Or get a volleyball game going down at his beach.

Hen's springy step fell like an anvil when he realized he hadn't yet done Tyler's bathroom. Ugh.

Why only now did he notice the bathroom door tightly shut?

Hen flung it open with a groan. And gasped, slapping a hand over his mouth and nose.

What the hell was that awful smell?

A strong chemical odor mixed with something else—something like disease. Urine, thick and dark, filled the toilet. Hen held his breath as he set the cover down and flushed, holding the handle until the bowl refilled. He tore open the shower curtain to inspect, thinking irrationally a dead animal might be there. It needed cleaning, sure, but it looked like any other dirty tub.

Ah, the garbage. Something gross must be in there. He pulled it from under the sink and carried it outside to empty in the bin. Couldn't help peeking into it on the way. Some plastic wrappers. Mostly used tissues. Some of them bloody. The disgusting odor couldn't have come from the trash, then. Was it his pee? What would make it smell so gross?

His steps slowed returning to the bathroom, this time armed with Lysol. He tackled the toilet, using more disinfectant than usual, holding his breath until he almost popped. He went on to the bathtub, moving as quickly as possible. Wanting to be done and out of this place more than anything.

By the time he got to the vanity, he felt calmer. The lemony scent of the cleaner filled his nostrils. As he swished the cloth across the counter top, it knocked something off onto the tile. Only then did he note Tyler's lack of toiletries. Just a toothbrush and paste. Maybe he'd stuck his deodorant and razor in a drawer. But what had fallen?

Hen reached behind the toilet to retrieve it: Tyler's meds.

The plastic orange prescription bottle went electric in his fingers. He studied the label. Talk about codes—Hen couldn't make sense of the ALL CAPS type describing the medicine. Impersonal and menacing, an order from an evil dictator. Its name, unpronounceable, seemed heavy with meaning. Evidence of Tyler's chronic and impossible sickness. Surprisingly, the bottle was weightless.

Empty.

His fingertips went numb on the little bottle.

How long had Tyler been without his meds?

A hollow fear crept into his psyche. All those horror stories he'd read about schizos attacking their families? The dude who stabbed his girlfriend, the mother who drowned her three kids, the lady who led her niece into the middle of the highway... They all had one thing in common. They hadn't taken their meds.

Hen slowly replaced the empty bottle alongside Tyler's

toothbrush and paste. A wave of sorrow filled him. And a biting rage. His thoughts raced as he finished up with the bed.

It was me! It was me!

He did it. He *fricking* did it! Screw the potential new suspect. Tyler had been off his meds. And he attacked his own mother.

He couldn't go to Wesley's. He had to get to the cops. Or that detective. Hen had his card somewhere. Where did he put it?

He shot out of cabin eleven as if the place could infect him. Left the sheets and everything out on the curb. And ran into the office to find the business card.

CHAPTER 22

"It's your lucky day."

Ty stared back, trying to decipher those words, his undigested breakfast churning in his gut. It took a moment for him to realize the guard was speaking to him.

He'd be released on bail today, the guard explained. The motel was now collateral and he couldn't high-tail it out of town.

They had him change into regular clothes and didn't make him wear handcuffs. The hallway stretched longer with each step. No security cameras hid in the corners. The door at the end had a window to the outside where Marcella and Bernie waited to take him back to cabin eleven.

Ty felt a little sick.

Outside, clouds gathered in big chunks, obscuring the blue and the sun. A steady breeze brought a chill to the air. He watched the clouds move around in layers of different dark shades.

"Tyler." A woman's voice. His mother's.

He adjusted his gaze back to earth. There stood Marcella and Bernie on the sidewalk not twenty feet away.

Wind blew back her hair, exposing her face. A cold blaze of horror flashed through him. Her face—always had been the prettiest face—had layers of different dark shades. Just like the clouds. Her eye was badly bruised. *Black eye.* A raw, red line with prickers sticking out—stitches—on her forehead. Looked like it still bled.

Ty's feet went hot. He turned back toward the door. But it was closed, locked. He spun back to face Marcella, gasping for air. She beamed at him, and one side didn't rise up like it should. A tear crept from her good eye.

"Oh Tyler." She reached to embrace him. And went to him when he didn't move.

He stood there like a piece of cardboard, his arms flat at his sides. She held him for a long time—what felt like a long time—before letting go. Then turned away quickly, shifting her hair to cover her bad eye. He wouldn't look at her again. But he could still see her face. Her pretty face that wasn't pretty anymore. *Ugly.* His insides squirmed, calling up the word.

"Come on, then." Bernie gestured to Marcella's car, parked behind him.

Like a robot, Ty put himself into the backseat. The firm, cool leather felt like a slap. Car doors slammed around him, and the wind cut out. Silence and still air suffocated him, and he went to open the window. Locked.

"Can you open my window?"

Bernie started the engine. "I'll turn on the A/C."

"I'd like to open my window. Can I please open my window?"

From the passenger seat, Marcella turned, showing her profile. Her good side, still so pretty. Her gentle voice. "I think there's too much wind, sweetie."

A glimpse of her perfect side, hearing her voice. It did him in. He lost it. A guttural sound burst from him, and tears gushed. He folded into himself, blubbering with sobs.

The car halted to a stop. Ty sensed Marcella and Bernie crane toward the backseat. But everything was squeezed shut for Ty, whose hands had become a mask. Keening, snot and tears broke through his fingers. And he heard his own, muffled voice, "I'm sorry."

A hushed argument, a wind gust as the passenger door opened. Then, Marcella by his side. Her hand on his back, rubbing in circles like she used to when he was a kid.

"Shush, sweetie. It's okay."

Bernie drove in silence. The hum of the tires told Ty they were on the highway. His head had found Marcella's lap, warmth seeping through her thin cotton dress. Her cool hand still circled his back. He stared at the dark tan interior of the car, his tears finally stubbed out.

"I'm sorry."

"Oh, sweetie. For what?"

For *what?*

For everything. For being born. For screwing up her life. For having a messed-up brain. For obsessing over Roxanne. For hearing aliens.

He choked. "I'm so sorry."

For Y2K and the computer viruses that will destroy the world. For allowing the wild to overcome the tech and the gorilla to steal into their lives and ruin Marcella's pretty face.

"I'm so, so sorry."

"Gol-darnit!" Bernie banged on the steering wheel. "Stop saying that."

"Bernard Hubbard, shut your mouth," Marcella said through clenched teeth.

"Well, my gosh. How's that supposed to land over here? You know where I go with that?" Bernie's hand flew skyward.

Where he goes with that?

"Stop it. Right now."

Bernie's voice got louder. "You want to tell us, Tyler? Your mother asked you and you still haven't answered. What are you sorry for?"

Ty slowly eased himself upright. His head felt like a lead ball.

What am I sorry for?

"All of it," he said.

Bernie pulled off the exit. "All of what?"

"Tyler, don't answer that. Bernie, be quiet. I'm telling you. Tyler's upset. He just got out of jail, for crying out loud."

A snort, gruff and unsmiling. "And we all know why he was in jail, right? Or have we forgotten?"

Ty's stomach sank. A vision of Sally Hubbard flashed, blood pooling from her skull, soaking her living room carpet. The television aliens had been there. Before they got sucked into the computers. That happened a long time ago. And now, while Y2K loomed, the wild thrashed through the tech and attacked.

Bernie thought he was the gorilla.

Was I the gorilla?

"No. No. No," Ty said. A darkness pooled in his blood as shame enveloped him.

Marcella said something, but it sounded like noise.

His face was stiff and tight from salty tears. His nose clogged. His breath fogged the window. As they pulled into the parking lot, Ty eyed cabin eleven across the lot. It seemed miles away.

CHAPTER 23

The sweeping views of the Adirondacks along the highway never ceased to inspire Detective Randolf. Alone in his car, he sang on the drive up 87, as he usually did on long highway rides. Nothing beat the acoustics of an enclosed vehicle.

No one in his division knew he had a Minor in Fine Arts, and they would razz him for days if they knew he sang opera. As a child, he'd always enjoyed singing. He had dreams of becoming a famous tenor since, at thirteen, he'd attended a wedding where one serenaded the newlyweds. When he heard this man belt Nessun Dorma, tears sprang to his eyes, and he believed he'd found the meaning of life. Turns out, he had a pretty decent voice. No Pavarotti or anything, but...

Law enforcement was in his blood, though, and there had never been any question what he'd do for a living. His parents had been clear since before grade school. They allowed his Minor in Opera as long as his degree led to a career in the police force with his father. Grateful for his twelve years as a detective with the force, he much preferred solving mysteries over walking the beat. And he kept up with his vocal exercises in private. Even his wife—ex-wife now—hadn't known about his true passion. It proved time and time again to be the best free therapy, if not the meaning of life.

He finished the last verse, and then sipped from his water bottle, satisfied. His thoughts went to the Trout case. He chuckled, thinking about those M&Ms he had bought from the vending machine. That kid—young man, actually—hadn't been asking for chocolate. He had repeated the license plate of the car spotted at the scene. Strange kid. Randolf had assumed autism but after studying his file and criminal record, he realized Tyler suffered from a more serious psychosis. Those cases always proved the most trying. And now, driving all the way to Minerva, he wondered if he chased a legit piece of evidence or a mirage invented by a psychotic.

A sigh escaped as he reminded himself it was part of the job, collecting crumbs. Even the stale ones.

The registered owner of the car with the license plate in question was a woman by the name of Paula Hugo who lived in a multi-family housing unit in Minerva. Pulling up to the address listed on the registration took the song right out of him. He'd thought he'd seen the worst of the rundown homes in the remote Adirondacks. This one gave new meaning to the term dilapidated.

He walked up the soggy wooden steps to what he assumed to be the front door. When he knocked on the broken screen, it sounded like clanging silverware.

No answer. He clanged again.

"Hello? Anyone home?"

Next door, a dog barked aggressively. Randolf quickly assessed the unit before him and determined no ferocious dogs lived within. Always a relief.

He knocked on the vinyl siding of the house which made a pathetic thudding noise. His nose hit the screen as he peered inside to some kind of storage room. Maybe they couldn't hear him?

He raised his voice. "Ms. Hugo? Are you home?"

A rustling. A flicker of movement.

Randolf's blood pumped in anticipation. He drew in a deep breath, readying himself. Stepped back from the screen.

A man came into view. He didn't open the door. Didn't speak. Tall, and so skinny he looked undernourished. His hair shorn so close to the scalp, Randolf couldn't tell its color. At first glance, he seemed to be middle age but after a quick study, he was clearly in his mid-twenties. He swam in his worn T-shirt, the Phish logo partially bleached out. Randolf prided himself on withholding judgment in these situations. The man's snake tattoo slinking up his neck made it difficult.

"Hello there." He flashed his badge. "Detective Randolf with New York State Police. I'm looking for a Ms. Paula Hugo. Does she live here?"

"Yeah. What's it to ya?"

"I have a few routine questions for her involving a case I'm investigating."

He sniggered. "Wha'd she do?"

"We're not at that point yet, just here for an interview with Ms. Hugo."

The tall man blinked at him, looking more youthful as his expression went blank. He seemed to be weighing his options, though Randolf could hardly guess why. Suspicion tickled, just a bit. He shrugged it off.

"Is she in?"

"In?"

"Is she home?"

Another beat. Then, "PAULA!" so loud Randolf startled back and almost fell off the step.

The tall man didn't even turn his head but screamed right at Randolf, "PAULA!" like an accusation.

Randolf decided to wait at the bottom of the rotting stairs. Some lawn chairs sat askew in the side yard. They could talk there.

Paula Hugo emerged looking like she'd just rolled out of bed. Her hair, colored an unnaturally bright red, hung lank at her neck. Black eyeliner smudged under her eyes. Her nose ring looked infected. Randolf sighed internally.

"Ms. Hugo?"

Her lips twitched, holding back a laugh. "Paula."

No sooner had they sat in the exact lawn chairs he had eyeballed than a car roared out of the driveway. A quick study told Randolf it was a black two-door, license plate 430-0MM. With the tall man who answered the door behind the wheel.

"That your car?"

"Uh-huh."

"Was that your husband driving it away or..."

Another twitch. "Husband? That's funny. No. Boyfriend. I guess."

"Does he use your car often?"

Blank.

He waited. A trick he'd perfected over the years, the art of waiting in silence. Let someone else fill the void. They always want to.

Not Paula Hugo, apparently. He tried again. "Does your boyfriend regularly drive your car?"

"I dunno. Guess so."

Randolf nodded, resigning himself to an interview with minimal dialogue.

"I'm asking because we have reason to believe that car was at the scene of a crime."

No response. Not even a non-verbal.

"Ma'am, where were you the night of June first?"

A shrug. If he blinked, he'd have missed it.

After a few full minutes, he asked again, "Ma'am, where were you the night of Friday, June first?"

"Oh, a Friday? Here."

"You were home?"

"Always on Fridays. I got my kid those nights."

"How old is your child?"

She picked at her cuticles. Stuck a fingernail between her teeth. "Four."

"Was your boyfriend home with you that night?"

She screwed up her face. "How am I supposta remember? I told you I ain't his babysitter."

He whipped out his pocket calendar. "Please try to remember. It was the Friday after Memorial Day."

She stared at the calendar as if she'd never seen one before. When she finally spoke, she sounded sad. "He doesn't stick around when Chloe's here."

"So, can we assume he was he out with your car that night?"

"Guess so."

His pulse quickened. His head turned reflexively in the direction of her car.

"I'm going to have to talk to him. Will he be coming back any time soon?"

Beat. Beat. Beat. "Who?"

He pulled his pen from his shirt pocket. *Click.* "What's your boyfriend's name, ma'am?"

"Who, Pistol?"

"His name is Pistol?"

"Pistol Pete."

"Pete, what? What's his last name, ma'am?"

"Bortello."

The name meant nothing, yet. He wrote it down.

"Everyone calls him Pistol."

He wrote that down too.

His cell buzzed in his pocket. He excused himself politely, which Ms. Hugo barely registered. Figured he'd wait in his car for Pistol to return. Take the call here. He didn't recognize the number.

To his surprise, it was the younger Trout son. Called himself Hen.

The kid's voice shook on the other line. "I have some new information. About my brother."

CHAPTER 24

As much as Marcella had looked forward to having Tyler home, she hadn't expected it to look like this. It was supposed to be a happy homecoming. Not this rancid stew of crap.

The car ride drained her. Her organs felt wrung out by nausea. Her head ached from suffering an extended bout of anxiety. Those physical symptoms seemed tepid compared to the searing emotional pain brought on by Tyler's reaction to her. His gut response at the sight of her. His persistent apology in the pained voice of a stranger. It literally felt like her life's blood had been leeched entirely. Her bad eye throbbed with a new, stinging pain. Her good eye felt worn out and raw from crying.

Tyler had gone straight to his cabin, shoulders drooping and head bowed, walking past Hen without acknowledging him. Marcella had watched her two sons, their non-interaction loaded with unspoken resentment, and sorrow filled her. A new worry for the future bore down, insurmountable, and she slowly trudged toward the house, feeling weary and much older than her years. Bernie said something in the background, which Hen swiftly mitigated. Their hushed voices faded as she ventured inside, vaguely aware of Hen taking off on his bike. She wanted only her bedroom. Her bed. The silk blindfold couldn't create the darkness she craved.

Now she lay in bed, her insides churning with exhaustion and sleeplessness, haunted by that voice: *I'm sorry. I'm so sorry.*

Hours passed in this fashion. Torture.

She barely noticed Bernie come in. His side of the bed dipped with his bodyweight. His familiar earthy smell of sawdust and motor oil found her senses.

She turned away from him. After his unacceptable behavior in the car, spewing that crap, she had no desire to be near him.

"Em, how are you feeling?"

After a bit, she whined, *hrm-mm*, which meant *leave me alone*.

The bed moved again as he lay down. The force with which his feet landed on the mattress told her he still wore his work boots.

She gritted her teeth and pain cut through her skull. Another sound came from her as she buried her face into the pillow, knocking her blindfold off-kilter.

"We should talk."

Her blood pressure spiked. "No." She'd explained more than once: since the accident, speaking brought physical pain. Why did he press her?

Bernie sighed. Minutes ticked by and nothing happened. Marcella felt her breathing settle a bit.

"I'm worried about Hen," he said quietly.

She opened her eyes to blunt darkness. "Why?"

"He's overworked. He's been doing everything. I think he needs help."

"You can help him."

He began unlacing his boots, lifting one leg up, then the other. It felt like a waterbed sloshed beneath her. He had the nerve to laugh. "You don't think I'm helping him? But he needs a different kind of help than what I normally do."

Marcella sighed. "I'm tired."

"If Tyler doesn't go back to work at Mini Chopper, we should put him to work here. He's an able-bodied man. There's no reason—"

"No." After the disaster of a drive home, Bernie thought it would be a good idea to put that poor boy to work? Now?

"He could do some of the grunt work that eats up all my time. It would free me up to do the books and—"

"Stop." If she didn't already have a headache, thinking about financials certainly would trigger a migraine.

Abruptly, Bernie got out of bed. Marcella seemed to levitate with the shift in weight distribution. Drawers opened. And telltale sounds of Bernie changing into pajamas.

"Are you really not going to talk to me? Come on, Em. It's me. Don't shut me out."

She took off the blindfold and turned. The bed hardly moved.

"What do you want, Bernie?"

"I just want to talk about stuff. Motel stuff."

"I don't want to talk about motel stuff."

Bernie's face changed. He looked right into her eyes. "Us then. I want to talk about us."

Marcella stifled a groan. "Oh, Bernie. Please."

"I know you're hurting. I know you're hurting in lots of ways."

She turned back to the window. "You have no idea."

"I do. I know you. I know you better than you know yourself."

She clamped her eyes shut to stop tears. Her voice wobbled. "That's enough."

A long bout of quiet. Nowhere near sleep for him, though, she could tell. His breathing, the way he rubbed his sore shoulder told her he was wide awake.

How convenient, so was she.

He spoke in a midday voice. Too loud. "You know, I did some reading about concussions. The way it affects a person's brain? Sometimes it affects their personality."

She huffed. "Now I'm Sybil?"

He scratched. It scraped her eardrum. "I wonder if we should've taken you to a neurologist. Maybe they could explain some stuff."

Sigh. "I don't need a neurologist. I'm getting better. It takes time."

More quiet. He turned toward her. She prayed he wouldn't curl up against her.

"I know it's got to be hard," he said, his mouth up against her ear.

She spun around with such force, the covers twisted around her torso. Bernie flinched back.

"What, Bernie? What do you think you *know* is hard?"

"Everything. Your recovery, of course. But also Tyler being home."

"Tyler being home is the sunshine in all this, Bernie. If you don't know that, you don't know me. And you don't know anything."

He nodded, placating. "I know."

"No, you don't! You *blame* him. You haven't forgiven him for what he did ten years ago."

"I'm working on it. I am. It's a process."

"And now you blame him for what happened to me. Admit it."

"Blame is a harsh word. I don't think—"

"How about you listen to me? How about you trust me?"

"Of course I trust you, Em."

"I need you to believe me. You, of all people in this whole thing, should be the one who believes me. Even if you're the only one."

"I do believe you."

"You do? You believe me when I say it wasn't Tyler?"

He shook his head, mumbling. He moved toward her. She pulled back. He obviously didn't believe her.

"Listen," he said. "you are my priority. You know I love you. I love you with everything in this world. I would do anything for you. I'm trying to protect you—"

She put up a hand. "Stop. Just stop. Please go sleep on the couch." His sappy sentiment made her feel ill.

"I'm not leaving this time. You need me here."

"No, I don't. I really don't."

"I'm staying."

His calm was maddening. "I don't want you. Here, I mean. I don't want you *here*, in bed." His face fell, and guilt pricked. "It's too hard to sleep with you tossing around," she added.

"See? This is what I mean. You keep pushing me away. We need to talk about us, Em. We need to stay together in all this."

"If you want to talk so badly, go see your therapist. Let him redirect your anger away from my son. Let him fix you."

The pause that followed brought a chill to the room. "We can't afford it, Em."

Now he wanted to claim Sally's money? Hen's inheritance? No, thank you. "Oh, but you want to send me to a neurologist that's not covered by our crappy insurance?"

His eyes dipped. "I'm just talking to you, Em."

"I don't want to talk! It hurts." She heard her voice crack, which pissed her off. "I told you before. It *hurts* to talk." She pulled the covers over her head, quickly, as tears started. "Please. Just go."

CHAPTER 25

Hen had to get away from the motel. Part of him wanted to run away to Alaska or someplace. After hanging up with the detective, he rushed back in to grab the empty prescription bottle, threw it into a Ziploc, and then—for lack of a better idea—stuffed it under his pillow for safekeeping. Sweating from nerves, he wasted no more time getting out of there. He would rather come face to face with Freddy Krueger than his brother, Tyler.

They pulled in right after he'd gotten his bike out. Hen froze, a foot poised on a pedal, as Tyler walked by zombie-like. After a few words with Bernie, Hen took off while Mom went inside.

He got to Wesley's, as promised, within the hour. So hyped on adrenaline, he barely remembered his bike ride down to Lakeside Inn. Wes waited on the bench outside the office, a bucket hat shadowing most of his face. Beneath it, a smile in a slice of sunshine.

But Hen wasn't much in the mood to joke around.

Wes didn't seem to notice. Just needed an audience.

"There's my man. Let's go."

"Where are we going?"

"Hardware store."

"I thought you had to stay here to watch the front desk."

"What—you checking up on me now? It's under control. And we need lightbulbs."

"Fine by me," he mumbled. "The farther from Blue Palms the better."

It felt good to keep moving. Although he'd rather play basketball than walk to the village, Wes proved a decent distraction.

"Next jogger who passes? Take a look at their face. That's what they look like when they're having sex."

Hen laughed half-heartedly. Until the next jogger went by, and they both cracked up. Felt good to laugh.

"You're a sicko. How do you come up with this stuff?"

"I'm prepping my standup routine."

Hen wiped laughter tears as they picked up their normal pace.

"So, you haven't asked about Bianca," Wes said, as if the mention of sex brought her to mind.

Hen's stomach swooped, hearing her name. He tried to sound aloof. "I'm supposed to ask about her?"

Wes whopped his shoulder. "Don't play dumb. I know Jay told you she went out in the boat with us."

Hen palmed the sky. "I don't need to know anything."

"Yeah, but. I want you to know." With each step, the air seemed heavier. "Keith was there too."

"Keith?" It didn't make sense. They weren't friends with Keith. Jay didn't mention... "How? I mean, what happened?"

"Bianca told him she was going, and he just showed up." Wes swallowed. His voice got low. "So, it got to be this thing. Like, Bianca made it a competition for her attention. Really annoying."

"I bet."

"But, in the end, I think it was good he was there. Keith, I mean. Because, well. He's an ass. We all know that. He was an ass that day too. But he was an ass who wouldn't let anyone touch Bianca." Pause. "You get me?"

Hen nodded. The whole thing felt wrong and Hen didn't want to be pulled in like this. He tried to think of something else to talk about, but Wes seemed determined.

"So, she keeps calling me and telling me it's over between the two of them, but I'm not buying it." A nervous glance. "I thought you should know."

"Not my business."

"Well, I wanted you to know. And she wanted you to know."

Hen's insides twisted, despite his slight relief. Why would Wes tell him all this? Did he want a medal for *not* taking advantage of Bianca? And why did Bianca want him to know she broke up with Keith?

Still, what Wes said didn't exactly ease Hen's conscience. So, would he have hooked up with Bianca if Keith weren't there?

He couldn't help asking. "Do you like her? Bianca?"

Wes flicked a hand at the traffic. "She came after me."

"Yeah, but. Do you like her?"

No answer. Wes wagged his head. "I dunno. Not really."

Hen held back from launching into it. *Come on, be a man.* The idea that Wes would even think about making a pass when he didn't even like her made his stomach turn. Bianca deserved better. Keith had nothing to do with it.

"Like I said. Not my business."

"Also, she wants to go by Bee now," said Wes. "Not Bianca."

"Also none of my business."

"Fine, man. Whatever."

Hen's sour mood intensified as the village crowd thickened with tourists, and the mood followed him into Lake George Hardware. The village was hopping. Hen felt guilty for leaving the motel. Who would take care of things if it got busy?

Pushing away some guilt, he waited up front while Wes shopped. The clerk made keys at the machine near the front counter, and Hen watched, transfixed. Hard to believe a strip of metal carved with bumps and grooves could unlock a door. Made him think about the master key and how it opens multiple doors. Speaking of, where did he put that thing? All the business finding and hiding the empty prescription bottle, he'd kind of lost track of it. Not in his pocket. Did he put it on the rack in the office? His neck got hot, worrying he'd misplaced it.

"I have an idea. Two actually." Wes held a two-pack of lightbulbs over his head.

Hen half-smiled. "I'd leave that one out of your standup routine."

Eager to get back—where was the darn key?—Hen stopped short when Wes turned the opposite way out of the hardware store.

"I'm thirsty. Let's hit the chopper."

Hen followed, feeling doubly anxious. First the key thing, and now he'd walk into Mini Chopper, Tyler's old workplace. He'd been in there a zillion times, sure. But had avoided it since Tyler had his meltdown. Hen had only heard bits and pieces, but even the wildest of scenarios wasn't out of the question.

While Wes went to the drink dispenser, Hen window-shopped the magazine rack. A fan of the old-school comic books, he spotted a Marvel—

"Hey," a voice behind him—female.

No way. "Bianca?"

She pulled her hair into a pony tail, showing the pale of her bare arms. "What are you doing?"

Hen shrugged, feeling hotter than the weather warranted. "Wes is back there getting a drink."

"So? What if I want to talk to you?" She smiled. A shy kind. Not flirty or anything.

"Okay," he said, mystified.

Dressed for the beach, her bathing suit straps were visible under her sundress. "Are you guys hanging around? Do you...want to hang out together?"

"I'm with Wes."

She had a really nice laugh. "I know."

"And we just came down to get something at the hardware store."

She bit her bottom lip. "And now?"

"I really need to get back. To the motel. Take care of things. You know." Geez, did he forget how to talk?

"Okay. Next time. Take care."

As she casually walked out, glancing back once, Hen trembled inside his shoes. What was that all about? His body had a clear reaction to her. Did he like her? Or had Wes put ideas into his head? He shook them away and went to the ice cream case—wanting cold.

Where the heck did Wes go? What was taking him so long?

Maybe he should get an ice cream.

An older guy in uniform did a double take on him, super obvious. Hen looked away, trying to brush him off.

"Hey, aren't you Tyler Trout's brother?"

Hen's heart rate kicked up, hearing his brother's name. "Uh, yeah?"

The guy wouldn't let up. "Do you know...how is he?"

"Oh, fine. Yeah. He's good. Thanks."

"Well, I know that's not exactly true." A sympathetic smile. "My name's Bill. I'm the manager here. I worked with Sheila Farris to get him a job here. Stocking shelves. I think you came in once with your mother during one of his shifts?"

Hen shrugged, hoping no one was listening. Especially Wesley.

Bill moved closer, shifted the box of whatever he carried to his other hip. "It's a bit of a revolving door around here. Not by design. I mean, we stay open all year. One of the few places in the village that does. So, when Sheila mentioned Tyler could potentially work here long-term, it was definitely an attractive offer. He was good at his job, you know? And he seemed to enjoy it."

Pause. Was this guy joking? "Yeah?" Hen scanned the store for Wes, desperate for him to interrupt. First, Bianca. Now, this.

"So, the abruptness of his leaving and the circumstances around him leaving, well, it's been a concern. Not only professionally but personally, for me. I have a soft spot for the kid. You know?"

"Sure. Yeah. I get you." Hen felt beyond uncomfortable with this conversation. This guy, Bill genuinely cared about Tyler, a new phenomenon. Did he know what happened at the motel? Did he know Tyler had been arrested for assaulting his own mother? Probably not. Hen felt swollen by the secret.

Tyler. Tyler. Now he couldn't get his brother out of his head.

"So, how's he doing?"

"Um, I guess he's okay. I mean, he's home."

"Okay, okay. That's good." Bill stared down a store aisle.

Hen's thoughts turned dark. Yes, his brother was back home, out on bail. Mom home too. Did he have his meds? Was he taking them? Who knew? Did anyone check? Dread sludged down to his knees as he thought the worst. Mom, probably in bed, a sitting duck with Tyler—off his meds—with zero control over his thoughts and behavior and feelings. No reasoning with the irrational. The only saving grace was Bernie being there too. Hen hoped against hope Bernie stayed home and didn't run some stupid errand.

Wes showed up, chugging Mountain Dew. Hen eyed his best friend, knowing the drink hadn't been paid for.

"What's up?" Wes wiped his upper lip.

"Oh, nothing. My brother used to work here." Hen started burning up again.

"Really?" Wes laughed for no reason.

Bill glanced at Wes, ignoring the open soda, and then he endeared himself to Hen again. "Will you please tell him I asked about him? And please let him know, he's got a job whenever he's ready to come back."

On the way back to Lakeside Inn, Hen was so distracted by the master key and Tyler and Bianca, he had zero interest in playing basketball. Which never happened. That truth made him uneasy, walking beside Wes, as if he was keeping secrets from him. As they got farther from the village, Hen felt himself relax. Until, out of nowhere, Wes asked, "Hey, did I see Bianca in there?"

CHAPTER 26

Detective Randolf didn't have to wait long for Pistol Pete to return. Twenty minutes, tops. He took the time to mull over the strange phone conversation with the younger Trout brother.

"Tyler was off his meds," he'd said, out of breath like he'd been working out.

"Come again?"

"My brother, Tyler Trout? You know he has schizophrenia? Well, that night, he was off his meds."

"And how do you know this?"

"I found the empty prescription bottle. In his room."

Randolf flipped open his little notebook and jotted down what Hen told him, verbatim.

Hen rushed to fill the silence. "You know, people with his condition have been known to do things...terrible things...that are out of character. You know, while off meds."

Randolf had held back a sigh. This kind of evidence, delivered in desperation by a family member, usually led to more problems. More unanswerable questions. Odd, though. This particular so-called evidence wouldn't help his brother's case, but make it worse.

He'd kept his voice neutral. "Okay. Where is this bottle now?"

A hesitation so pronounced, Randolf heard Hen hold his breath. "Oh, I have it. I mean, I can get it."

"Okay."

After a while: "So, what does it mean?"

And here, the detective had heard regret. He'd explained a bit about the process of interviewing the medical professionals who had treated Tyler in the past—in his usual carefully vague way. Hen, not Randolf, had ended the call with an abrupt "gotta go."

Now, Randolf flipped his phone open and closed, meditating on what Hen told him. Minutes later, the rust-bucket two-door pulled up alongside the dilapidated house. When Pistol got out, he stared at the detective, challenging him. One hand weighed down as if the six pack of beer were a kettlebell.

Randolf waved him over. "Can I have a word?"

Since Paula Hugo still sat in a lawn chair trimming her nails with her teeth, he invited Pistol to sit on the hood of his car. The easy way Pistol joined him, handing him a Coors Light, zapped any suspicion away.

Pistol lit a cigarette. "'Sup?"

Randolf patiently asked the standard questions, referencing his pocket calendar. Turns out, Pistol had indeed used the car the night in question.

"Yeah, we went down to Dudley's."

Randolf straightened. "In Lake George?" Dudley's Tavern happened to be right down the street from Blue Palms—the scene of the incident.

"Yeah. Me, Flat Eric, Bacon, and Flake."

Randolf stopped writing. "Are those real names?"

"Just Eric."

He wrote the names down as he heard them. He knew Dudley's proprietor, who could get him access to their security cameras.

"Was the car at Dudley's all night?"

Pistol nodded, exhaling smoke slowly, so it filled all the crevices of his skeletal features.

"And you were the only one who drove it?"

He scratched his ear and made a face. "Bacon went out to smoke some hooch. Used the car for it. Said he stayed in the parking lot, but I think he took it out."

"Why would you think that?"

"Parked in a different spot." Pistol drank some beer. Smoked a little. "Took a while to find it when we wanted to take off."

"Is that something Bacon does often? Take the car without permission?"

Pistol looked at Randolf like he'd spoken Swahili. Randolf changed tack. "How did he get the keys, anyway?"

"Keys? Keys stay in the car. Who's gonna steal that piece of crap?"

Randolf waited, thinking there was more to the story.

Sure enough. "Yeah, Bacon was off that night. I remember. We don't go down often. As soon as we hit the village, he was all jumpy."

"Really. Why, do you suppose?"

Pistol shrugged. "Not like me and him are super tight. Who knows?"

Maybe Bacon had unfinished business in the village...at Blue Palms? The familiar rush in his chest told Randolf he was close to something. "I'm going to need Bacon's real name. First and last."

Pistol looked blank. "Bacon?" Then he shouted across the street. "Paula, what's Bacon's name?"

Paula bobbed her foot, still working on her nails. "How am I supposta know? He's your stupid friend."

Pistol threw down his cigarette with a shrug, a puzzled frown amidst the smoke. "Whatever. From the get-go, he's Bacon."

Randolf chuckled. "You seriously don't know his real name?"

Pistol heaved off the hood of the car. "I know where he lives."

"Well, then. That will be great. I'll take it from there." He jotted down what became more like directions rather than an address. Randolf hid his frustration. Nothing about today had been straightforward. All part of the job.

Minutes later, though, alone in his car, he didn't feel like singing. He didn't even play the radio as he navigated the impossible, circuitous route to Bacon's residence not a half-mile away.

CHAPTER 27

"Yo, Hen, wait up," Wes called from behind.

Hen picked up his pace, not caring if he annoyed his best friend. All he cared about was getting back to the motel to check on Mom. What the hell was he doing, roaming around the village with his Mom in danger? Tyler, like, ready to pounce? He could scream, he was so mad at himself.

"What's your deal, man?"

"I gotta get back."

"All of a sudden? I thought we were gonna hang."

Hen only shook his head.

"You're funny."

"Stop saying that. I'm not funny."

"No, like...you came down to Lakeside all like eff that and eff Blue Palms and eff my brother and stuff. Now you're rushing back?"

"I wasn't 'eff' anything."

"You know what I mean."

Hen stopped walking and forced himself to breathe. Felt it deep in his lungs.

Wes came around and stood right in front of him, blocking his way. "Why such a rush to get back?"

"I think I forgot something is all." Hen didn't know what else to say. He wanted to make sure Mom was okay. But he also wanted to forget about Bianca for a little while. Hen didn't understand why she kept popping into his head. But he certainly didn't want to talk to Wes about her.

"Like what?" Wes's bucket hat looked like a giant saucer. When Hen didn't answer, Wes wagged his head. "Wrong way, my man. You're going the wrong way."

"What do you mean?"

"Like, I think the problem is you're too wrapped up in that stuff over there. And it hasn't exactly been a smooth ride."

"What are you talking about?"

Almost to Lakeside Inn. Hen could see his bike poking out of the carport. Practically home. Relief doubled down when he found the master key in his bike pouch.

"You keep getting deeper into the bullshit over there, man. You need to pull yourself out of it."

Hen didn't answer. But he listened.

Wes kept talking. "After graduation, you should get the hell outta Dodge. Move away. College or not. Doesn't matter. You just need to go. Do your own thing."

"Whatever. You don't know what you're talking about." At Lakeside now. Hen pulled out his bike, hopped on.

Wes straddled the front tire, his knees a vice grip. "Sure, I do."

"I couldn't leave my mom."

"Yes, you can. And you will. Come with me. I'm going out west. And if you're worried about money, I can help."

Hen chuckled, fiddled with his bike gears. "Money isn't an issue."

The air stilled around them. Why had he said that? Wes's hardened gaze was too serious under the floppy hat. "Money isn't an issue? Oh, really? Do tell, Daddy Warbucks."

"Nothing. It's nothing. Can you move out of the way?"

"No. Tell me about all your money, man. What—did your father set you up? Win the lottery? Tell me."

A jolt hit Hen's gut at the mention of his father. He'd never known his dad, the deadbeat who left Mom before Hen was born. He decided a long time ago not to waste time thinking about that ghost.

"No. Not my father. Not the lottery."

Wes waited, his lips parted like when he listened to his favorite music. Hen felt himself smile. Wes, his best friend, could be trusted. Right? The yearning to tell him this big thing overwhelmed his better judgment. Telling Wes suddenly seemed crucial.

Hen's words were quick. Like passing a hot potato. "A family friend...when she died, she left me her estate. I get it when I turn eighteen." It felt so good to say it aloud.

Wes's eyebrows shot up. "How much?"

"I dunno. Like, a million-five. Something like that."

"A mil-five? *Something like that?* Are you for real?" Wes laughed heartily, kicked the tire sideways. Hen caught the bike frame before it hit the pavement.

"Not a big deal."

Wes laughed in his easy way. "Oh, yes, it is."

"Yeah. I mean, it is. But it's not like it's going to change my life or anything."

"Oh, but it could, my man. This is exactly what I'm talking about."

Hen's grin went to his ears. Somehow, getting home didn't seem as urgent as before. "What exactly are you talking about?"

Wes stretched his arms as wide as his dream. "Me, you, going in on our own thing, together. Out west. I'm thinking big. I'm thinking Colorado."

Hen's way no longer blocked, he was taken by Wes's dream and in no rush to leave. But, unlike Wes and most other kids who grew up in the Adirondacks, Hen hadn't learned to ski. Or snowboard. Basketball filled his winters. "What the hell would I do in Colorado? You know I don't ski."

"Right. I'll be the ski bum." Wes gave his signature, open-mouthed grin. "But our job would be hotels. You know, do what we know. We run our own resort. In Boulder or somewhere cool. You and me. Big time, my man. We'll be big time."

Wes's wide grin was contagious. Hen felt something tingly move from his toes into his chest, and it had nothing to do with Bianca Chase.

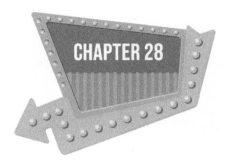

CHAPTER 28

Cabin eleven smelled like ammonia. The stiff bed sheets reminded Ty of rehab. Hen cleaned it, Marcella had said. "A good, thorough cleaning."

The first night back he slept on top of the slippery comforter. So slick it felt like slime. He tunneled under the blankets in the middle of the night. Sally visited then, standing at the foot of the bed, eyeing him like she used to years ago. Disapproving. Still there even when he pulled the covers over his head. But she stayed quiet. Sometimes, she didn't have to say anything.

It took days for the smell to go away. Not sure how many. By then, Ty only got out of bed to use the bathroom or to eat something. He ate the same thing all day long until it was gone, then went on to the next thing. It didn't matter what went into his body as long as he stayed full.

The next day, Sally spoke to him. *It's coming for you.* A stern warning. He knew she meant the Y2K crisis, but she didn't get specific. Still, he couldn't help imagining the ticking time bomb that would lead to the end of the world—all controlled by tech. Danger lurked everywhere.

So, he stayed in bed.

Darkness found him even there. Like the bed would swallow him up.

A knock at the door.

"Who is it?"

"It's Bernie. Your ma wants me to take you to see Dr. Asner."

Ty shouted to be heard. "That's today?"

Bernie shouted too. "Yahp. You decent?"

"What?"

"Can you open up?"

Ty didn't want to get up. He especially didn't want to open the door to the outside world. His curtains had been shut tightly since his return. The mere thought of looking out the window made his knees squiggle.

But then, like magic, there he stood, the sun playing in, warming his tube socks, Bernie silhouetted in the doorway. Fresh air stung. He squinted against the too-bright light.

"Do you want to put some proper clothes on?"

Ty surveyed his outfit, his old gray sweats.

"Or you could go like that," Bernie said. "Don't matter to me."

Ty stared at the carpet. It hurt to look out, with the sun.

"At least put some shoes on? Come on. We'll take your ma's car." An about face, and Bernie headed for Marcella's car without looking back.

Ty knew what to do. He got out of his sweats, pulled on jeans and a T-shirt. Found his sneakers under the bed. Grabbed his baseball cap to shield the sun.

Outside.

He left the door unlocked so he didn't have to worry about the key. Kept his eyes on the gravel at his feet. A hundred steps to Marcella's car, felt like. The muscles in his legs seemed out of practice. He slunk into the backseat, exhausted already.

"What, am I your chauffeur?"

Ty glanced up. "Huh?"

"Never mind," Bernie mumbled. "Probably better this way."

The car hummed along. Ty closed his eyes, on the brink of sleep when Bernie started talking again.

"You plan to get back to Mini Chopper? To work, I mean?"

Ty came to, just enough to process the question. Bernie asked if he would go back to work at the store? Ty had no answer. He didn't want to see Roxanne again.

Bernie went on. "Because if you don't, we could use the help around the motel."

Ty looked out the window, the highway median so familiar it seemed sad. Carved into a huge forest with two wide lanes of pavement, leaving a big blotch in the middle. Do animals live in there, in the trees, trapped in the median of the highway? Have to cross for food and water. Seems like a pretty crappy habitat. How do they survive? How will they survive after Y2K takes their small patch of habitat away? What will it look like then? All pavement and lanes and electric cars? Will animals continue to exist anywhere, no less the narrow patch of wood between two roads. Ty trembled, watching the blur of trees out the window.

"What do you say to that?"

"Huh?"

Bernie studied him in the rearview. "Your ma didn't want me talking about this with you. But it's just a friendly chat, right? Can't go the whole way to Glens Falls without talking, right?"

Confusion filled the car like dust particles. Ty didn't like sitting in the back seat now. In the narrow rectangular mirror, he could only see Bernie's sunglasses. What if he were a spy for the Y2K tech...all this time? Marcella trusted Bernie, but could he?

"Getting a lot out of these sessions with Dr. Asner?" Bernie asked after a bit.

Ty shrugged. "Been a while."

"Right. But, are you going to be talking about what happened that night? What happened to your mother?"

Ty tore his eyes from the sunglasses in the mirror. Heat flooded his veins.

"You're gonna tell the truth, right?"

Ty nodded, turned to look out the window. No more trees in the median. Just dead grass. Only bugs lived in there, probably.

"Cause we're all dying to hear it."

Bernie used a strange tone. Ty had heard it before. He sank into the seat cushion, unsure really what Bernie was talking about anymore.

Ty SAT on the musty loveseat, waiting for his session to start. Dr. Asner sat across from him on another loveseat. She waited. For what? Did she already ask a question?

He stared at the rug—all the paisley and flowers and swirly designs. Old-timey style rug. From the Orient. He played a game and tried to find a face inside the pattern. But the one that appeared—menacing and deformed—made his heart clench. He averted his eyes. Set them on his hands in his lap, but he still felt the misshapen face staring.

"Tyler," she said in a sing-song.

He glanced up at her. She wore jeans and a cardigan. Her hair pinned back at the sides. She looked different from the last time he saw her.

"How is it to be home?" She'd asked this question earlier. The one he'd missed.

He shrugged.

"Please use words, okay?"

"Okay."

"How do you feel, being back? With your family?"

"Don't see them much."

"You stay in your room?"

"Mostly."

A hint of a sigh. "Okay, Tyler. Before we get into what happened, and I will let you guide us on how you'd like to speak about that, there's some business we should clear up."

A long pause. Ty tried not to look at the face in the rug and who might have put it there.

"As you might remember, Sheila Farris, your social worker, and I have been working on getting you into that day program, where you could not only socialize in a safe environment but also learn valuable life skills—like balancing a check book and how to write a resume and useful real-world things. We had been extremely lucky Bill Loftus agreed to hire you on a trial basis."

Another long pause. Ty flicked his eyes again to restart her lecture.

"But your arrest changes everything. You're no longer eligible for the day program, and your mandatory meetings with me take a greater weight, so to speak. I'm required to report to the authorities after each session. Do you understand?"

Ty nodded, a numb feeling descending.

Dr. Asner gave a slight smile. "You're a good person, Tyler. I know that in my heart. I will do whatever I can to help you. It's always been my goal to help make you a whole person. Do you know what I mean?"

Ty shook his head quickly—wanting to get rid of the question. It sounded icky. The face in the rug laughed at him.

"What I mean is, I want you to be able to stand on your own two feet. I want you to gain independence and live your best life. What that looks like very much depends on you."

She got quiet then, still with a small smile.

Clock's second hand went around almost an entire revolution.

"Unfortunately, this recent setback might undo all our progress. But I refuse to give up on you. I want you to know that. You have a lot of people willing to help you."

"Okay," he mumbled.

"But you need to help us too." Now she seemed sad.

Her next question sounded like soft clouds. "Do you want to talk about what happened with your mother?"

Ty hung his head. A deep sadness found him. "She's getting better. Sheila said she was getting better."

"Your mother's improving." Not a question. "That must make you happy."

"Her face is different."

"She's still your mother."

"Marcella."

"Right. Her name is Marcella. And she's your mother."

A giant wave of fatigue struck. He knew he couldn't meet Dr. Asner's eyes again. She seemed to know this too.

"All right. When you're ready."

Silence stretched so long, Ty's neck started to cramp. He wanted to hide inside Dr. Asner's throw pillows. How long had he been sitting here?

A panicky swirl in his gut reminded him about the important information he gave to Hen and the lawyer and the detective. What happened with it? Why didn't anyone talk about it? Did they get it to tech? He opened his lips to ask, but—

Another soft cloud: "How about the store? Did you like working there?"

The store? Ty didn't really want to think about the store. He nodded and shrugged at the same time, his feelings a jumble of cereal boxes and Roxanne Russo. But he didn't want to think about Roxanne. He forced something else into his brain.

"Bernie asked me that too."

"He asked you?"

"If I was going back. If I wanted to go back."

"Oh. And what did you say?"

"He wants me to work at the motel, I think."

"Bernie does?"

Tyler nodded.

If experience taught him right, her next question should have been, *How do you feel about that?* But it wasn't. "What about Hen?"

"What about him?"

"Have you seen him?"

"Yeah. I think so." Did it matter?

"Is he still working at the motel?"

"I think so."

She nodded. Jotted something down. "We had talked about your stay at the motel to be temporary. Your job at the store was a way for you to make money in your own right so you can eventually get a place on your own. But considering all the changes of late, working at the motel might be a good option."

She sounded so hopeful. Ty wanted to feel it too. She shifted, re-crossed her legs. "Yes, I think it's a very good option, now that I think of it. Especially considering Hen's situation."

Ty frowned, tried not to look at the rug.

She kept talking. "He won't be working there much longer, as you know."

Something bubbled up. Ty felt it in his throat. "Why not?"

"Well, he's almost eighteen. He'll graduate and claim his inheritance and then—"

"What? His what?"

Dr. Asner's face went blank. "The money Hen is due to inherit. You know about this. Sheila told me before we got started. Your mother—"

"Money? Hen's getting money? From where?"

It was a trap. A dirty trick. Ty's family had no money. The Y2K people were playing some kind of game, getting their hooks into Hen.

She looked at him hard. "You've forgotten. It is not my place to say—" She fidgeted, looked away.

Ty levitated over his seat, felt like. "How much?"

She studied her fingernails now. "That's something I couldn't disclose even if I knew."

"Is it cash or electric money, like in a computer?"

She flicked lint off her jeans, her face going red. "You should really talk to your mother about this. I'm sorry I brought it up." She

166 | J. D. SPERO

locked eyes with him suddenly. "This money should be a non-factor in your situation."

Ty stared at his shrink, who looked like a stranger. "Hen's money."

"Right. Hen's money." She glanced at the clock over the door. Her neck was red too. "Time's up."

CHAPTER 29

Marcella timed it perfectly to be downstairs when the dryer stopped. Pulling out warm towels, she inhaled the scent of her favorite laundry detergent. How many afternoons had she hidden down in the basement, folding linens? For once, the unending laundry that accompanied motel life seemed a blessing. Down here, where she couldn't tell if it were sunny or cloudy or rainy or what, she lost herself in a brainless, repetitive task and pretended the rest of the world didn't exist. Neither did her problems.

She wished the same for her memories.

Young Marcella, in the driveway of her babysitter's home, wouldn't let go of her mother's leg. She'd been dropped there before, but this time felt different. Mom had been unusually quiet on the way. No pep talk or false cheer as she clutched the steering wheel. At their destination, she shook her leg as if to shoo Marcella away, barking a laugh in a single, bitter note. Dread filled young Marcella's heart, hearing her mother laugh like that.

"Don't leave," she'd whispered.

"Don't be silly," her mother said. And then to the sitter, "Come and get her, will you?"

Her sitter—named Carolyn or Caroline?—had to pry Marcella from her mother, muttering assurances that fell on deaf ears. Her mother didn't say goodbye. Not even a wave from the car. Marcella's fear was too great for tears, but it clogged her up inside so that she couldn't eat or drink or watch television. Hours passed as she stared out the window. It seemed certain her mother would never come back for her.

But she did. That day, she did.

Now, a sudden thundering down the bare wood stairs shocked her alert. She hugged a towel to her chest on reflex.

A man approached. Every muscle in her body went rigid as his silhouette gradually found the circle of light in which she stood.

"Tyler?" A wave of relief. "What are you doing down here?"

"Bernie said you'd be here." He looked around, perhaps for a place to sit.

She had the only chair. If she gave it up, she'd get queasy. "Is there anything wrong?"

"No. No. No." Tyler shuffled in place, agitated.

Grateful for the dim light of the basement, Marcella kept the bad side of her face in shadow. "Did you just get back from your appointment with Dr. Asner?"

A slight nod.

"That's great, sweetie. I'm so glad."

She finished folding the towel she held. Tyler frowned at the ground. A spider crawled out from under the rug covering the cement floor. Black and round—so small it could be mistaken for a beetle. She thought for sure her son would squash it with his foot. But he didn't seem to see it.

"I was thinking about calling your lawyer. What's his name again? Mr. Haas?"

Tyler blinked at her, a dullness in his eyes.

Now she spoke to herself. "Maybe I'll try the detective again. What was his name? Randolf, I think. He's probably closer to the investigation, anyway. I can't wait to get all that business behind us. You know? So we can focus on getting you back on track. Like, into that program or whatever." She raised up a smile and then turned back to the dryer. She took her time folding a few hand towels, half expecting Tyler to leave.

He didn't. He stood there, staring at the cement floor where the spider had been. Marcella wanted to fill the silence but didn't know what to say. Once again, she felt out of her league. She wished for someone to tell her what to do.

Then, out of nowhere: "Is Hen getting money?"

Marcella swallowed a hiccup of surprise, then caught herself. "You mean, for the housekeeping he does? Yes, of course. Not a lot, mind you. More like an allowance." She grabbed the last towel. Regretfully, it had cooled. She folded it quickly and set it on her lap.

Tyler didn't say anything, just frowned at the dirty rug. Marcella fought a niggling shame for having spent so much time down here in this dank place. And for liking it so much.

Then, Bernie's words from the other night came to mind. "Does this have to do with... Do you want to talk about working here, at the motel? Did Bernie put you up to this?" She stacked the linens in her arms.

Tyler's eyes stayed on her. He struggled for words. "No. No. No. An inheritance. Dr. Asner said he was getting money."

Marcella allowed a sigh. So many emotions flooded her at once. First and foremost, irritation at Dr. Asner for speaking out of turn. Flustered, she handed Tyler the towels. "Here. Bring these up."

Tyler's limp grip on the pile matched his expression. She walked by him, following an urge to be aboveground. "I have to go lie down."

Deep fatigue pressed down on her. Up the stairs painstakingly, she pulled on railings, hoisting herself up each step. Ty followed. Too closely.

"Please. Please, give me some space."

Her breath grew ragged. At the top, a wave of humid air struck her—and she thought she might faint. In the kitchen, Bernie stood, fists on hips, apparently waiting for her. She moved past him, in no state to entertain his mood du jour.

Bernie's voice boomed. "Did he go down there? What did he say?"

Marcella sat at the table, trying to catch her breath. "Would you get me a glass of water?"

Tyler stood at the entryway, holding the pile of towels, staring at her. Why did he have to stare at her like that? Gave her goose bumps. Those bright blue eyes of his, just like his late father's.

"What?" she snapped.

Her water appeared. She took a long drink. Bernie sat next to her. Tyler still stood with the towels, looking ridiculous. The towels, useless props, did not convey Tyler's health and competence as she'd hoped. On the contrary, they seemed to highlight his irrelevance. His weakness. His instability. As if he held an empty box. She could barely stand the sight.

"You can put those in the linen closet, sweetie. Right down the hall."

Tyler didn't seem to register. "Is it a secret?"

Bernie: "Is what a secret?"

"Nothing!" Marcella drank more water. "Go ahead and put those towels away, Tyler. Thanks so much."

Tyler didn't budge.

"What did he ask you?" Bernie said, his mouth too close to her ear. She felt the tingling itch of a coming migraine.

"Nothing. I need to lie down." But she didn't make a move to get up. She shooed them both. "You two, go do something. Go busy yourselves somewhere."

"He didn't say a word on the ride home," said Bernie, as if Tyler weren't standing there. "Except that he wanted to talk to you. And I warned him—"

She turned sharp eyes on Bernie. "You warned him? Of what? Tyler has every right to talk to his mother. If he needs something or... whatever. I don't need to remind you of that, do I?"

Bernie's jaw fell open and then knocked shut. He swung his gaze to Tyler. "Go ahead then, talk."

Tyler with his towels. "Hen's inheriting money."

Bernie wagged his head toward Marcella. She refused to look at him. Stared at the inch of water left in her glass.

"Well, well, well," he said under his breath.

She ignored Bernie and focused on Tyler, feigning courage. "Yes, that's right. I've told you this before. I'm sure of it."

"I didn't know." Tyler sounded like a child.

Her war-torn smile felt its wound. "Oh, of course you did."

"How much?"

She felt Bernie tense beside her. "It doesn't really matter. Does it? It's going to be Hen's when he turns eighteen. When he's an adult. And he's probably going to spend it on his college education. Although we haven't figured it all out quite yet. Or, *he* hasn't." She laughed stupidly. "There's still time."

Tyler's eyes got bluer as he stared, the light from the window making them glow. "Where did it come from? The money?"

Bernie let out an insolent laugh. "Go ahead. Tell him. He's a grown man. He can handle it." In bitter, uncharacteristic sarcasm.

Marcella glared. Tyler being a grown man had nothing to do with whether he could handle *it*, as Bernie was well aware. She took a shaky breath. Her nerves had no place here. She changed tack. "Why don't *you* tell him, Bernie?"

"Sure!" Too loud. Falsely upbeat. "See, Tyler. You remember my ma, Miss Sally? Of course, you do. Well, it turns out she had a lot of money. One-point-three *million* to be exact. And she put it in a trust for none other than Henry Trout, your baby brother, to inherit when he turns eighteen. Just because he's such a peachy kid. Isn't that wonderful?"

Marcella rolled her eyes. Didn't he know Tyler couldn't detect sarcasm? Didn't he know how cruel he sounded? She forced a lighthearted atmosphere. Or perhaps she meant to belittle the truth Bernie just spewed. "Geez. Let's not get crazy." As soon as she said the word, she wished she hadn't. Her chest filled with heat.

Ty opened his mouth but nothing came out. Did he think she referred to him?

Marcella mashed her lips together. Could she not do anything right?

Bernie ranted on. "Now, if you're thinking you have any right to that money, think again. Or should I say, over my dead body." He laughed, and Marcella bristled.

Over my dead body. Did he really just say that...to Tyler?

"That's enough." She pressed herself up from the table, sneering at Bernie. "I'm going to lie down."

"No. No. No." Tyler, still with the towels. "I don't want money. I just didn't know. I don't like secrets."

"Well, now you know," Bernie said.

"There's no conspiracy here, Tyler. Don't jump to that. Really, this has been in place for many years and if you'd forgotten...well, I'm sorry for that."

Tyler wrinkled his brow. Did he understand any of this? Had they made things worse? She shouldn't have used that word, crazy. Or that other word—conspiracy—which was reserved for Dr. Asner and other professionals looking in on Tyler's illness. The objective perspective, so to speak. Marcella felt drained and ticked off at another failure in her repertoire. *Please, someone tell me what to do here.*

She touched Tyler's shoulder as she passed him. It felt soft and weak beneath the thin cotton fabric of his T-shirt. The word *pulpy* came to mind, and she took back her hand. "Let's not say anything to Hen about this," she whispered. "He's got a lot on his mind. It's a big responsibility, you know."

She waited for Tyler to nod. It took longer than it should've.

Pure exhaustion settled in her bones. All the activity—the talking, the stairs—had made her woozy. She worried she might faint right then and there.

She left the two of them in the kitchen with all their unhealed wounds and unresolved issues and stubborn grudges and the stack of clean towels and her dirty water glass and went to bed. They could figure out what to do with all that stuff.

"COME ON, Tyler. Put those towels away so you can help me out with something."

Bernie pushed down his resentment and went outside, assuming Tyler would follow him to the pool. The Macaulay family from cabin four had just gotten out and were drying off. Bernie gave a friendly wave and overheard them talking dinner plans. Soon, the pool area would be empty. Perfect.

The Macaulays latched the gate behind them as Tyler came out. He moved soundlessly, hands balled up in his pockets. Bernie tried not to look at him. It was easier that way.

"Okay then. I'm putting you in charge of the pool. Every evening it needs to be skimmed. Skimmer's over there on the fence." Before he could finish, Tyler fetched the skimmer. "Scoop up all the floaties —y'know, the pollen specks and stuff—off the surface." Tyler had already started. "That's good. Good."

Bernie cooled, bitterness floating off him like steam. Maybe this would turn things around for all of them—putting Tyler to work like this.

"And once a week, the pool needs to be shocked and vacuumed."

Tyler kept skimming. Bernie had to admit, he did a pretty good job.

"Okay, take a break from that and let me show you where I keep all the pool stuff."

He led Tyler to the shed which housed the pump as well as the giant bin of chlorine tablets. Next, he showed Tyler how to use the vacuum which reminded Bernie of a sea creature. "It's like any other vacuum. But you're moving through water and sometimes it doesn't want to follow your lead, you know what I'm saying?"

Tyler looked blank, but nodded. Bernie chose not to be skeptical and continued with instructions. "Here are the chemicals to shock the pool. Just open one of these bags and dump it in the water."

He wandered back to the pool. Tyler followed. "It keeps it a nice blue, the water. If you notice it's looking a little green, it needs to be shocked. Depending on how much activity is out here, it may need it more than once a week. But no one can swim for about twenty minutes after, so you want to time it right." Tyler nodded, the pool ripples reflected in his eyes. Blue on blue.

"You want to vacuum at a time when no one's swimming too," Bernie said softly. "Like, maybe at night."

"I can do that. I can do that." Tyler's words were quick. Took Bernie off guard.

"Yeah? You think you can handle this? Like, all of it?"

"Yes. Yes. Yes. I can do it." He grabbed the skimmer and got back to work. Bernie watched him a while and the tangle of feelings loosened and smoothed out. Tyler looked tired. His hands unsteady but driven by a surprising determination. As if skimming the pool were of utmost importance. Bernie softened and tried to take him as if he'd just met the kid. Like all the baggage and stuff between them didn't exist. Swollen beneath his jeans and T-shirt, battered by everyday life. Bernie felt sorry.

But he couldn't bring himself to say so.

"Okay then. You're officially in charge of the pool. So, go ahead and finish that up and on Sunday we can vacuum and shock. I'll help you the first time around." He waited, but Tyler didn't respond, fixated on the wide screen of the skimmer as it slowly filled with bugs and seeds and maple keys. "I'll be inside doing the books." He paused, then mimicked Hen. "They're kind of a mess." He laughed, knowing Tyler didn't get it.

He left him out there with the skimmer, pleased to cross pool maintenance off his to-do list. Until he sat before the screen, faced with baffling Excel spreadsheets, and missed the fresh outdoor air, the calming effect of the water, the strong chemical smell of chlorine.

Quiet settled in the house. He watched Tyler through the window. He skimmed for a long while, his shoulders hunched and his gaze never leaving the pool. After a while, Bernie noticed Tyler's lips moving. Not the first time he'd witnessed him talking to himself.

Now, though, with the dappled pool lights reflecting on his once-handsome face, it looked freakish and pathetic and sad.

Bernie tore his gaze away, back to the computer screen, a lump crawling from his chest to his throat. A yearning to be close to Marcella struck like a gale force wind. Maybe he'd do the bills tomorrow.

CHAPTER 30

Randolf sat in the tiny backroom office at Dudley's Tavern, poring over security camera footage from the past few weeks. He blinked away fatigue and considered ordering a coffee even though he craved a nice glass of scotch.

He hadn't felt like singing on his return trip from Minerva to Lake George. But then, the song had risen up out of the silence as if the radio had turned on, filling the car. It took him by surprise and made him realize his singing was subconscious—and he spent the remainder of the hour-plus trip pondering how many times he'd embarrassed himself at the station.

That and, well, the Bacon ordeal.

After waiting forty-five minutes at Meadowbay apartment complex for Bacon to show, a local cop had pulled up responding to a complaint about a suspicious man loitering on the property. And even though he'd flashed his badge and explained the situation to the officer's satisfaction, the experience proved to be the straw that broke the camel's back, as they say. It was always irksome to be interrogated by one of your own.

As curious as he was to meet this Bacon character—what kind of guy allows himself to be called Bacon?—at that point he wanted to be done with Minerva.

Plus, in the back of his mind, this footage could vet the whole Bacon-as-suspect idea, anyway. Could be a dead end.

By the time he'd gotten back to Lake George, it was the perfect time to pay Big Dudley a visit before the restaurant got too busy for the night.

He'd forgotten how boring parking lot security camera footage could be. While the scratchy images flickered over the screen, he went over the facts of the case. Tried to organize all the chicken scratch notes in his little pad.

1. Marcella Trout, 49, attacked the night of Friday, June first at approximately 10:19 pm at her home and motel property office at Blue Palms in the village of Lake George.

2. Motive for attack unknown.

3. The victim described her attacker as an overweight man wearing a black hooded sweatshirt. No facial description provided. Trauma serious but non-life-threatening. Victim unable to work, recovering from concussion. Victim unable to provide detailed account of attack.

4. Tyler Trout, 27, the only witness and son of victim, became primary suspect when his statement of interest to the police—*It was me!*—was deemed a confession.

5. Witness/suspect Tyler Trout, convicted felon (involuntary manslaughter) suffers from paranoid schizophrenia. May have been off medications at time of incident. (Evidence: empty prescription bottle found in motel room)

6. Tyler Trout described a large man ("a gorilla") attacked his mother. (Though his view obstructed by tempered glass of the office, description corroborates victim's testimony "overweight man.")

7. Attacker's car described as a rusted two-door, sports-car style. Make: Mazda. License plate 430-0MM. Potentially made skid marks at driveway entrance— though non-conclusive. (Marks have since been obscured

by other tire marks.) Car said to have been in Lake George (Dudley's Tavern) the night of the crime. Car's owner: Paula Hugo, not currently a suspect. Car's driver: Peter (Pistol) Bortello, not currently a suspect. Pistol's friend, Bacon (?), may have had access to car at time of incident.

Hmm...that's where things got murky. Bacon apparently went out to the car to smoke pot. Maybe took it for a drive, maybe not. Pistol claims the car was moved, but how reliable was his word after a night of drinking and recreational drugs?

Still, Randolf's gut told him the Trout kid didn't hurt his mother. But, of course, his gut wasn't going to hold any kind of weight in court. The more he thought about it, the more this Bacon character was a person of interest if not a bona fide suspect in the case.

Not a dead end at all.

A knock on the door. Dudley himself, with a platter of chicken wings. "Extra spicy for my ol' pal?"

Randolf's stomach lurched at the smell of bubbling hot buffalo sauce. "Aw, wow. I'm famished. Thank you."

Dudley winked and handed him a can of light beer. "Good luck," he said, and shut him in with the beer and the wings and a pile of napkins. No use trying to rewind or fast forward the tapes with hot sauce on his fingers. Randolf let the tapes play while he ate. Closest thing he'd had for a dinner break in some time.

His mouth on fire, the platter lay piled with picked over bones when his cell phone rang. He wiped his hands as best he could. Still got orange sauce on his phone.

It was the Trout woman. Marcella, the victim. Pity rose at the sound of her voice, and he felt foolish eating party food. Such a shame, what happened to her. An attractive woman, permanently scarred. He hated when bad things happened to good people. Still precarious to discuss the case, though. He cleared his throat and got his collection of canned non-committal responses ready.

"I wanted to check to see how the investigation was going."

"I'm glad to hear from you, Mrs. Trout. Have you been able to recall any other details about that night?"

"Um, only that I did see the car. It was black." Pause. "I think you have the license plate? Were you able to find the owner of the car?"

It was black. Gee, thanks for that.

"The investigation's still under way, ma'am. I don't really have anything to report right now."

Something caught his eye in the grainy, black and white video playing across the screen. There it was, the black two-door. Parked right there in the second row. He squinted to make out the license plate. Yup, 43O-oMM.

How could he have missed its arrival? He rewound the tape. But a lot of cars came in at once and the stutter of the video made it hard to make out. Still, four guys—one apparently very large—had to have piled out of the car in question at some point. They didn't magically teleport into the bar. How could he miss it?

Mrs. Trout had to repeat her question twice. "Will there be a trial?"

His eyes remained glued on the fuzzy images of the cars. He pulled a canned non-committal out of nowhere and hoped it answered her question. "Too early to say, ma'am."

Impatient now, he fast-forwarded a few minutes. If the attack occurred at approximately 10:19 pm that would mean—

"Is my son still a suspect?"

Whoa—what was that? Randolf stifled a gasp as he watched a large, overweight man rush back to the car alone, pulling his hood up over his ears. He bounded side to side, his generous body mass apparently difficult to manage. He moved like an animal. A large, wild animal. Kind of gorilla-like.

It had to be Bacon.

Randolf's feet got hot and prickled like they'd fallen asleep. He watched as Bacon pulled the black car out of the lot, and turned in the direction of the highway...which also happened to be toward Blue Palms. He cleared his throat again. "I'm sorry, ma'am?"

"No, I'm sorry. Is this a good time? Do you need to call me back?"

He rewound and watched it again. Had to be Bacon. Now he felt silly to have left the apartment complex in Minerva. Part of him felt like driving back up there right now. Bring him in for questioning. Put this thing to rest.

"Detective?" Her voice, such a mom's voice, made him come to. So passionately adamant of her son's innocence, she seemed to have developed a kind of tunnel vision. Clearly, there were holes in her story. What could he do to help nudge her conscience into remembering? Maybe if she saw something to trigger the details that were missing? They might just get their guy.

Might be this Bacon guy.

Quick thinking gave him an idea. "Um, Mrs. Trout? How are you feeling these days? Would you be well enough to help us with this case?"

"Yes. Absolutely." No hesitation.

"I think we might need you to come in and identify your attacker...from a lineup." His mind raced. Would be easy to get three or four overweight guys to stand there. Supposed to include all the suspects, of course, but it would be problematic bringing in the Trout boy. In more ways than one. Maybe a lookalike? A plan fell together in seconds.

"Do you think you're well enough to handle that?" He barely got it out before—

"Yes. Absolutely."

CHAPTER 31

M arcella felt grateful Bernie didn't make conversation on the way to the municipal center.

She'd been asked to identify her attacker in a lineup. Oddly, the task felt disturbingly familiar. Another layer peeled back, she saw her authentic self once again, driven by her duty as a mother. For catharsis' sake, she forced herself to remember that awful time, ten-plus years ago, when she had to take the stand during her son's trial for the murder of Sally Hubbard.

Something a mother should never have to do.

As painful as the memories were, she didn't want to forget that time. Not just to hold on to her dear friend Sally who had helped her so much with little Hen. But she didn't want to forget what she'd learned during the trial. Namely, the inner workings of the US legal system, how best to argue a trial, what counted and what didn't count as evidence in a court of law. She'd seen how crucial the collective role of a jury was. How everything hinged on the judgment of a group of strangers with absolutely zero legal training. She'd learned about narcotics—specifically, cocaine—and how drug abuse destroys families. How it destroyed *her* family. She'd learned how surreptitious an addiction could be. To this day, she was miffed. How could she not know her own husband abused drugs?

She'd learned about schizophrenia.

Her biggest regret still ached deep in her soul. How could she be married to someone and not know he suffered from such a terrifying mental illness? How could she have a child with that person and not realize that child suffered from the same mental illness? How could she have lived with Tyler—raised him!—for all his seventeen years and not see it?

She forced herself to think of these things, to remember the terror that struck her family, to claim responsibility—painful though it was. A dark aura swam at the base of her skull, threatening to pull her under. If she allowed the gloom to swallow her, she'd never recover.

But she had to remember. Recalling those dark times ensured they would never happen again. Admitting to herself what she'd let happen so many years ago was a step toward healing. Sort of. Or a step toward punishment. Either way, she'd long ago accepted her past had become an integral part of who she was as a person.

But her past could also inform what was to be. Who she would become. Though a hard-fought battle, she always worked to be a better mom.

Bernie pulled off the highway. "You okay?"

Marcella wiped tears from under her huge black sunglasses. "Sure. Just a little queasy. You know, from the car ride."

"Sorry. Tried to be gentle."

"I know." Squeezing his hand, she forced different memories forward, as important as the others, like how selfless and kind Bernie had been. How reliable he was, how loyal. How he'd been by her side for nearly twenty years and hardly asked for anything in return. How he never pressured her to marry, even though she knew he desperately wanted to.

"Thank you," she said, forcing a smile. She didn't like the ugliness that had come between them. The anger, like a stubborn weed she couldn't uproot. It had been there since the accident. Possibly before. Come to think of it, she'd been upset with him since Tyler moved home.

Why couldn't she let it go? Bernie had every right to his feelings toward Tyler. Why couldn't she accept that he had to work out his grief in his own way, as her therapist reminded her again and again? Forgiveness wasn't a straight line. It was a process—the regressions as important as the progress.

Goodness, trying to rationalize all these emotions gave her a headache.

Maybe if she could separate Tyler from Bernie in her mind and love them individually, each in his own right, all the ugliness would vanish. Was it possible? Was it smart?

She made a mental note to call her therapist. It had been too long since her last appointment.

Still, by the time Bernie parked the car, she felt more herself than she'd felt for a long time. And ready to feign confidence with this whole lineup thing.

"I'll walk you in."

She took a breath, nerves sprouting. "All right."

Her insides quivered—a new level of nausea which had nothing to do with the car ride. She was grateful to have Bernie's arm.

"You can do this," he said, as if reading her mind.

They had to wait in the lobby longer than she'd anticipated. And the minutes stretched long and weary. The hard chair beneath her, the travel sickness, the fatigue, sapped her energy—energy she desperately needed to do this big thing in front of her. To save Tyler. To bring justice to light!

Her eyes closed. Her head found the sheetrock wall behind her. Who did she think she was? How could she make a difference here? She didn't even remember everything that happened that night. She couldn't summon her attacker's face in her mind's eye no matter how hard she tried. How could she possibly pick him out of a lineup?

"Marcella Trout?"

Bernie started, reaching for her hand.

She brushed him off and lied, "I'll be fine."

Another deep breath didn't bring enough oxygen into her lungs. She palmed the walls for support down a narrow hallway, praying she didn't pass out.

The door opened and there stood Detective Randolf, dressed casually, his badge dangling from a lanyard. The sight of him made her feel better somehow. Stronger. She could do this.

She followed him into a small, dark elevated room behind a one-way mirrored glass window. Through the window, a brighter room with large number decals marking the wall and the floor. Exactly like in the movies. Almost laughable how similar to the movies.

"So, it's pretty straightforward. If you see your attacker, pick him out for us. But if you're unsure, let it go. The way these things work, it's usually an obvious, immediate reaction. Understood?"

She nodded and folded her arms so he didn't see her hands shaking. He offered her a chair, but she chose to stand. It made her feel important, standing.

In a moment, men began filing in to the bright room, and stood on the numbered floor-decals. Each wore a baggy black hooded sweatshirt. She huffed a laugh at the costumes, the childish charade.

But then, the man on number two. She clucked her tongue at Randolf.

"Really? You put a Tyler lookalike up there?" A flash of anger appeared. "Were you trying to trick me into accusing my own son?"

"Checking all the boxes ma'am. And, honestly, hoping to trigger something from that night."

"Well, at least you had the decency to leave Tyler out of this. With his mental state, this would throw him into a panic attack. Still, if you really thought—"

Her words cut out as her eye caught man number six in the lineup. And a violent pulse coursed through her, rocking her to the core.

"Oh, my..." The words, a breath. All air got sucked from her lungs. She floated to the chair behind her as a numbness traveled up her legs. Dizzy, she blinked at number six. It couldn't be.

"Six!" She clamped a hand over her mouth, feeling she might vomit. "Number six." Muffled now.

"Six? Are you sure?"

She nodded, swallowing bile. Unable to rip her eyes off him. The size of him might be mistaken for strength, but she could see it for what it was—weakness—his bulbous gut and the round plumpness of his shoulders.

But something else struck her.

Horror sank like an anchor as she realized he looked familiar in another way. Not only from that night. Someone from her past. A tingling behind her eyes told her she *knew* him. Impossible. Couldn't be. Did she truly recognize this man?

She didn't want to ask, but she had to know: "Have him take off his hood." She had to see his face.

Randolf gave instructions to the guard through the intercom.

Like slow motion, number six pulled his hood away. Marcella's jaw dropped as she stared. Yes. She knew this man. As changed as he was, she recognized him easily.

There he stood. She couldn't believe it.

He frowned into the fleshy folds of his neck. Black eyebrows hinted at his hair color even though his head was shaved. Still him.

It didn't make sense. He couldn't possibly be here. No way he was a free man.

His eyes flickered to her as if he could see through the mirror. A shiver ran head to toe, and a gasp escaped.

No, she was wrong. Not who she originally thought. Not Leon, but his son.

Tyler's best friend. The one who got him in trouble ten years ago. The one Miss Sally warned her about. She could hardly believe it.

Derek Hogg.

CHAPTER 32

Two years earlier

In the eight years Derek sat in prison, he spoke to Pop maybe only the last three. Quite a feat since they both rotted in Comstock. Could you blame him? Pop had gotten him into this mess way back when, making him work at the diner since third grade—a big fat *screw you* to child labor laws—and then sending him on drug runs as soon as he got his driver's license. Thought he was king of Schroon Lake, which wasn't the grand metropolis Pop had bragged about. More like the middle of no-man's-land. What thanks did he get from serving his pop? From being a good boy and doing what he'd been told?

Effing prison, that's what.

Possession of illegal substance with intention to distribute: guilty.

Drug trafficking: guilty.

Money laundering: innocent (Pop took all of that).

Eight to ten years and a whopping ten-K fine. As if he had that kind of dough. Pop always had a hold on all the money, obviously. Who knew where it ended up after they were both thrown in the can?

But years behind bars changes a kid. Derek grew up in prison. After a few years of blatant eff-you, he started to at least acknowledge the ol' bastard. A nod hello, a "hey" here and there.

But the real turnaround came when Derek went to see about

changing his work assignment. Having worked for the first few years within the Compound Department—a fancy name for scrubbing bird shit off rec yard sidewalks—he went to see the Staffing Administrator about switching. He'd heard you could make bank doing laundry. Who knew?

The Staff Admin's name was Jordan Blanchard, Derek knew. What he didn't know and what he learned only after he went into the staffing office? Jordan was a *chick*. A brute of a chick, but still. Long story short, Jordan not only denied Derek's request, she took away his stash of cigarettes. For no effing reason. Now, ask any inmate how to get in their craw and they'll tell you—take away their smokes.

What did that have to do with Derek and his Pop?

Only that it brought out the true blame for Derek's fate. Not fair to lay it on Pop. When he stopped to think, problems started well before him working at the diner in third grade. Matter of fact, Pop wouldn't have put him to work if his own mum stuck around. Her dying in a car wreck when he was a toddler? That set every other bogus thing in motion.

Derek learned she'd had a few DUIs under her seatbelt, so even if no proof existed, she basically killed herself. Which meant she abandoned Derek and left him with a big mess he had no chance to clean up. Too young to hold memories of her, his prison-infected mind imagined her taking on the appearance of Jordan—thick-boned and androgynous and full of attitude.

It was all her fault. He hated her like he hated his mum.

He happened to know Pop hated Mum, too. He never loved her to begin with and then she went and died on him. Their mutual hatred brought them together at the chow hall. Not exactly family bonding, but, by then, Derek's steaming boil had reduced to a low simmer. All directed toward Mum. And Jordan and every other chick on the planet. They all sucked.

Anyway. Now, the time had come for Derek to cut loose. And he'd be done with Jordan forever, and that other ass-brute in charge of phone call privileges, and the other chow hall ass-brute serving food with the shower cap on her head.

Pop was another story, whose parole was a few years out. Derek hedged his bets Pop still had contacts in their hometown.

"Pop. Who do I call, you know, to pick me up?"

"Huh? Pick you up?" Pop wheezed as he sat down. Had to catch his breath before eating. He should've quit smoking years ago. But who was Derek—the walking chimney—to talk?

"Tomorrow's my date. I'm out. Who do I call?"

Pop shoved food in his mouth. "That went fast."

"Eight years."

"Huh. My parole ain't for another year then."

"I need to call someone for a ride."

Derek had phoned his high school friend Don last week, asking. And would rather forget that call ever happened. Don stumbled for a millisecond and then pretended not to know Derek. Like he was a telemarketer. For real. Pissed him off so much, he slammed the receiver—nearly broke it—which took away his phone privileges, thanks to the aforementioned ass-brute. So here he landed at the last hour trying to figure out how the heck he'd get home.

He wouldn't speak the other option—to go to the halfway house. No way he wanted to be shut up in there being babysat day and night with a bunch of other low-lifes. Might as well stay in prison.

"I need a ride, Pop," he said again. "Can't walk from here to Severance."

Pop didn't say what they both had to be thinking. What's in Severance for them anymore? Bank claimed their house. Foreclosure. Auction. Probably the whole neighborhood had changed over. Didn't want to think about their immediate neighbors, the Trouts. Too much baggage there.

"No, guess not." Pop scraped his fork around his empty plate. Never enough food for him. Derek neither, for real.

Derek hated feeling desperate. "Pop, come on. Help me out here."

Pop rolled a napkin between his hands. "I gotta cousin in Minerva. My cousin's kid, actually."

"Yeah?"

"I guess you could call him." Pop closed his eyes a sec. His next breath took some effort. They'd been sitting for a while.

"You okay, Pop?"

Pop glared, wheezed some more. "Name's Freddy Mesowicz. Only met him the one time when he was just a tyke. Probably in his thirties now." His laugh turned to a cough.

"What if...I can't get 'im?"

Pop shrugged.

Derek waited before asking the next question. "Do you think he'd put me up?"

Pop's eyes flickered to his. Glaring.

"Just temporary," Derek added.

"I have no frickin' idea, kid." Like trying to get rid of a beggar on the street.

Derek's spine prickled. *Could be me. I could be on the streets.* For the first time, he thought maybe it would be better to stay here in this sucky place.

Did Pop sense his fear?

Pop stared hard, breathing in Derek's face. Flakes of spit came out with each exhale. "Listen. There's some things we should talk about before you blow this joint."

"Yeah?"

"Some things you should know."

Derek leaned in, the fold of his gut cutting into the table. Pop seemed to embody his own personal prognosis: fat, wheezing, pathetic. "Okay. Go ahead."

"I'm sick."

Derek noticed yellow in the whites of his eyes. "Sick?"

"Yeah. Been to the clinic for some tests. Somethin' with the lungs."

Derek felt his knees buckle, even while sitting. That personal prognosis rang like a siren between his ears. Pop's wheezing, coughing, out of breath all the time—even sitting. No wonder.

"Can't cure me, they say. Only treat it. Whatever they's doing ain't working, seems like." He dropped his balled-up napkin onto his plate. "Might not make it to parole."

Walls fell down around him. "Pop, you kidding? You gotta be kidding."

A shrug.

"You're only—what, fifty-somethin'?"

"Sixty-three. But my lungs aged ahead." His laugh brought up mucous. Derek looked away as he got rid of it, embarrassed for him. It turned around in his mind, Pop being sick. Serious sick. And stuck in this cage. Derek didn't want to care but the sudden weight in his chest told him otherwise.

Pop went on, even though it clearly hurt. "But listen. You're getting out. And there's some stuff you need to know." Pop wagged his head, his eyes scanning the entirety of the chow hall. As if someone might be listening.

Derek learned long ago, no one gave two effs. He straightened a little and smelled his own sweat. "Other than you being sick?"

Pop heaved himself up. Blood rushed to his cheeks, and he panted so hard, drool slid from his lips. Painful to watch. How had Derek never seen this before?

"Find me tomorrow. Or tonight. Better alone." Like he used to years ago at the diner, he knocked on the table, his finger so swollen the knuckle was undetectable.

Could be me, Derek thought. Fat and wheezing and pathetic... and dying.

One big difference. He'd be out on the streets if he didn't figure something out.

LEON *HAD* BEEN king of Schroon Lake. The outpouring of support during his trial proved it. They led a freaking parade in his honor, right down Main Street. Handmade and professionally designed posters taped to store windows: *Save Leon's Diner!* or his personal favorite, *Leon Hogg—Community Hero!*

So, it surprised him that his fall from grace was a sudden and lonely drop. After his arrest—a freaking free fall. As soon as he was found guilty—*BAM*—everyone disappeared. He was shut out. No letters came fighting for justice or touting his worth. Just the opposite, some hate mail came in. Blaming him—shaming him—for Derek's imprisonment. *It's one thing to let yourself waste away, but to put your child at risk is ABUSE!*

That was one of the milder ones.

Only Gary Walsh, his car dealer buddy, stayed in the game. First, his breezy, brief letters talked about the Giants' season. Then, they got deeper. Almost poetic, truth told. Seems Gary chronicled a kind of midlife crisis in the letters, with Leon stuck as his sole audience. In one, Gary talked about changing careers to become a postal worker. Another waxed on about the benefits of meditation. And another came in ALL CAPS complaining about how he'll never be able to retire and *we gotta stick it to the big man, blah, blah, blah.*

Leon never wrote back.

Not until recently when Gary, in a letter about erosion in the Adirondacks and how it reflected the demise of his soul *blah blah blah...* As an aside, he mentioned Marcella Trout had moved to Lake George.

That got Leon's attention.

Marcella Trout, his former employee and his own personal Liz Taylor. Drop-dead gorgeous woman. Really unfair how gorgeous, to be honest. The kind of beauty that held power. It always ticked him off.

According to Gary, she and that Bernie Hubbard character went and bought a *motel* of all things. Just seeing the Hubbard name in Gary's scrawl gave him an itch he couldn't scratch. The mother, Sally

Hubbard, single-handedly ruined Leon. Destroyed his diner while alive. And in a cruel twist of irony, her death drove him and Derek into the clink. It was a train wreck—or a perfect storm or whatchamacallit. Ol' Sally was murdered. And her murder made national news. But Leon? Leon had *nothing* to do with it. Tyler Trout pulled the trigger, so to speak, when his brain went haywire. But somehow, he and Derek rotted away in here while Tyler got sent to preschool for the brain (aka psychiatric rehab). How was that supposta be justice?

Messed up, for sure.

But the rage had left Leon long ago.

Still. Gary's letter brought it all back, what he'd blocked out for nearly a decade. That freaking letter. It was the PS that really got to him, though.

Oh, and did you hear about her kid Hen inheriting the entire Hubbard fortune?

That was it. One line. And it became Leon's life raft.

Freddy Mesowicz turned out to be Derek's life raft. At noon the next day, on the dot, he waited at the south fence, as instructed, in his truck.

"Thanks, Freddy."

"They call me Flake."

The name seemed apt. A slight, thin-haired man whose freckles made him seem no older than fifteen, Flake's eyes were perpetually downcast. The blond fluff of his eyelashes surely made his vision a blurry sliver.

Derek sank into the passenger seat and the truck seemed to tip in that direction. Flake offered him a cigarette and pulled out without further comment. His thin hands on the steering wheel looked almost feline, his fingernails like claws. Derek wondered how he could possibly be related to this guy. Even twice-removed or whatever.

But, whatever. Flake was driving him away from Comstock. That's what mattered.

So freeing, watching the world pass by from a moving car. It had been so long but everything looked pretty much the same. Part of him had expected some things to change. Grass, mountains, all same. Disappointment pinged until Derek reminded himself this was a new beginning and all that junk. Trees budding leaves told him it was spring. He sprouted new leaves too.

He'd expected to say goodbye to his old man. But this morning, Pop was a no show at breakfast. And then Derek skipped rec per guards' orders. Paperwork, they'd said, for his release (Derek saw not a scrap of paper, by the way).

No worries. Derek figured he'd be back. He'd talk to Pop again. But the farther Flake's truck traveled from Comstock—Minerva was frickin' far away—the reality of getting back to visit Pop faded like denim in the dryer. Surprising how sad it made him.

"Why do they call you Flake?" Derek tried to make chitchat.

"That's my name." He sounded annoyed. Or bored or something.

Derek studied Flake's flat profile and concluded he didn't have much to say because he didn't have much going on upstairs. So, they sat mostly in silence the whole way to Minerva.

A quiet car ride worked for Derek, who still reeled from what Pop told him last night out at the rec yard about the Trouts...

Marcella Trout had been the only mother figure he'd ever known, and she'd flicked him away like he was a beetle crawling up her arm. For real. Came to a head at his trial—the truth about how she felt about him. How many times over the years had his mind replayed her testimony while he sat in his cell?

Sally Hubbard had warned her, she'd said. How she wished she'd have listened, she'd said. He had seemed like a regular *Bam-Bam* kind of kid growing up, who'd have thought he'd turn into such a vile, double-dealing person with no conscience? *Ah*, she'd palmed her heart, tears starting, how downright treacherous it had been living right next door to such a person! How reckless and unsafe!

And to think he'd befriended her precious and vulnerable son, Tyler...

(who, by the way, had confessed to killing her friend and neighbor Sally Hubbard and was thereby sent to an institutional psychiatric rehab for who knows how long. But she failed to bring up all that).

Like an avalanche, her testimony had gained power as it carried on...

Oh my, she'd said. To think how Derek had given her timid and helpless son drugs, gotten him good and addicted, so he could be his lackey and commit crimes for him. Where was the charge for that, she'd asked? Drug trafficking wasn't enough. What about child endangerment? What about physical and mental abuse of his friend —his friend who didn't have the mental fortitude to determine right from wrong (she had to have rehearsed that one)?

Derek should be locked up good, she'd said. He should never be allowed to see the light of day again, she'd said. Just imagine the damage he could do, the lives he could ruin, if he remained free?

And want to hear the real kicker? Marcella had been the witness to save him, they'd thought. Derek had effing *chosen* her as a character witness, per his lawyer's request. Supposta sing his praises. Instead, she thrust a knife into his back.

How he hated her.

No argument about how pretty she was. Not the point. Though she couldn't be considered an ass-brute in the looks department, she was beyond ugly inside. He learned that much. Every chick on the planet sucked, not only the ugly ones.

Still effing pissed him off. Derek punched his palm—*SMACK*— making Flake start.

"Sorry. Sorry."

"S'okay. I'd be mad too."

Derek sniggered inside. Flake thought he punched his prison time.

Funny, though, thinking about her looks department. She'd been the object of desire for Pop and all the men in the Schroon

Lake area. No one denied her beauty. And all these years, Marcella had been a frozen fixture in his mind. How she looked at his trial and what she said there. Any time he thought of her, that's what came up. Her sitting there, not in her rust-colored waitressing uniform, but in a sharp navy dress and fitted jacket—office attire—like a costume for one of those courtroom dramas. All those tender things she used to do for him when he was little went *poof*. And any sort of image of how she lived her life these days—what she looked like or how she spent her time as a middle-aged woman—all blank.

Eff her.

So, it took some time to wrap his head around the idea she owned an effing motel in Lake George—called Blue Palms, just beyond the main drag—with that dishwater excuse of a man, Bernie.

As much as he hated Marcella, pooling her in with all the other ass-brute women who'd made his life a living hell, that's not what got his nose out of joint.

The other thing Pop told him...

Effing *Hen*. Don't get Derek started on that kid. *Chicken*, Derek used to call him. What a snot-nosed, spoiled little shit. What Pop told him about Hen blew his brain to pieces. Effing kid had been named as the sole beneficiary of Sally Hubbard's estate. Apparently, he'll inherit the funds when he turns eighteen, which—Derek couldn't believe—was coming up. A year or two, if Derek did the math right. Pop said it was a load of cash. Could be in the millions.

Millions?

Effing millions.

Unreal. First, Old Mother Fricking Hubbard had that kind of cash. Second, Hen Trout was almost a grown man. A *rich* grown man.

Snot-nosed, spoiled little shit.

The injustice of it all made his blood boil.

But then.

Last night at the rec yard, Pop not only dumped the 411 on him—

giving him news about the Trouts that hurt his ears and his eyes and every part of his being—but he also asked a favor.

An effing favor.

What Pop had asked him to *do* about it? That brought up a feeling Derek hadn't felt in some time.

Fear.

Flake pulled into the grungiest apartment complex Derek had ever seen.

He didn't apologize as he let them into his place, despite the rodent droppings lining the floorboards. "Stay here if you want," Flake said without lifting his fuzzy blond eyelashes.

Derek had wondered why Flake had agreed to pick him up without any real arm-twisting. And now he invited him to stay?

Made sense though. Flake didn't have any family. And he was simple. Miracle he'd been living on his own at all. He needed a companion or an aide—someone to take care of him. Obviously, he needed help.

Derek sighed, assuming the job. You know, with his new sprouting leaves and all.

In Flake's fridge, Derek found seven cans of tuna, a case of chicken-flavored ramen noodles, a single green pepper, and value-sized yellow mustard. Putting his ol' diner skills to good use, like riding a bike, Derek whipped up a casserole that blew Flake's small mind.

By the end of the week, the pair had settled into a roommate situation that worked for both. Not by conscious choice, Derek fell into a domestic role—putting himself in charge of meals (but he refused to clean house. That shit was reserved for ass-brutes).

In between job searches, he introduced the four food groups to Flake, whose awe grew with every meal.

Friday night, Flake brought Derek out to "the fields" to drink beer with his two buddies. An abandoned baseball field across town, the perfect place to drink on the cheap and see friends, suppose-ably. Two guys, one super skinny, the other with a beard, pulled up in a junky black sports car.

Derek wondered how Flake would fold him into the group.

He kind of didn't.

His feline fingers made a gun pointing to the two guys, one after the next. "Pistol, Flat Eric."

"Hey," Derek said.

"What do they call you?" the skinny guy, Pistol, said.

Before Derek could answer, Flake piped up. "Bacon." Completely serious.

Derek barked a laugh. "What?"

"That's what we called your dad," Flake said without affect.

Derek bristled at the dig on his last name, Hogg. It had always been a sore spot growing up. Constant source of teasing. "Oh, I get it."

He wanted to ask who the *we* meant—*That's what we called your dad*—and learn more about his family tree. Baffling still how he could be related to this willow of a dude. But, honestly, he couldn't muster the energy.

No one asked his real name. No one cared. Derek decided he didn't either.

Bacon.

He chuckled internally at the stupid nickname. Then he got to thinking. Maybe this could be a good thing. Maybe this was his new leaves.

Did he really want to be Derek anymore?

Derek was the dude who did drug runs for his criminal of a pop. Derek helped supply a tiny Adirondack town with enough cocaine for a small country. Derek had a best friend who killed an old lady. Derek went to prison for eight years. Derek had a record. A convicted felon. An ex-convict.

But Bacon?

Bacon could be someone else. Bacon could be the dude who does the right thing. Makes things better. Bacon could close the door on the past and open the window to the future. Hallmark movie crap. A future with a stable job and a group of friends and a decent reputation. Why not him? Bacon could be a good guy. After all...

"Who doesn't like bacon?" he said with a grin.

The guys laughed with him. Must be a sign.

They drank beer and smoked cigarettes and weed on the splintery bleachers, watching the sun set past the trailer park where Flat Eric lived with his mum. Once in a while, a car went by and they stared as it slowly passed—four heads turning as it chugged away. Like, sizing it up. Had to freak the driver out, Bacon thought. Nothing else to look at, though.

The twelve-pack went fast.

That became the routine. Every Friday, they'd meet at the fields. Eventually, Bacon learned bits and pieces about the guys.

Like, the skinny one, Pistol, was the only one with a girlfriend—Paula, who worked as a receptionist at the health clinic in North Creek. She owned the junky black car he drove and had partial custody of her daughter, Chloe, who Pistol described as "a mean little wench."

Flat Eric, with the beard, had driven a plow truck for the town until an accident hurt his arm three-plus years ago. He'd been collecting disability ever since.

Flake, Bacon already knew, worked as a garbage collector—the "best job on the planet," as he put it. "Out in the fresh air." *Fresh?* "Riding at the back like hopping a train." *A train going in circles.* Flake tried to get Bacon on his route. Thankfully, his efforts failed.

They all accepted Bacon without question, as they did Flake. Like a brother. Actually, more like a helpless child. If Bacon had been raised to be sentimental, he would've thought it touching. Instead, he cooked for him. It wasn't a job, per se. But it was a start. A start at being a good guy.

Pop,

How are you? Been a few months. You doing OK?

Sorry I don't visit yet. No jobs here and still no car. Feel bad asking Flake to drive me (that's Freddy). Everybody here gets a nickname. Mine's Bacon. Get it?

Flake says they used to call you that, so I let them call me that too.

I guess you could say I made some friends.

Haven't done that thing you asked yet. Not sure how without my own wheels. Working on it.

Also working on being a good guy.

R you getting ready for your parole?

Use Flake's address. I'm crashing here for now.

-D (Bacon)

WEEKS PASSED. No letter from Pop.

CHAPTER 33

"You stink!" Chloe wrinkled her nose at Bacon.

He didn't respond. He had no business babysitting—period—and resented being stuck here at Paula's place with the kid. But she got called in to work on her day off and Pistol begged a favor. And Bacon had a new start at being a good guy.

Chloe didn't look anything like her mother. Not that Paula was any kind of looker. She didn't qualify as an ass-brute but appeared weather-beaten, almost sickly, like something hanging at the thrift store. On a cheap wire hanger.

Chloe, on the other hand, had the potential to grow into an ass-brute. For a young kid, she had unusually manly features. Dark, bushy eyebrows clashed with her mousy brown hair. Close-set eyes on a wide face. And how could a four-year-old have a double chin? Must've gotten her pop's looks.

Bacon would've felt sorry for the girl if she weren't such a mean little wench. Pistol had been right about that.

"You gwoss." She poked her finger into his arm. Embarrassing how much it sunk into the flesh. "Fat!"

The TV showed some annoying cartoon with lots of singing and whiney voices. The colorful, blobby creatures danced across the screen to catchy music. Bacon had no memory of watching anything like this as a kid. Chloe didn't seem to care about the show, but Bacon didn't know what else to do with her.

The clock must be broken. Only an hour had passed. It would be a long day.

It made him think about babysitting Hen (or Chicken) with Tyler, back in the day. The only one to call him Chicken, he didn't see why no one else caught on. Really, how perfect could a nickname get? He didn't tease him with it. Not really. Maybe a little.

But he didn't always hate the kid. Bacon had tried. He joked around with him. That one Halloween...the last Halloween, he'd told him he should dress as a chicken. Get it? Then, when Chicken said he didn't have a girlfriend, Bacon offered to get him some *chicks*. Get it? It was *funny*. Hilarious, really. But Hen's reaction—the hate in his eyes—still rubbed at him, even now.

Hen had these huge eyes—a creepy hazel-green color—that saw right inside you. Or *through* you. And the kid didn't say anything. Hardly ever. All he did was stare you down like he had some kind of magic power coming through his eyeballs. Bacon swore his stare made things happen, made people do things or not do things. And the fact that he didn't say a word—his lips would be totally sealed shut—made it even more freaky.

Yeah, kids can be shitheads. Just because they're kids doesn't mean they're good or nice or deserve anything special.

Especially a spoiled, snot-nosed little shit like Hen.

Also, this mean little wench.

Bacon studied Chloe's profile on the sly. Yeah, an ugly kid.

"Do you have a nickname?" He tried to get her talking, out of sheer boredom.

She didn't look over. "No."

"What if I call you Chicken?"

She scrunched her nose again. "Why?"

"You know, a nickname."

"Dumb nickname." Zero eye contact. Exact opposite of Hen.

"Could be fun."

"You dumb." She glanced over, stuck out her tongue. "I'm going outside."

Water drops lightly tapped the window pane. "It's raining."

"No, it's not." She turned off the TV. The room felt colder with it off.

He really didn't want to go outside. "It's sprinkling."

"Spwinkwing's not waining." She shoved her feet into rain boots with yellow ducks printed all over them. "I'm going."

He spoke louder. "I don't think so."

She didn't listen, but skipped across the room and—no hesitation —opened the front door and...gone. Her giggles faded as she bounded off.

Bacon scrambled to get up, but his size made big movements difficult so it was slow going. By the time he got to the door, out of breath and sweating, the kid was nowhere in sight.

Shit. Shit. Shit.

Out he went. The screen door clanged behind him like a warning bell. The worn wood steps bowed under his weight. He made his way around the perimeter of the house, searching.

Driveway, clear. Side yard, clear. No sign of the kid.

"Chloe!" he yelled, cold fear creeping in. She may be a mean little wench but he couldn't lose her, for shit's sake.

What to do? Soft rain blanketed his hair and shoulders, and he pulled up his hood for cover, which only created more heat.

"Chloe!" On the street now, he headed toward the dead end. Maybe she went into the woods. Like boys would? He used to go off and play in the woods with Ty all the time. But would girls? Did little girls climb trees and play with sticks and stuff?

No clue.

He never moved so quickly in his entire life. Wheezing like Pop, his head throbbed from exertion, his heart pumping so much it hurt. At the edge of the wood, he shuffled back and forth, searching, needing this to be over. His calves cramped. His feet swelled inside his shoes like they'd burst. His ankles were broken, for sure. He stared into the thick swath of trees, at a loss.

She wore pink pajamas, right? She'd stick out. Right? She should. Like a sore thumb.

Right?

His vision went wonky, he stared so hard.

Nothing.

Shit. Shit. Shit.

He spun around, blood rushing to his ears. Where was the fricking *pink?*

At the other end of the street, beyond the stop sign, the road with a yellow line down the middle. Route 28. More cars, more traffic on that road. His entire being gasped with panic. No. Is she near 28?

Shit. Shit. Shit.

"Chloe!"

Ignoring the spikes of pain in his feet, ignoring the pressure in his chest—surely the nibble of a heart attack. Ignoring the rock in his lungs which made breathing near-impossible, he ran.

Holy shit, he ran.

An echo of Pop's prognosis floated somewhere in the back of his brain. Running would kill the ol' bastard, for real. Might kill Bacon too. Still, he ran like the cops were on his tail.

Chloe!

He should call her. Yell her name. He wanted to scream but saved his breath for breathing. His head pounded in time with his shoes slamming the pavement.

At the stop sign, he looked right, then left, frantic.

He panted so hard he started to dry-heave.

Right, then left again. His hood fell back and raindrops pelted his forehead, matted his hair. Rain came down harder now. He blinked against the rain. It blinded him.

Where'd she go? Which way?

Pink pajamas, in the road...

Duckie boots splashing in puddles.

There she was! About fifty yards away, in the middle of 28—

"Chloe!" He found his voice. Didn't matter because the little girl in pink pajamas didn't hear. Or wasn't listening. There she was, in the middle of the fricking street like it was a playground, stomping in rainwater. Giggling. Not a care in the world.

He ran hard, pumping his arms, finding strength in his thick legs he never knew he had. He chanted her name with each step, praying no cars would come. For sure they'd be blinded by the rain, too, and then...and then...

Oh, no.

"Chloe!"

Closer now, very close. She heard him, and turned, a sour look on her pinched, wenchy face.

"What?" she snapped. And something snapped inside Bacon.

He grabbed her arm and swung her off her feet, pulling her to the side of the road. A car whooshed past less than a second later. He held tight to her arm, his blood charging through his veins like river rapids. He was shaking. And he shook her.

"You almost got hit," he said between chunks of breath. "You can't go in the road." Bile filled his mouth. Bacon wheezed the next word: "Dangerous." He coughed, dry heaved. He felt he might puke, and it pissed him off.

"Lemme go!" She tried to wrench herself free, and it pissed him off even more.

He gripped her arm tighter. Gritted his teeth. "What the *hell*."

His feet. His chest. Nothing worked anymore. He felt broken all over. Still, he held tight to her arm even though she pulled and tugged, screeching her puny four-year-old scream.

By the time they got back to the house, they were both rain-soaked. Chloe had kicked off one of her duckie boots outside—lost along Route 28, probably.

Bacon felt like he might die. He never thought it possible, but his lungs actually hurt. He imagined them as big balloons filled with blood, about to explode.

This was it. The end. After years rotting in prison, this was how it would go down. Prognosis, shmognosis—he'd die before Pop.

Survived eight years rotting in prison only to die from a lung explosion chasing a mean little wench around fricking Minerva.

He bolt-locked the door, even though Chloe looked more wiped out than he did. Tears—or rain?—streaked her apple-red cheeks, and she sniffled and sneezed a few times. Probably caught a cold out there. Bacon fell onto the couch, his body giving way. A vague awareness of Chloe fetching her purple blanket and curling up on the bean bag—soon asleep.

Good. They'd both sleep. He let his eyelids shutter closed, tried to pray.

And if I die before I wake... He didn't remember the rest.

BACON AWOKE to two pair of beady eyes glaring. And he corrected himself: Chloe did in fact look like her mum. Like her mum, when she was ticked off.

"The hell's wrong with you?" Paula snapped. She wore a polyester dress with lace at the collar. Her arms crossed at her chest, she tapped her foot. Steam shot from her nostrils. Like a fire-breathing dragon.

Chloe stood next to her. The two of them like a little effing brigade. Bacon blinked the girl into focus. She stared at him too, her pinchy wench face all screwed up at him. She stood straight and still, holding onto her arm like she'd gotten a flu shot at the doctor's.

"What?" His voice was groggy.

Paula pointed at her daughter, who flinched from her mum's hand. "You want to tell me what happened?"

Bacon sat up and winced. His whole body screamed in pain at the movement. Out the window, the world looked like it just got out of the shower.

He stifled a yawn. "Still raining?"

As if offended by the question, Paula kicked off her heels. They soared across the room. Bacon jumped when they smacked the wall near the couch.

"You think it's okay to manhandle a child like that?" she screeched. "Shit's sake, she's only four freaking years old!"

He shook away a sleepy feeling. And the whole charade came rushing back: Chloe running out of the house in her duckie boots, splashing puddles in the road, him trying to save her. Heck, he *did* save her.

"Wait a minute," he said. "She was in the middle of 28. She coulda got hit."

Paula didn't listen. "Did you see her arm?"

He squinted at her. "Wait. Just a sec. She left the house. Wouldn't listen to me. I tole her not to go outside. And she—"

As he talked, Paula pushed up Chloe's pajama sleeve to show a huge red welt, beginnings of a bad bruise. In it, Bacon made out the shape of his own hand.

"I could have your ass thrown back in jail for this. You put your hands on a child? They torture guys in the cell who hurt kids, you know."

Bacon tried to laugh. "No, it's not like that. It wasn't—"

"Something funny?" Paula's face went red hot. "Do you see what you did to her arm?"

"Yeah. Yeah, I do. But—"

"I don't want to hear freaking excuses. There's no excuse for this."

Bacon went quiet, stared at the floor.

She leaned closer. Her Jean Naté singed his nose hairs. Her voice got really low. "What else did you do? Did you touch her? Are you some kinda pervert?"

Whoa. Felt like a gut punch. He was the bad guy here? "What? No! Paula, she took off, outta the house. I ran to the woods, no sign of her. I ran in the other direction and—"

"You *ran?*" Half her face wore a snotty grin, the other a glare.

Chloe hid a giggle behind her hand. Still ugly.

He decided he hated them. Both of them. "Yes, I ran. And nearly had a heart attack."

A snicker. "I bet."

"She was in the *middle* of the fricking road!"

"So, you vio-lated her?" The way she enunciated the word told him she didn't know its meaning.

"What? I saved her life. Frickin' A." He dropped his face in his hands.

"I don't want to hear anything from you. You are a fat, stupid idiot. You might be Pistol's friend, but I don't want to see your face here ever again. Got it?"

"Got it." As if he planned to. Whatever.

"And you go nowhere near my daughter. Never again. You understand me?"

"Yes, ma'am." Easy promise to make.

"Don't *yes ma'am* me, you freaking loser. Get the hell out of my sight."

Both mother and daughter stood motionless, waiting for him to leave. *Watching* him leave.

It took way too long to extract himself from Paula's couch, and then her lousy house. Embarrassing.

On the stoop, he remembered something. He spoke through the screen. "Um, you were supposta give me a ride home?"

A laugh, for real. "Fat chance, Fatty. You all braggy about running today? Go ahead. Run home."

Chloe's tiny voice, like air screeching out of a balloon. "Yeah. Wun home, Fatty!"

"Can I use your phone, at least, to call—"

"Get the hell outta here!"

If Bacon thought it hurt to run, the walk home was downright excruciating. Slow, agonizing torture. Each step killed him. Not just his feet, his whole being throbbed. And though it made zero sense, even now while his lungs were actively dying, he wanted a cigarette. Stupid. He railed at himself for it since he couldn't smoke, anyway.

Wouldn't have the strength to pull in the nicotine. Wouldn't have the strength to hold the thing to his lips, even. *Maybe I'll quit*—a fleeting thought.

Not only physical pain. His being pulsed with outrage. How dare she accuse him of hurting her daughter when he really and truly kept her safe? Her kid could've died if he didn't pull her out of the road. So what if she got a boo-boo on her arm? Would she rather have a bruised kid or a dead one? That witch—how could Pistol stand her? The way she sneered at him. The disgust in her face. How he despised her.

One foot in front of the other. Each step seemed a gargantuan feat. If he moved any slower, he wouldn't be moving at all. At this rate, he wouldn't be home until midnight. He stuck his thumb out a few times. Gave up when a driver flipped him the bird.

What the hell? He couldn't get over it, what Paula said. He did the big favor to watch her kid, and this was the thanks he got. And the mean little wench, with her ugly pinched face and asinine way of talking. She's nothing but a brat. The way her mum treats her, coddling her like that? She's a spoiled little shit, she is.

Just like Hen.

That gave him a whole 'nother thing to focus his rage on. The whole fricking basket of Trouts.

He made tracks in the gravel, dragging his thick feet. His empty stomach cramped from hunger. He felt he might faint from thirst. One step. And another. And another.

After a few blocks, everything went numb. At some point after the sun went down, the black of night fell over him and everything looked different. He stopped caring about Paula and her dumb kid.

But he couldn't stop thinking about Hen and how his family destroyed his life. Pop had been on to something with that favor. For a start.

Bacon had some other things in mind.

CHAPTER 34

B acon woke up the next morning angry at the world—angry at the chicks of the world—and determined to fix his fate. It had been months since his release, and still no job prospects. *Stay in your lane*, he'd heard somewhere once. Going back to school? Not an option. He'd never be a corporate dude. Heck, he couldn't even swing a job as a garbage collector. No one wanted to hire him as a cook because of his record, they said. But the way they looked at him said it was his size.

What else could he do? What else did he know?

Fricking drugs.

Screw trying to be the good guy. Where did being the good guy get him? Accused of violating a little girl.

He had to stay in his lane. And his lane was covered in dung. Fricking Skid Row.

He got himself into the shower—it had been a few days—and lost himself in the rush of the water, trying to think it out.

He had to take control. Sick of mooching off Flake and the guys, waiting around to drink cheap beer at the fields. This wasn't him. Not what he got out of prison for. This wasn't the vision of freedom he'd dreamt about.

He had to make money. He had to go back to selling drugs.

Was cocaine still the drug of choice? Or was ecstasy the way to go? That supplier in Rensselaer still in business? Or did he get sniffed out when he and Pop got nabbed? He should know this stuff. Maybe he did once. But in prison, he'd made it his job to forget. Even though prison was its own circus of vices. Pop and he steered clear of the low-lifes dealing inside.

Moving on. He had to find a way to sell again. If he could figure it out, he could forget the big favor Pop asked for and make his own effing money.

He didn't need Hen's money.

He didn't want to need Hen's money.

Hen had been dead to him for years. The whole effed up Trout family had been. He would do it on his own, the only way he knew how. He just needed an intro.

In the back of a kitchen cabinet, he found a jar full of quarters. Forgotten treasure? He filled his pockets and walked down to Stewart's where stood the last remaining pay phone on the planet.

Who knew? It took a massive amount of quarters to reach Comstock.

Pop wheezed on the other end. Didn't even say hello.

"Pop? Hey. How ya feeling?"

Lots of gravely breaths before: "Like shi-ite."

"You get my letters?"

Long pause.

"Pop? You still there?"

"Yah."

Forget the small talk. Bacon couldn't waste any more quarters. "Pop, hey. Do you still have that guy down in Rensselaer? Is he still, ya know—"

"The hell, D. You outside now. You wanna get thrown back in here or what?"

"Hey, I gotta do something. Can't get a job. No job, no car, no phone. Effing ridiculous. It's like I don't exist."

"Aw, poor baby."

"Serious, Pop. I don't know what else to do."

"I *told* you what to do." The spite in his voice surprised him.

"No, I know. But I need a car to do it, right?"

Another long pause. "Sheesh. Just figure it out."

Bacon's body overheated, even as his fingers went numb holding the receiver. "What about your parole? You getting out?"

"Who knows?"

"I hear getting a lawyer can help."

Pop coughed. Then laughed a little. "You are one stupid kid, arentcha?"

"What?"

"Money, you dumbass. Need money for a lawyer. Like I need money for meds. You get me?"

"I know. But Pop. How am I supposta—"

"Like I said, figure it out. I'm running out of time over here."

"What do ya mean?"

"I'm dying, D. Don't you know—"

Click. Line went dead.

Out of quarters. Just like his luck.

On his way back to Flake's, he walked through sludge. After all this time, Pop threw him this? No help. No tips on how to. Just an order to his pony boy.

Made no sense, what he asked for. Premature or something. Pop hadn't thought it through. Or had he?

Like, didn't they have to wait until Hen got the money before robbing him of it? Bacon thought hard about time. Years passed. How many? He, at twenty-seven, Hen had to be eighteen by now. Right? He wished numbers made more sense to him. But he'd barely been able to keep track of his own age. How was he supposta keep track of some snot-nosed, spoiled little shit he cared nothing for?

But if Pop asked, it must be possible. Hen had to be eighteen by now.

Already a rich bastard.

FLAKE WAS STILL on his trash route when Pistol showed up at their apartment, toting a six pack. As he moved through the doorway, Bacon caught a whiff of marijuana. A lightbulb went off. Maybe Pistol knew someone.

"You really screwed up, didn'cha?" He handed Bacon a beer. The clock read 8:47 am.

Bacon cracked the can and chugged it down in three seconds. It took some concentration to recall what the heck Pistol was talking about. Oh yeah, the mean little wench. "You think?"

"What the hell, man? Wha'd you do?" Pistol followed him into the kitchen.

"Want some eggs?" Avoidance tactic.

Pistol scratched a rash on his forearm. "Nah, man. Paula sent me over here. I'm supposta tell you where the dog died."

Only four eggs left. He scrambled them in a cereal bowl. "Oh, yeah?"

Pistol's long exhale reeked of morning breath and beer. "Hey, I don't really care either way. But you gotta admit it's kinda effed up."

"What is?" Eggs sizzling in the pan. Bacon wished they had bacon.

Pistol took a long time answering. He scratched and scratched until blood came. Bacon lost his appetite. He put the whole batch of eggs on one plate in front of Pistol who stared at the fluffy pile a few seconds before picking up his fork. Like he didn't recognize it as food at first.

"Whatever. Don't really want to talk about it."

"Yeah, me neither."

Pistol ate like a bird. Pea-sized bits of egg as if they hurt going down.

Bacon started feeling hungry, watching him eat so slowly. "Wanted to ask if you knew anyone, ya know, with a connection."

"What kind of connection?"

"Like, a hookup?"

Pistol did the eyebrow thing. "I got weed. Want some?"

"No, I mean, to sell."

Pistol's face went sour, all the pockmarks filling in red. "What the hell? You kidding me?"

Bacon shrugged. "Just asking."

"Paula, man, she's so pissed." He shook his head. "Almost called the *cops* on you. But I held her off. So, consider yourself yelled at, okay?"

She almost called the cops? Heat built in his chest. "Okay."

"And don't go near Chloe again." He ate a few bites. "Or Paula."

"Don't plan to."

Chloe. Paula. The names felt toxic. Bacon had a visceral reaction. Made him want to hit something.

His mind reeled while Pistol ate. Fury coursed through him in a way he hadn't felt in years. Paula almost called the cops? She could've ruined his life. Still could. She had the power to ruin him.

Pissed him off so bad, he had to get up. Get away from Pistol. He paced the room.

What the hell could he do? Stuck here in fricking Minerva with no job or money or any kind of life besides going to a stupid field to drink beer with a bunch of misfits. One, currently eating eggs in his kitchen, who held his lifeline in his hands. He hated for anyone to have anything over him, no less a fricking mean little wench.

Pistol pushed the eggs away. He'd barely eaten half the pile. "Anyway, we ain't going to the fields this Friday."

"No?"

"Nah. Going to Lake George. Hit the bars down there in the village."

Bacon's antenna went up. "The village?"

"Yeah, you been?"

"Not for years."

Pistol sweetened the deal. "Got a fresh stash of weed too."

Bacon didn't need a sweetened deal. He'd been waiting for a way to get down to the village since he got out.

"I'm in," he said, taking Pistol's fork and shoveling down his cold, leftover eggs. Eagerness bubbled up and clogged his ears. Plans for Pop filled his thoughts like a shopping list. In his head, he'd been keeping the name on repeat lest he forget: *Blue Palms. Blue Palms. Blue Palms.*

Right there in the village.

CHAPTER 35

Present, summer 2001

Hen yearned for a childlike, carefree whimsy he'd seen in Wesley and the rest of his peers. It had never been that way, for him. An old soul, Mom used to say. Supposed to be a compliment.

Sometimes he just wanted to be a kid.

Earlier tonight with Mom, he begged off with the excuse of being tired but really, he needed time alone to process what she'd told him. Sitting on his bed, he stared at the random junk in his bedroom which had always been part of his life—suddenly unfamiliar. Like he'd been planted in the middle of some dirtbag yard sale. On his dresser, plastic chachkies from the arcade stood next to his deodorant and hairbrush. A binder from school he planned on reusing in the fall. An old library book he bought at a red-dot sale but had yet to read. The cheapo full-length mirror fastened to the door had been there when they moved in. It distorted his reflection. The pink rug at his feet signaled a girl used to live here. He hadn't cared at the time. But now, he was almost an adult. And his bedroom still had a pink rug and a warped mirror. The Larry Bird poster over his bed did little to elevate his cause.

So many feelings filled his chest, he couldn't make sense of them. Did he want to cry? Hit something? No use trying to solve it, so he sat and stared into space.

Mom had waited a day to tell him. Probably because she had to process it herself. Still, did she really have to ask, "Do you remember him?"

Seriously? How could he forget?

Yo, Chicken. I'm talking to you. HEY!

He'd nodded to his mom. Muttered something about being wiped out. Like a zombie, he slunk to his bedroom, the loud voice of the bully from his childhood ringing in his mind.

The facts fell hard in his brain. Derek Hogg was out of prison. And he'd found out where they lived. And he came here and attacked his mother. A raw fear moved through him.

He came here and attacked his mother.

His hands made fists and his eyes watered.

Why did he do it? What was he after? Why attack Mom, of all people? She never did anything but be nice to him. Even when he wasn't nice back. Growing up, Derek was constantly at their house, sharing their dinner table, lounging on their couch. Heck, Hen remembered he'd come to his birthday dinner at Flanagan's that one year. Maybe more than one year. Always around. And Mom embraced him—welcomed him—like another son.

Until everything changed. That awful thing happened next door, and sweet Miss Sally was gone. Tyler sent to psychiatric rehab, and Derek sent to prison. His father, too. Hen was little still. He hadn't thought much of it, but Mom told him not to worry. Both Derek and his father received long prison sentences, Mom had assured him. The Hoggs would never bother them again. Derek would never get another chance to bully him.

Hen started shaking. He shook so much, he scared himself.

He could hardly believe it. Derek *attacked* his mother? He could've killed her. It was Derek. THE Derek.

Noises from the hallway told him Mom was headed to bed. Poor Mom. He felt her pain so acutely, his heart ached. Still not fully healed, and now having to deal with another blow, this one from the past.

His phone buzzed. Wesley. He shut it down, mentally shutting out his best friend. He couldn't remember the last time he felt so alone. No way could he tell Wes about this, about Derek, about what had happened all those years ago. He wondered—did his best friend really know him? He raked a hand through his hair, wishing he hadn't told Wes anything about the money—it being so intimately tied to his past, to Derek and Tyler. Wes didn't have it in him to understand these things. Ski bumming in Colorado seemed like such a childish, stupid pipedream.

Hen stayed in his room until he heard Bernie go to bed and then decided he couldn't be in his room any longer.

He moved silently through the dark house.

A nighttime ninja, he used to pretend. The memory made him sad. He had been so young when everything around him crumbled. Part of him wanted to go back in time and protect that little boy.

If he'd known then what he knew now, would things have been different? Would he have been able to do anything about it? If he could magically go back to that time and do it over, could he possibly change the trajectory of their lives?

Maybe he could've helped Tyler choose a different best friend, get therapy and treatment for his mental illness sooner, and the awful thing with Miss Sally would never have happened. What would their lives be like now?

What he wouldn't give for that do-over. He'd trade his entire inheritance for it. He didn't even want Sally Hubbard's money.

Out at the pool, the water so still and unmoving, it seemed like glass. Like he could step right onto it and not fall through. Specks of dust and crap floated on the surface, though, and his interest for swimming waned. Looking over the edge, his reflected image was mostly shadow. And even though the water seemed to be still, his shadow undulated and stretched beyond the bounds of nature. A slight breeze made the water ripple, and Hen felt a stirring in his chest.

Deep breath and—*plunge*—head-first into the deep end. The

shock of cold only lasted a moment, and then the water felt like a bath. Another deep breath. But he still felt knotted up inside.

He did a trick he used to do after moving here whenever he felt scared or confused. Hen swam down to the bottom and held himself there. He opened his mouth in a silent scream, letting out all the air, feeling it scrape his vocal cords. Hardly audible. Just a burst of air bubbles floating to the top. But he felt the sound in his lungs and his throat and all over. And as he rose to the surface, the cool air felt glorious. And tension seeped from his body.

Until he saw someone standing there near the ladder, watching him.

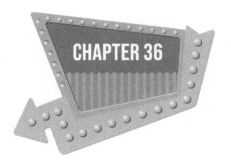

CHAPTER 36

Detective Randolf was pleasantly surprised at how easy it had been to get cooperation from Bacon once he finally caught him at home at the Meadowbay complex in Minerva.

That, apparently, was the extent of his cooperation, however.

As soon as Bacon came out of the lineup room, Randolf descended on him and read him his rights. His size prevented his hands from reaching behind his back so he had to be handcuffed in the front, and Randolf was the unfortunate recipient of a death glare. Rarely was he fazed by a look after all his time on the force. This one, though, gave him a chill.

Into an interrogation room to complete the paperwork and officially charge him. The whole while, Bacon kept those devil-eyes on him. Randolf felt it like a wave of heat. He weighed his options. Throwing him in a holding cell would be safest, but Randolf's gut told him if he didn't get a confession right away, he may lose his chance. Using a controversial tactic some considered dangerous, Randolf removed Bacon's cuffs.

"We can be adults here, can't we?" He hoped his gentle tone garnered trust.

It had the desired effect. Disarmed him, so to speak. Bacon instantly calmed.

Randolf took up a pen. "Your legal name, please?"

No answer. But his loud, labored breathing could almost be considered a voice.

"Derek Hogg, I believe?" He paused. "If you don't say otherwise, I'll assume that's correct."

Bacon rolled his eyes. "You don't say it like that. Not like the pig."

"Oh, really? My apologies. How do you pronounce it, then?"

"HOAG." Like a dog's growl.

"Ah, a long O. I get it."

Bacon shrugged.

Randolf smiled, tried to ingratiate himself. "You've probably had to correct people your whole life on how to pronounce your name. I bet teachers made that mistake all the time." Part of him wanted to ask why he allowed his friends to call him Bacon, but decided against it.

Good decision. Bacon had already started to withdraw.

"Listen, you're being charged with assault, and although you have a record, your previous felony was non-violent. So, assuming your full cooperation, you could be looking at a reduced sentence here."

Bacon stared, his face blank.

"Do you understand what I mean by that?" Randolf figured he'd have to do most of the talking. He slowed his speech and tried again. More direct this time. "Okay. If you confess, there will be no trial." He waited for Bacon to look up. "It's better with no trial, believe me. And your cooperation will be much appreciated. And rewarded with a lesser sentence. I can pretty much guarantee it, since you don't have a record of violence."

Bacon blinked a few times. "How long?"

"Your sentence? Oh, I'd say five to ten. Five with good behavior. You know the drill."

"Yeah."

"So, I can assume your cooperation?"

No response.

"You're willing to confess?"

Bacon shrugged. But for the first time, emotions played on his face. His bottom lip quivered and his eyes got moist.

Randolf felt for the guy. He used his gentle tone again. "I'll need a verbal response to make it official. So, I'll ask again. Are you willing to confess to assaulting one Marcella Trout at her home on Friday, June the first?"

Bacon tensed, and the chair beneath him creaked in protest. He nodded backwards. "Was she here? Did she see me?"

Randolf cleared his throat, weighed his options how best to answer. "You were identified by the victim, yes."

"What did she say? Did she say anything about me?" A flush of red on his neck.

A strange series of questions. Randolf maintained composure. "No."

He spoke louder. "She knows me. She's known me my whole life. She didn't say anything?"

"Even if she did, I'm not at liberty to say."

Bacon wagged his head, muttering something under his breath. His hard frown creased irritably, tugging at all his features.

Randolf waited. He'd have to wait until Bacon calmed again. When the lines in his face smoothed. Perhaps removing the handcuffs wasn't the smartest idea.

Curiosity always got him at this point in the process, once they found their guy. Why did he do it? What was he after? But he put his questions aside, for now. He knew they'd be answered in good time. He hoped they would, anyway.

Randolf counted to ten, and when Bacon still hadn't settled down, he went to twenty. He got to a hundred before Bacon reclaimed his aloof, impassive persona. He added another ten for good measure before asking, "Are you willing to confess?"

Bacon took his time answering. A few shaky breaths. "Yeah, okay." He wiped his eye. His thick hand was filthy. "Can I make my phone call now?"

"Okay, sure." Randolf paused. "One more question, though, off the record? Curious since there's clearly some history there. She's known you your whole life, you say?"

Bacon nodded. Barely.

"So...why?"

Minutes ticked by and Bacon seemed to have shut down. And then—

"Off the record? I didn't go there for her. I didn't expect her there. But there she was, and..."

"And?"

A hefty shrug, weighed down with regret maybe. His wide face drooped with it.

Randolf waited a while. He waited until it became clear Bacon wouldn't say anything more. Then he led him to the phone in the hall.

CHAPTER 37

Hen treaded water, trying to move as little as possible even though he panicked inside. Who stood there at the side of the pool? He blinked away the sting of chlorine, trying to regain focus.

"Tyler?"

"Pool's closed." He held the skimmer as if set to cast a spell over a giant cauldron.

"Tyler, it's me. Hen."

No response. Just started skimming.

Hen let out a small laugh. "You can't really clean the pool when someone's swimming in it."

Skimmer out, he tapped the net by his feet, soaking his tube socks. His next, choppy breath sounded like a grunt. "I'm supposed to clean the pool now. Pool is closed. No swimmers at night. That's the rule."

"I know. But it's me. It's okay."

He slammed the net hard on the concrete patio. Raised his voice. "No. N-n-no swimmers at night."

Hen scrambled out of the water. "Hey, it's okay. Okay, I'm out, see? It's okay. Really. No worries."

"You shouldn't be swimming."

"Okay, I'm not. I'm sorry." Hen saw the plastic rim of the skimmer, broken. Tyler had busted it when he'd slammed it down. Still, he pushed on, trying to collect all the dust and nubs off the top.

He didn't seem to notice it was broken, the screen bent and ineffective. He didn't see the stuff going right through.

Hen glanced around, realized he'd forgotten to bring out a towel. He shivered, hugged himself. "Hey, you wanna put that down and talk?"

No response.

Hen's teeth chattered. "All right, listen. I'm going in to grab a towel. When I get back, let's sit down and talk."

"Need to clean the pool."

"I know. I'll help you. After we talk."

Inside, as Hen took a towel from the linen closet, he imagined Mom carefully folding them down in the basement, pausing to smell the Tide. It made him smile.

Tyler was seated by the time Hen got back. His shoulders drooped and his face drawn, as if he wanted to fold into himself and hide. He still wore those stained gray sweats and now-wet tube socks. Hen had planned to talk about the whole Derek thing, but hesitated now.

He looked at the sky, dark as a chalkboard. "Remember what you used to tell me about the dark?"

Tyler's eyes flicked to Hen's. A splash of blue. Just for a moment.

Hen hoped Tyler saw him smile. "Remember how you used to tell me when it's dark it's dark for everyone, so I shouldn't be afraid?"

Tyler stared at his socks.

Hen softened his voice. "You don't even have to hide, you'd say, the dark hides you."

Tyler's face stayed blank. "That's not really true. There's technology. Like, infrared glasses that detect movement and heat. Police use them when—"

"Right. I know." Hen's laugh echoed over the water. "But I didn't know that as a kid, even though I taught myself all about nocturnal animals having night vision and stuff. But what you said made me feel better about the dark. You helped me not be scared."

Tyler didn't say anything. Didn't move a muscle.

"So, thank you."

Still nothing.

Hen played it cool, like Tyler's non-responsiveness didn't matter. It felt weird, though, he couldn't lie. He leaned back in the lounger as if getting ready to sunbathe. He let out a sigh and hugged his towel tighter around his shoulders.

After a few seconds, Tyler went to get up. "Gotta clean the pool."

Hen started. "No, wait. There's something else I want to tell you."

Tyler scratched his head and sat back down.

How long had it been since he'd been this physically close to his brother, for this long? When had they last really talked? As a kid, he'd given Tyler superhero status. Like all kids do with their big brothers. Back then, Tyler could do no wrong.

Until he did.

Hen shook the thought. Decided to abandon the whole Derek topic. More important things came between him and his brother. Hen had been holding something there, blocking Tyler's entry into the family. Maybe as a kind of shield.

If he didn't allow Tyler in, who would?

Hen took a big breath, unsure how he wanted to say it. "I-I think I owe you an apology."

He waited for his brother to stop scratching, but no luck. He spoke louder to compensate. "I heard you say it. I came up and heard you—*It was me! It was me!*—with your hands in the air and everything. And then, I found your meds...the bottle, empty. What was I supposed to think? I mean, what can happen without your meds?"

Tyler looked up then, and his eyes were clear—clearer than the chlorine-sanitized pool or crystal waters of the lake. So blue, his eyes. Startlingly blue. It gave Hen pause. When did they last lock eyes?

Hen remembered Tyler's father had the same eyes. Tyler's father, Hen recently learned, suffered from mental illness too. So unfair. Sadness welled up in him, and he wished so hard for that do-over. For Tyler. He wished he could rewind and make it better for him.

He waited what seemed a lifetime.

"You thought I hurt her?" Tyler's voice sounded so pained, it brought a whole new layer of guilt.

"Tyler, I'm sorry. I'm so sorry." What else could he say? He talked fast. "But you had the code—you know, the license number. Turned out, the license plate was the only thing that led them to the guy who did it. You did that, Tyler. You really helped."

Tyler stared at the pool, brooding, silent. Hen had wanted to make it better but maybe he made it worse?

"Sorry, Tyler. I just...I didn't..." He trailed off.

"I would never hurt her," Tyler said.

"I know."

"I would never hurt you, either."

Hen's throat filled. "I know."

They sat for a long while. The moon rose high, and the stars shone bright in the sky. No longer a chalkboard sky, but glossy black like an old-timey record. Crickets and frogs croaked in the distance. The pool calmed to stillness again.

Hen, now fully dry, felt a chill with the damp towel around him. He wanted to go inside and change and finally go to bed—maybe he'd even sleep—but didn't know how to extract himself. It was like he and Tyler had entered a cave, and a light shone at the end of it where a forgotten treasure waited for them. But neither had a map.

"I'm me." Tyler's groggy voice sounded like he'd been sleeping. Or crying.

"What's that?" Hen asked, automatically. He'd heard him but it didn't compute.

"Without meds, I'm still me."

"Oh. Yeah, okay. I know."

"I know I'm sick. But I'm still me."

Hen felt something leave him. The night sky pressed down on his chest. Tears started. "I know."

Tyler got off the patio chair, stepped over the broken skimmer, and left the pool area through the gate and walked across the crushed stone part of the parking lot to cabin eleven. It took a while. Hen sat there. He had plenty of opportunities to stop him and apologize again. But he didn't. He stayed there, shivering in the lounger, watching Tyler trudge to his lair, his last words hanging there like a wet bathing suit.

Without meds, I'm still me.

I know I'm sick. But I'm still me.

What Tyler didn't say but Hen was sure they both were thinking. What had slipped away from Hen's heart through all this mess:

I'm still your brother.

CHAPTER 38

The phone rang too many times. *Supposta be a well-run facility. Pick up the damn phone.* Bacon shifted his weight to his other leg, wishing for a chair. *Who puts a phone in a hallway?*

He ran through what he'd say when he finally got Pop on the line.

Good news, first. He found out where they lived. He saw Marcella.

That threw him off, seeing her. Aside from the obvious—she'd gotten older—her shorter, graying hair and baggy outfit made her seem a different person. This woman who used to have every guy drooling had let herself go. The word *dowdy* came to mind. Unrecognizable. Only when she spoke and he recognized her voice did he realize she was *the* Marcella. This frumpy woman sent him to prison with her stinging testimony. This pathetic excuse for a mother pointed the finger at everyone else but her own son—the one who'd confessed and who'd already been convicted. This woman who stomped all over his little-boy heart. This *chick.* This ass-brute in disguise. There she was. Standing right in front of him. Looking like a hobo.

And, like fixing a blown fuse, something ignited inside him. His muscles tensed and his blood pumped and his lips quivered, making out the words he'd rehearsed hours earlier.

But she'd gotten in the way.

And he'd forgotten why he came.

It was her fault, what happened next.

Whatever. Pop don't need to hear his personal sob story. He'd skip the sentimentals.

Bad news, after. About getting pinched. How he took a deal and confessed. Prison-bound, awaiting sentencing. Hopefully back in Comstock soon.

Hey, he thought, bad news was kinda good news. Father and son reunited. They could take their time and meet up at the chow hall. They'd cook up a plan to get this thing done together.

If Pop didn't already make parole. Bacon re-jiggered his script to ask about that first.

Abruptly, the ringing stopped.

"Comstock." Sounded like a dude but Bacon knew it was that ass-brute. Never learned her name.

"Need to speak to Leon Hogg."

He waited. Nothing on the other end except a bunch of background noise.

Bacon tensed. "Yo. You there?"

"Yup."

"I need to speak with Leon Hogg." He yelled Pop's name.

"Who's calling?" She sounded bored.

"Derek Hogg. His...son."

A big sigh on the other end. Annoyed or tired? Maybe something else. Who cares? Do your job and get my pop.

He heard some pages flipping.

"You used to be an inmate here?"

"Yeah. I'm...out now. But I need to talk to my pop."

Another whopper silence, then, "Hate to be the one to tell you this, but Leon Hogg expired two nights ago."

"Huh?"

"Sorry 'bout that."

"Expired?"

Another sigh. "Dead. He passed two nights ago."

He huffed a laugh and got dizzy. "Wait a minute." His knees

buckled. The floor dropped out from under him. "He was supposta make parole."

"Sorry, kid. Got the paperwork right here. Leon Hogg, deceased."

"Wait. No. That's not..." Everything bubbled up. He broke out in a cold sweat. Who is this bitch, telling him this crap? He shouted, "Hey, screw you!"

"Excuse me?"

She's got an attitude? The nerve. "What the hell? Where is he? Why didn't I get a call or nothin'? I'm fricking next of kin, ain't I?"

But the line had cut out. Dial tone sang its lonely note in his ear. She'd already hung up.

He slammed the receiver.

"And you don't fricking say it like that," he yelled at the top of his weak, susceptible lungs. "We are *not* PIGS!"

CHAPTER 39

Marcella thought she'd been dreaming. But no. Wide awake, surrounded by darkness. She felt the mattress beneath her, the top sheet cool against her skin, Bernie's warmth beside her. Though safe in her bedroom, she braced herself against an invisible danger—or the dream that haunted her. She couldn't escape it.

Derek Hogg, in her home. He'd turned into such a big brute of a man, so much like his sad excuse for a father. That terrible night, the office had filled with the odor of cigarette smoke. So pungent, like someone blew smoke in her face. But it came from his clothes, his oversized black sweatshirt—so worn that the hood had stretched out of shape, flopping down over his eyes. And his skin—she could smell the smoke on his skin, mixed with body odor and dirty laundry. Reeked like a vagrant, he did.

How odd that's the first thing she noticed. The stench.

The second thing she noticed? His eerie silence. He stood there, breathing, staring at her, his face hidden by his hood. Like some creepy villain in a horror flick. Freaked her out.

"Can I help you?" She hated the weakness of her voice.

Then he said something. What did he say?

Do you have any vacancies?

No, that wasn't it.

I need a room.

No, not that either.

She'd thought she couldn't remember. Hardly gave any details to the detective. Shamefully hid the fact that she'd blacked out. But it seemed so obvious now—what happened—since realizing she knew the intruder.

How convenient, she thought bitterly. Now that her memory didn't matter, it was all she could think about.

A cruel darkness churned inside her as the night replayed...

"Where is he?" he'd demanded, ending the strange silence between them.

"Pardon?" she'd said, trying not to breathe—he smelled that bad.

"He home?" He tried to shove past her. She blocked him at the entryway, the door to her home ajar behind her. Why had she left it open? She was always careful to close it.

The mass of him nudged against her as he pressed forward. He took up too much space. "Where's that spoiled little shit?"

"Excuse me. You're not allowed back there." She put her hands up, hoping it would be enough. Hoping not to touch him.

His eyes flashed beneath the hood. He pushed closer. "Who are you to tell me where I'm allowed to go? Who are you to me? You are *no one* to me! You are nothing."

His words so harsh. So unnecessarily vicious. At the time, she'd been taken aback, shocked and offended. Perhaps she should've recognized his voice. But it had been worn down by smoking and age and poor health—nothing like the boy next door she used to take care of. Her oldest son's best friend.

Here, he was a stranger, bearing down. His mere size could swallow her. She felt suffocated.

"Please leave. Now."

He stuck a fat finger in her face. It grazed her nose, and she flinched as if he'd slapped her.

"You are nothing."

His voice. So cruel. So full of rage, it chilled her veins.

"Get out." She meant to shout, but it came out a whisper.

His fat finger disappeared. And in its place, his face came fully into view. She had told the detective she'd never seen his face. Couldn't describe his features. That his hood obscured it, covered it in shadow. It wasn't a lie. She hadn't remembered at the time. But now, she saw it, clear as day.

His features were sunken. But his eyes bulged, the whites showing, quivering. The flab of his cheeks shook, his scruff an uneven, unkempt beard. His teeth, gritted and stained. Fury emanated from him.

Had she recognized him? She couldn't say. So unlike the child she knew years ago, so unexpected—a shock—that he stood there before her, threatening her, infecting her personal space.

In self-defense, she blocked his girth with a forearm, her other hand searching blindly for the cordless phone on the podium desk. "Get off my property, now, before I call the police."

Did she say that? Something like that.

Like a raging bull, steaming rancid breath in her face. What did he say next? He kept mumbling. Disgusting and horrifying. She stopped listening. All she could think of was, *Get away from me!*

Frantic, she slapped at the desk, knocking over the pen jar, ripping pages of the register. Where was the darn phone? Finally found, she lifted it overhead, her movements ignited by panic. With a piercing shriek, she slammed the receiver down on his head.

Like a mouse kicking the toe of an elephant.

Next thing she knew, he threw her body back, smacking the wall. She fell onto the overturned roller chair. Tangled with it on the tile floor.

The disgusting ogre hovered, a huge black cloud, his arm raised like she'd done with the phone. She braced herself but her arms were like uncooked spaghetti—frail, useless defenses. She screamed so loud it hurt, squeezing her eyes shut.

She didn't remember how it felt when his fist found her forehead, and whatever had been in his hand that tore her face open. Everything had gone black by then—completely.

That much had not been a lie.

SHE DIDN'T REALIZE she'd been crying until Bernie turned on the light. "Hush now, it's okay. Just a bad dream."

Rattled, she blinked against the sudden light and tried to sit up. "I still can't believe it was him. I can't believe he found us." Tears started. She trembled. How cruel for a middle-aged woman to feel so much like a weak, frightened child. "I don't feel safe. I don't feel safe."

He rubbed her back, her shoulders, her hair—his hands a balm. "I know, Em. I know. But we are safe. Derek's being held. They've got him and he's going to be put away again."

"You should've seen him. If you had seen the raw hatred in his eyes." She hugged herself against a sudden chill. "It's a terrible thing, to know someone hates you like that."

"I thought you couldn't see his face?"

A long pause. "Some things are coming back."

"Oh, Em." He held her. "Hey, you're still getting better. You still gotta take it easy now. Be sweet to yourself now."

She buried her face in his neck, breathed him in. "Bernie. I-I've been upset with you." She pulled away to meet his eye. Such grief there, still. "I haven't been thinking about you. About how you feel. I don't want to be angry with you. I don't want to be angry anymore."

He swallowed, held his chin high. "It's okay."

"No, it isn't. You don't deserve that. You deserve—"

"What's that word—deserve? It bears no meaning in our lives." His voice unusually forceful. "We start thinking we deserve something special in this world, we're in for nothing but disappointment. Did my ma deserve to die the way she did? No. Did Tyler deserve to have his brain turn on him? No. But still. We have to deal with what we got."

"But Bernie—"

"Listen, I don't want you to be angry either. Especially not with me. But you know what? I probably deserve some of your anger because I've been plenty angry myself. It's a bad emotion, you know? Unhealthy for the one feeling it."

She dabbed her tears with a tissue. "It is. It hurts."

"Sometimes you might think you can't help feeling it. But you can. You can choose."

She smiled. "You sound like your therapist."

Bernie grinned at the ceiling. "He's given me a few good lines."

It felt good to laugh. She leaned against him and let him stroke her hair. After their talk, she couldn't find a trace of anger in her heart toward him. Or anyone, really. No, that emotion was gone. In its place? Sadness, confusion, and fear—yet exhaustion played over it all. She had no strength for anything. Too tired to cry. Too tired to sleep, even.

After a long while, she found words. As if they washed ashore from the depths of the ocean. "He used to love me, you know, like family. I was like a mother to him. The mother he never had. I took care of him. How could things change so much? How could someone who loved me turn on me with such hate?"

"I honestly don't know. Thinking about how much love I have for you, I couldn't imagine it ever changing."

Her cheeks rushed with heat. "That's different."

"Maybe. But they caught him. That's the good thing."

"But he could come back when he's out, right? What's to stop him? Do we have to move away? Change our names and stuff?"

"Oh, it's not going to come to that. Let's not worry about that. I don't think—"

"And that's the thing. It's not like they got him right away. He had time. He could've come back and finished the job, you know? Why didn't he come back for me?"

"Oh, gosh. Let's not think about that."

She straightened, alert now. Fear overcame everything. "But really, why? If he hated me so much..."

"Maybe he doesn't hate you. And, you said yourself, he came here for a reason. He was after something."

"Right. He kept asking 'where's that spoiled little shit?'" She swiveled toward him. "He meant Hen, didn't he? Why would he be looking for Hen?"

"He doesn't know about the inheritance, does he? Hen's money? He couldn't know about that."

"Oh no, Bernie. The son of Leon Hogg? I'm sure he does." Another sob filled her throat. She nodded, almost wishing she didn't know. Wishing she could go back to not remembering. "That may have been what brought him here. But once he was here? Once he saw me? It was all about the hate. And I was his target."

"I don't think—"

"I could see it in his eyes, Bernie. I could feel it. He wanted me dead." She took his hand to stop hers from shaking. "He wanted to kill me."

CHAPTER 40

A new night terror visited Ty.

Derek Hogg.

Like a ghost, he appeared as Ty remembered him from high school. Sitting in the armchair inside cabin eleven, laughing like he saw something funny on TV. Ty couldn't go to the bathroom without passing him. So, he stayed in bed and thoughts piled up, crowding his mind.

He didn't believe it at first. The secret code went into the super computer and Derek Hogg came out. It had to be a trick. But people kept telling him. Marcella, Sheila, Dr. Asner—all said the same thing.

It was Derek Hogg. He drove the black car to the motel that night and attacked Marcella.

The detective thanked him.

But it didn't match up. Derek drove a black truck. He was Ty's best friend. And he loved Marcella.

It had to be part of the Y2K ruse. Tech had changed Derek, programmed him to make Marcella weak. The first step of many in the process, probably. No use trying to make sense of it. But that didn't mean he couldn't try to stop it.

Hen would tell him the truth.

Ty poked his head out when he heard Hen cleaning cabin ten. "They say it was Derek Hogg."

His little brother paused, dust rag dangling from a gloved hand.

His sweat-soaked shirt looked like he'd been in a water balloon fight.

"Yeah," he said, "Unreal, right?"

"Yes." *Unreal*—exactly the right word. "What did he want?"

Took a while for Hen to answer. He threw down the rag and peeled off his gloves. "I don't know, Tyler."

"Where is he?"

"Who, Derek? He's in the county jail right now. Probably headed back to Comstock eventually, though."

"Have you seen him? Are you sure it's him?"

A kind of laugh. "It's definitely him. But no, I haven't seen him." Hen wiped sweat from his chin. He changed his feet so he faced Ty straight-on.

Ty stepped back.

"Do you want to see him, Tyler?" Hen tilted his head to the side like Marcella did sometimes.

Hen didn't know, though, Ty had already seen Derek. And saw him all the time now. The last time while cleaning the pool, he'd seen Derek drive by in his black Ford truck playing Nirvana on the car stereo and smoking a cigarette.

A strange feeling had come over Ty, like he belonged in that truck with his best friend. Not only in the truck, but inside Derek too. Like, they were the same person. He part of Derek and Derek part of him.

At times in his childhood, he'd felt closer to Derek than he had his own mother. Derek protected him when school became a circuit board maze—got him around and stuff. And Derek had been there at Sally Hubbard's all those years ago when they narrowly escaped what Ty had thought was an alien abduction but really was tech prepping for the Y2K takeover. Derek was the only person who knew what happened that night, but for some reason he'd been taken away and Ty couldn't see him for a long, long time. They had said he went to prison but Ty saw him here. The gorilla took over tech right there at the motel.

But they were part of the same person. Ty felt it in his bones.

"Yes, I need to see him."

BACON HAD no clue who came to visit. Pop, dead before a chance at parole, didn't leave a trace of a spirit to watch over him. Bacon felt his lack of presence so acutely, he got why folks called it a loss. Did it count as grief? Was it the sticky stuff that slowed the flow of blood in his body and the beat of his heart? He wondered, because he couldn't say he felt sad, really.

With Pop gone, Flake would be the only person who might bother to visit. His roommate, the only person he could call a friend, lost his phone line shortly after Bacon moved in. But Flake wouldn't make his way here without a direct instruction. He felt some guilt about leaving Flake behind. Leaving him to his cans of tuna and mustard and ramen noodles.

He'd called Pistol once, and wouldn't try again after getting an earful from Paula. He didn't have Flat Eric's number at his mum's. Now that he thought about it, he'd shared less than two words with Flat Eric in the months they hung out at the fields.

How could it be, after nearly three decades on this planet, he was so completely alone?

Bacon didn't recognize the two guys waiting for him in the visiting room, one a kid. He sized them up as he walked over. The kid's looks got his attention, like a surfer model. You know, those guys who don't even comb their hair but somehow look all put together? Bacon's quills raised, seeing him there. He never trusted good-looking guys.

And the other dude? Could only see the top of his head. He was curled up like a snail. But obviously tall and had the kind of out-of-shape build skinny guys get when they gain weight. Somehow, they're still skinny with a potbelly and a bit of fluff. Not like Bacon, who got big everywhere. Even in his fingers. In prison, he'd gotten bigger than Pop had ever been. Never thought it possible.

As Bacon got closer, the fluff dude lifted his head, and their eyes met. Like a bright blue laser, it struck him. Familiar. Where did he—wait, no way.

Bacon slumped into a chair. "Ty?"

"Derek."

A long, big quiet.

Hold on, if Ty was here, that meant...

He turned to the model-kid. "Chicken? You gotta be kidding me."

"Hi, Derek."

Effing kid says *hi*?

How did he get grown up? All this time he'd been planning to rob Hen of the Hubbard's fortune, he'd imagined that annoying, creepy little kid who used to stare him down all the time. Suddenly, Pop's grand plan to take this kid's money seemed absurd. And embarrassing.

A weird, shaky sensation passed through him, and he had an urge to run back to his cell. Or throw his fist through the table. He huffed a few times like the big bad wolf until it passed, steam rising off his neck.

And then another feeling came, and his head clogged and his eyes filled. With all the crap in his life lately, he had to admit a huge chunk of his past had been somewhat okay. As a kid, almost happy. And these two had been there. Ty and Hen were his childhood.

The wave of emotion surprised him, and Bacon looked away. "What do you want?"

"I see what you mean about the gorilla," Hen said to Ty, laughing a little.

Sweat coated Bacon's neck. He didn't like the brothers talking to each other in front of him. About him? Leaving him out. Not that it made any kind of sense.

Ty didn't seem to register anyway, which reminded Bacon of the truth about Ty—what came out at his trial. A schizo, he had to be sent away. Probably put into a straightjacket and padded room and stuff.

All those years, Bacon had been right. Ty had a screw loose.

Bacon saw him now as a meek nothing. Weaker than a chick,

even. Someone he could easily take down if he wanted.

But the other set of eyes on him gave him willies. One glance at Hen was all he could stand. The kid did the staring thing again. And like old times, his eyes held magic power. Some voodoo crap. Bacon felt it zing into his bloodstream, and he leaned back as much as his dumb chair would let him. Effing kid.

No way. He wouldn't let this spoiled little shit get to him. He put on his best mean face—not hard to do—shooting all his pent-up fury through his eyes. Right at Hen.

The kid surprised him. "I'm not scared of you anymore," he said, calm as a spoon.

And just like that, Bacon was disarmed. He turned away quickly, cramped with a sudden need for the toilet. Had to take a dump. It pressed on his tailbone, for shit's sake. He looked to the guards for help. No luck.

"Dammit," he muttered.

A silent plea to Ty—*just go*—but their signals crossed. No surprise there. What did he think—Ty had any clue about anything anymore? Drugged up on meds now. Worse off than Flake, probably. Worse off than when he was all coked up, for sure.

Clearly agitated, Ty broke a world's record in the fidget category. Did he even know where he was? What the hell was he doing here?

"What the hell are you doing here?" he said aloud.

Ty locked eyes with him then, still shaking like he went through withdrawals. Made Bacon squirm, seeing him so jittery. Ty opened his mouth, but no words came.

"What?" he spat.

A hand slapped the table. Ty's? In a split second, the shaking stopped. Ty leaned closer, speaking low. In the voice of someone who had nothing to lose:

"If you go near my mother again, I will murder you."

Bacon scoffed. This was kinda funny. "Oh, yeah?"

It shouldn't have, but what Ty said next shocked him. "I've done it before."

CHAPTER 41

U p on the ladder, Bernie installed a security camera surveying the office entrance. He'd spent his morning changing the door's lock to make it automatic, so folks would have to be buzzed in. A bit of an investment they couldn't rightly justify, but he didn't care about going into more debt if it made Marcella feel safe. Some things you can't put a price tag on. Why hadn't he done this stuff before? His heart could burst with so much love for that woman, he felt like he could fly.

Since Derek's arrest, something freed up between them and he felt closer to her than he had in months. Probably since Tyler's moving back. It didn't matter. They were back. He didn't care why or how, he loved her so much.

Marcella's car pulled up as he screwed the last bolt and was down off the ladder before Hen and Tyler got out. He wanted to hold onto the light and joyful feeling he'd had all morning, having done those small acts of love. Approaching the boys, he wanted to put things right with them, too. He wasn't sure how, but seeing Tyler stand hunched beside the car in his usual sheepish way spurred him into action.

"Hen? Do you mind if I have a moment with Tyler?"

Hen's eyebrows shot up slightly. He studied Tyler a moment before responding. "Sure thing. I have to catch up on cleaning, anyway."

After Hen skipped off, Bernie sat on the bench facing the parking lot. No one ever sat here. It was more for decoration. Rickety and worn, probably the most uncomfortable seat on the property. But Bernie didn't care. The slats cutting into his thighs felt like penance.

He waited for Tyler to sit but he stayed in the harsh sun, hanging his head.

"At least come out of the sun, Tyler."

He shuffled into the shade.

Bernie fiddled with his hands, unsure how to start. "I can bring you to your appointment with Dr. Asner tomorrow."

"Okay."

"And the pool looks great. You've been doing a good job. Thanks."

"Okay."

A few beats passed, and then Tyler turned toward his cabin.

"No, no," Bernie said. "Hold on. That's not... I wanted to talk a bit."

Tyler turned back. Said nothing.

"So. I'm not sure how to say it so I'm just gonna jump in." Bernie felt a revving energy in his chest. Is this what courage felt like? Courage and determination. The new Bernie.

Deep breath. "You know, ten years ago your little brother—gosh he was only, what, seven at the time—he asked me a very important question. Always been a clever kid, that Hen. Anyway, he asked me something that got me thinking. And I've been thinking about it all these years."

Was Tyler listening? Bernie couldn't tell. Pushing aside doubt, he forged ahead. Felt like scaling a cliff. "Anyway, Hen asked me how I could forgive you."

He paused to let it sink in.

"...for killing my mother." Such hard words to speak.

Bernie's next breath trembled out of him. "At the time, I told him how much I love your mother, and I love everything she loves. And that I'm working on forgiving you because that's what my ma would have done. All that's the truth. I didn't lie."

Tyler looked up. They met eyes. Bernie was first to turn away.

"Forgiveness is a tricky thing, though. All those years you were away, I thought I was in a good place about the whole thing. I thought I had forgiven. Or at least, made peace with it. But when you came back, it was clear I hadn't. But I guess you knew that."

Tyler shuffled his feet. Tiny stones danced on the pavement under his shoes. He seemed uncomfortable. Couldn't blame him. Bernie felt plenty uncomfortable himself. And it had nothing to do with the darn bench.

"I have to be honest with myself and with you. And your mother. Seeing you brings it all back. Every time I look at you, it's like I relive the whole thing. I've made a choice not to be mad, but some things are easier said than done. I'm still pissed."

He swallowed hard.

"And I don't know if I can ever forgive, really."

Tyler stopped moving his feet. His head hung lower. Bernie could only see the top of his head, his thinning hair.

"But I'll keep working on it. Promise." He wiped moisture from his face, surprised to find tears. "I'm sorry, Tyler."

Tyler snapped his head up and his eyes—so blue, like little lights inside—took Bernie off guard. He wanted to look away but didn't. He held eye contact, man to man. And waited.

"Why are you telling me sorry?" Tyler said, his voice like the gravel at his feet. His words stuttered out, clearly causing him pain. "You have nothing to be sorry for. I'm the one who's sorry. Every day. Some days, it's all I think about."

"Ah, Tyler. I didn't mean for—"

"No. Just, let me. Just... I'm sorry. Okay? I'm so, so sorry." He blinked at the ground. This time, when he turned away and headed for his cabin, Bernie didn't stop him. He didn't get up from the bench either. He sat and sat, long after Tyler had closed himself into his room, letting what that young man said wash over him.

Talk about courage. He had nothing on Tyler.

CHAPTER 42

M arcella awoke to a dull thud. A germ of a headache? She blinked against the flat afternoon light filtering through her blinds.

*Thud...thud...thud...*methodically, like someone's head banged against the door. She sat up, too quickly, triggering a wave of vertigo so strong she almost howled. Her face fell into her hands.

"Who's there?" Muffled through her fingers. She uncovered her mouth. "What is it?"

The door opened a crack. She squinted at the shadow, a niggle of fear creeping in. "Hello? Is someone there?"

Door creaked open halfway to show Tyler standing there.

She palmed her heart. "My goodness, sweetie, you scared me half to death."

"Sorry." In the entryway, still as a sculpture.

"Come on in. Everything all right?" She had an urge to scoop him up in her arms as if he were still little.

He shuffled in like an elderly man. Finally, he sat in her vanity chair. It took ages.

She waited.

He waited.

She rubbed her forehead. How long had she been in bed? The mattress had seemed to become part of her. "What time is it?"

"Two-forty-five. Bernie said it would be okay. He didn't think you'd be asleep."

"Oh, it is okay. It's always okay."

Two-forty-five meant nothing. Weeks ago, it may have, but time had become abstract. She'd slept so much since the accident, part of her needed confirmation this wasn't a dream. "What's going on? Did you want to talk about something?"

Long pause. He knotted and re-knotted his hands. "It was Derek."

She went rigid, hearing the name. Especially from Tyler's lips. "Yes. I'm sorry. He was your friend."

"No. Not my friend."

Her chest ached as she forced air into her lungs. "I know it's been a long time, but he was. He was your best friend. You must remember that."

He went to the window and fingered the blinds. A slice of sunshine fell across his chest. "Yes. But I don't want to."

She laughed. "Wouldn't it be nice to be able to choose our memories?"

Still holding the blinds, he turned to her. Light shifted, catching his profile. His father's square jaw. "What?"

"Never mind."

The room went dark again as he shoved his hands into his pockets. "I'm mad at him."

She took a moment to build energy, unsure she could manage Tyler's emotions on top of her own. Her words were careful. "Sure, you are. We all are. He did a terrible, hateful thing."

"He hurt you."

He looked so much like a little boy right now, pouting as if he didn't get his way. She patted the mattress. "Tyler, sit. I'm okay. I'm going to be just fine."

After a few moments, he sat. And the mattress hardly shifted with his weight. He whispered. "It was me too. I'm so sorry."

This would not do. She wouldn't replay that awful car ride. If he never said sorry again, she'd be glad. She took his hand, which felt like putty in hers. "No, Tyler. It wasn't you. You have nothing to apologize for. It's not your—"

"I won't let that happen ever again."

The determination in his voice surprised her. "Listen, sweetie, you don't have to worry."

"I took care of it. I went to see Derek, and I told him...and you don't have to worry or be scared or anything anymore." He sounded uncharacteristically confident.

A swell of pride found her—inappropriate, perhaps. Yet a boost nonetheless. It took a moment for what he said to register. "Wait a minute. You went to see Derek? Tyler, why would you—"

"Hen took me. I went with Hen."

Her eyes went wide. "*Hen* took you?"

She tried to picture it: her two sons in the car, going on an adventure together.

A memory arose of the two boys, as kids, venturing out together in the woods near their home in Severance. Hen had painted a bat box and Tyler promised to help him hang it. They nailed it to a tree so it faced Paradox Lake, Hen had reported excitedly. Even Tyler couldn't erase his smile, seeing the joy it gave his little brother. This would be a memory she'd choose to keep.

They never could tell if any bats visited Hen's box. After a while, he lost interest. Marcella wondered if it still hung there, faded and weathered and alone next to Paradox Lake.

She ran her hand along her comforter's stitching, thinking of her boys. Together. And she felt something big and weighty leave her—freeing her—giving it up to her children. Part of her wanted to keep it. Part of her didn't know herself without it, though she couldn't say what it was exactly.

"You and Hen, you shouldn't have done that. It could've been dangerous."

"No. It wasn't."

"It's in the hands of the law now. Tyler, everything's taken care of. I don't want you getting any ideas."

"Don't worry. I'm not gonna do anything crazy."

Awkward pause. She froze, staring at the covers, her whole body going hot. That word had been banned in their home for years. Slowly, she lifted her gaze to meet his—and found an impish grin on his handsome face. His blue eyes shining.

"Gotcha," he said, and let out a big belly laugh. She hadn't heard him laugh like that in over a decade. A glorious sound.

EPILOGUE

2 Years Later

Common App college essay by Henry A. Trout

My mom used to tell me I was born an old soul. As a kid, I didn't know what she meant. But I thought it might have to do with my concern for wildlife. I loved all animals but mostly those found in the wild. And in my little mind, I believed I could save them. Much of my childhood was spent trying to help endangered animals whose habitats were vulnerable—building makeshift habitats in my backyard out of sticks and mud. Or a bat box out of plywood, a bee sanctuary with sugar water.

But then tragedy struck, making me see the world differently. What happened in my family showed me it wasn't wild animals who needed help, but people...specifically, my brother.

My older brother suffers from paranoid schizophrenia. Before he was diagnosed at age seventeen, he had a complete psychotic break that ended in a tragic loss of life. Sentenced to psychiatric rehab, where he spent the next ten years, my brother began what would become lifelong treatment for his condition. The problem was, though, after he came home, getting the help he needed proved to be extremely difficult, if not impossible. His weekly mandatory appointments with his psychiatrist became more medication management as the red tape to the transitional program—the program which would safely integrate him into society—became thicker than the Great Wall of China.

Why was it so hard to get my brother help? Clearly, he was sick. No one would deny he desperately needed support to acclimate to society and the real world. After ten years in institutional rehab, with only a pill a day to help him reintegrate into a normal life, he fell into post-psychotic depression that turned him into a zombie-like presence no one wanted to be around. Even to me, he seemed hopeless.

But he was still my brother.

The tipping point, for me, for him, was 9/11. My brother had always been wary of advances in technology. When the news began reporting on the Y2K scare in the late nineties, he became fixated on computers controlling people, and believed we'd see the end of the world. Even after the 2000 new year, he waited for the worst. Then, 9/11 happened, which confirmed my brother's paranoia. He had such a severe breakdown, he had to be hospitalized for over six months. During this time, I took over for my mother as his primary caretaker. Only then did I begin to understand my brother's courageous and overwhelming struggle—and my life's purpose. I decided to use my inheritance to start Miss Sally's House.

Right now, Miss Sally's House is a transitional day program for the mentally ill based in Saratoga Springs, New York. We provide many services here, mostly volunteer-based, like counseling, group therapy, music and pet therapy, also meal programs and coffee hours geared for socialization. I'm proud to say, not only is my brother a member here (we don't call them patients), he's also a volunteer—in charge of our food pantry. Since working here, he stands a bit taller. And smiles. I hadn't seen him smile for years.

The members of Miss Sally's House are similar to my brother in a lot of ways, but, of course, each person has his or her unique needs. One thing they all have in common, though, is a basic human need to feel accepted, productive, and loved. Which makes them not all that different from any one of us, if you think about it.

I'm applying to your psychology program as a stepping stone to become a clinical psychiatrist so I can help people like my brother. My goal is to expand Miss Sally's House to include substance abuse rehabilitation and psychiatric care.

I would be honored to pursue my education at your university.

B ee looked up from the essay, her eyes brimming.

Hen tried to read her expression. "Do you think it's good?"

"Do I think it's good?" She came around the desk and wrapped him into one of her signature hugs. She gave the best hugs.

"You like it, I take it?"

"Like it? No, I don't like it. I love it." Her voice sounded strange. Was she getting choked up?

He tried a laugh, soft and bashful. "That's a relief. You're the first person to read it."

"Tell me about that time. What happened to him after 9/11?"

Hen shook his head. "I don't like to think about it."

Bee waited. Touched his arm so a jolt of warmth shot up to his shoulder.

"I don't know how to describe it," he said. "I mean, it was a textbook breakdown. It happened like you'd imagine it happening. He went completely off the rails."

"But what did he do?"

"Pretty much destroyed cabin eleven. Smashed the TV, threw it into the parking lot. That's what got our attention. By the time we got the police involved, he was so worked up...just kept yelling about the Y2K thing. Nonsense, you know? But he kept yelling. Aw, man. The other renters—there were only a few since it was September—they came out to see what the big to-do was. One of the cops tried to restrain Tyler. Big mistake. Ended up biting his hand to get away. It was such a cluster. The ambulance finally got there and gave him a shot that basically knocked him out. And off he went. My poor mom. It was too much for her. She was screaming too. Seeing her in such pain all over again? It made me realize I had to step in, for real. To protect her. She's too fragile for this. Thinking back, she never really had it in her to take care of Tyler."

"Not many people do."

A laugh. "Right. I wonder if I do."

"Of course, you do."

"I wonder sometimes."

A memory struck Hen. On a visit during Tyler's last stint at the state hospital, they went for a walk on a trail around the adjacent pond. With his eyes on the dirt and sticks at his feet, Hen had the guts to ask, "How does it feel, you know, being sick like that?"

"Schizophrenia?"

Almost a shock to hear his brother say the word. "Yeah. Do you mind if I ask that?"

"No."

They rounded the pond. Got to a flat spot and started skipping stones. "So?"

"I dunno."

"Is it scary?"

After a few beats. "Yes." The word seemed to weigh a thousand pounds.

And then the magic happened. Hen would never forget it, the feeling. He looked up above the tree line. And it was like the clouds and the sky met the dirt path at their feet, and an energy lifted them airborne. Flying, guided by a cosmic force—like safety and love and pure goodness.

Miss Sally.

It sounds unreal, but she spoke to him. Like, he clearly heard her voice. And he hadn't thought about Miss Sally for years. But in this spiritual moment, she gave Hen the best gift. She told him what he needed to do, how to spend her money. Once she said it, his path seemed obvious. He started planning the very next day.

Bee looked up at him now with her doe eyes and her full, bow-shaped lips. It made it hard not to kiss her. "Thanks for telling me," she said. "I wish I could've been there for you. We were in our senior year of high school, remember? I had some important things to do, myself."

Hen gave her a knowing smile, grateful his path included her. And then he did kiss her—soft on the lips.

After 9/11, everyone in school had noticed the transformation of

Bianca Chase. Like, night and day. Not only did she dress differently, more modestly, but she dropped the whole flirtatious vibe. And, thank goodness, that jerk Keith, too. She joined student council and started going by "Bee." Her biggest achievement, though, was an after-school scrapbooking program. Sounds hokey, right? But it became a kind of peer therapy, with this cool creative outlet. Seeing what she'd done at school, it was a no-brainer to bring her on board when Hen started Miss Sally's House. He didn't find out until months later that Bianca's mother suffered for years from clinical depression. Another few months after that, he learned how she felt about him. By then, she had long become someone he respected. Admired, even. And no one could deny how adorable she was.

So, yeah. He liked being her boyfriend.

He took his essay back. It looked so official, all typed up. "Do you think I should make any changes?"

"Well, you could talk about yourself more. Like, how you've always wanted to help people." She tilted her head and her hair fell to the side. "Like me."

This had been a recurring topic between them. "I didn't really help you. All I did was walk you home."

"But that walk home saved me. I've told you that before."

"Yeah, but—"

"And, it took me a while to realize it, but that was also when I fell in love with you."

Hen's face filled with heat. It's not the first time she'd said it, but still. "Geez, Bee. Come on."

"You're so cute when you blush." She kissed his cheek. "Come on. It's time to close up shop and get to your mom's. Can't be late for her birthday."

Friday was game day, so Hen knew the front room had a zillion board game pieces littering the place. Also, snack remnants. They had about twenty members visit today, eight of whom were part of the state program. Hen still battled through a tome of paperwork to offer Miss Sally's House services to state hospital patients. It was a grueling process. Grateful every day, though, Tyler was healthy enough to avoid hospitalization. And Hen could care for him.

"Is Tyler ready?" he said.

"Who do you think's closing up shop?"

Hen hugged her again. He could hug her all day. "We better get going."

She shoved him, laughing. "Get your hands off me, then."

HEN DROVE AND, as usual, Bee rode shot-gun while Tyler sat in the back. Right in the middle, so he could see out the windshield. Early signs of agitation started with Tyler biting his nails. He had made huge strides in the past year. Though no longer withdrawn and solemn, he seemed to get agitated more easily.

Hen tried to calm his worry. "We'll get there at a perfect time."

"It's her birthday, though, right?"

"Yeah. Well, technically it's tomorrow but we're celebrating today."

Quiet filled the car, but it had a rigidity to it. Bee shot Hen a look, holding it until he nodded. In the rearview, Tyler rocked in his seat.

"What's up, Ty?"

"Where's her present? Did we get her a present?"

"It's okay. She doesn't want one. She told me, all she wants is for us—"

"No. No. No. She has to have presents. And balloons. It's a birthday party. Why didn't we get her anything?"

Hen wracked his brain on how to stop Tyler from escalating. But couldn't think of anything to say. Tyler slapped the seat beside him and repeated himself, louder. Then he pulled at his seatbelt strap as if trying to make an escape.

As experienced as Hen had become, these situations still made him nervous. Especially while driving.

"Tyler, really, I promise you. It's okay." His words trailed off. His brother had stopped listening.

"You know what?" Bee to the rescue. "We're actually early. The party doesn't start for almost an hour. We have plenty of time to stop at the market and get balloons and a card and... I know!" She spun toward the backseat. "Tyler, how about if you and I go in and pick out a nice bouquet of flowers? What do you think?"

Like magic, Tyler calmed. A nod. A trace of a smile. Hen saw it in the rearview, and he felt a layer of stress melt away.

"You think we can pull off to get to the market, Hen?" Bee asked, knowing the answer.

"Oh, sure. Of course. Next exit, we're off."

Hen stayed in the car, watching Bee take Tyler's arm into the market. He didn't think he could adore her more.

He phoned Mom on his cell.

"Lakeside Inn."

"Hi, Suzy. It's Hen. My mom around?"

"She's already down at the beach. And don't bother trying her cell. It's here at the front desk."

"'Course it is." Mom always forgot to keep her phone with her.

This huge change—Marcella and Bernie now owning Lakeside Inn—had also been triggered by 9/11. The tragedy made Wes's parents realize they didn't like motel ownership (or each other) and they put their resort on the market the same day they filed for divorce. Pretty much a turnkey thing, Hen used a portion of his inheritance for the down payment and gifted it to Mom (and Bernie). The resort proved so profitable that the down payment was all she needed. Amazing how a motel not a mile away could be so much more successful because it sat directly on the lake. Not only was the place at full capacity all season—at higher rates!—most rooms were full even in the off-season. Mom could afford to hire a cleaning crew and part-time receptionist (aka Suzy), as well as take a tropical vacation last winter.

As for Wes, well. He made good on his dream to become a ski

bum in Colorado. He didn't own a resort—far from it—but bartended at one. Part-time. He and Hen stayed in touch for a bit, but more than distance drove them apart. As Hen's goal to build Miss Sally's House grew, he outgrew Wes. But Hen would always be thankful Wes helped broker the Lakeside Inn deal.

Bee had been right. They got there in plenty of time for Mom's party. The three of them each had their arms full as they made their way down to the beach where bundles of balloons tethered to the picnic tables. A guy with a guitar crooned from the dock platform. A perfect beach party. Even the weather cooperated.

"Hey guys!" Bernie said, his wide smile in full effect. He looked good, wearing a navy-blue polo and fresh jeans. And, was that cologne? "Hi, Bee. Let me take that stuff off your hands."

While Bee and Bernie made room for their gifts on a picnic table, Hen stayed with Tyler and searched the crowd for Mom. He saw Mike and Sue from next door. Phyllis, who owned the breakfast place down the street. Sheila and Dr. Asner waved from the shoreline.

Then, like from behind a curtain, Mom appeared. And, seeing her, Hen felt the wind leave him. So beautiful, she wore a wrap dress which showed her ballerina figure, the same navy blue as Bernie's shirt. Hen couldn't help his grin, she looked so much like her old self, how he'd remembered her. Even if his memory transformed her diner uniform into a cocktail gown, he'd always seen her with royal elegance. Her hair fell in loose waves at her shoulders, and she wore a sheen of makeup that sparkled in the sunshine. Her scar had faded, undetectable but for a shiny, moon-shaped speck on her eyebrow. He understood why she made heads turn—even now as she turned fifty-one. Made him proud.

Not as proud, apparently, as she seemed to be. Her smile was brighter than the summer sky. She looked at them—Tyler and him—with such love in her eyes, it made Hen shy. She airplaned her arms wide. "My boys." And pressed them into a three-way hug.

Hen and Tyler shared a look and a smile as they both towered over Mom. Hen could smell Mom's orange blossom lotion—the kind she used to wear all the time when he was little. And it transported him to that small brown house in Severance near Paradox Lake—their street like a patchwork quilt.

"Happy Birthday."

Hen closed his eyes and hugged back—one arm around Mom, the other around Tyler.

NOTE TO READERS

Schizophrenia is a serious mental illness. Although there is no cure, with proper medication and treatment, it can be managed. If you or anyone you know exhibits symptoms, please contact the National Alliance on Mental Illness at 1-800-950-NAMI (6264) or go to mentalhelp.net

DISCUSSION QUESTIONS

1. "Challenges of forgiveness" continues as a theme from *Boy on Hold*. In this book, nearly every character is faced with it. Consider each. Do they achieve it? How do you define forgiveness? Have you ever found it impossible to forgive?

2. How has Hen changed from the first book to the sequel? Is it in the way you expected?

3. Hen has been described as an old soul. At one point, he regrets that he can't just be a kid. Why can't he be both? Do you know any kids who fit the description of an "old soul?"

4. How could Hen's inheritance become a problem, as Marcella suggests?

5. Choose your friends wisely, the saying goes. Is Wesley a good friend to Hen?

6. Is Hen a good brother to Tyler?

7. Tyler's presence in this book triggers a range of emotional reactions from different characters. Some could say his

presence acts as therapy, encouraging others to express their feelings and acknowledge wrongdoings. Thoughts?

8. Tyler faces a huge challenge to reintegrate into his community (and family) after ten years in psychiatric rehab. How does he fare?

9. Do you remember the Y2K crisis? Did it affect your job/life? What about 9/11? How do these two events get mixed up in Tyler's mind?

10. Though Bianca is not a major character, she changes a lot throughout the book. From what we know of her, what inspires the change?

11. Bernie says that anger only hurts the person feeling it. Do you agree or disagree?

12. How has Marcella changed since the first book? Have your feelings toward her changed?

13. Do you believe Randolf is a good detective? How would you rate his handling of the investigation?

14. Upon his release, Bacon seemed determined to start over and become a "good guy." Was he able to? Why or why not?

15. Why did Bacon attack Marcella?

ACKNOWLEDGMENTS

First, thanks to the fans of *Boy on Hold*. Many ideas for the sequel emerged from your thoughtful comments at book club discussions. I hope you enjoy this one as much as the first.

On that note, so many readers have opened up and shared personal, often heart-breaking, stories about a loved one suffering from a serious mental illness. Thank you for your courage and honesty. And your trust in me.

This book would not have been possible without the generosity and brain-power of some awesome individuals:

My father, James R. Davies, Esq. (retired)—my go-to legal counsel.

My friend and fellow yoga instructor who also happens to be an attorney, Sheila G. Duerr, who shared details of her concussion recovery. *It hurts to talk!*

My brother, Dr. Jim Davies of Carleton University Cognitive Science Department, whose *Minding the Brain* podcast provided valuable information regarding hallucinations, trauma, and concussions.

Family friend and retired psychiatric nurse, Kate Relling, shared stories of her forty-plus years working in the field. *One thing they all have in common is a basic human need to feel accepted, productive, and loved.* Thank you, Kate, for your enthusiasm for Tyler's story.

My neighbor and friend, Maria Custer, has my utmost admiration for her selfless role as her brother's caretaker. Thank you, Maria, for reading and re-reading this book, and for sharing your day-to-day reality navigating the mental health system. Your brother is lucky to have you!

The amazing and talented team at *Immortal Works*—Beth Buck, Holli Anderson, John Olsen, Rachel Huffmire, Ashley Literski, Jason

King, Megan Nerdin, Staci Olsen. I'm so grateful to be part of the IW family!

Special thanks to my parents, Jim and Janet Davies, and my in-laws, Mike and Robin Spero, Judith and Sam Basile.

Endless love and hugs to my biggest fans, my boys, AJ, Adam, and Chaz. Thanks especially to my "old soul" AJ. You were my model for teenage Hen.

Anthony Spero, you are the one, the only, the real deal. I love you more than Bernie loves Marcella.

ABOUT THE AUTHOR

Johannah Davies (JD) Spero's first release, *Catcher's Keeper*, was a finalist in the Amazon Breakthrough Novel Award in 2013. Her young adult fantasy *Forte* series has won recognition from National Indie Excellence Award (2014, 2016), Adirondack Literary Award (2015). *Boy on Hold* was a 2020 Book Excellence Award winner and a 2020 IPPY Gold winner for Best Mystery/Thriller ebook. Having lived in various cities from St. Petersburg (Russia) to Boston, she now lives with her family in the Lake George area, where she was born and raised.